Modern Means of Extinction

We had just come out of the Hall of Small Mammals, leaving behind the roar of the crowded dining area, into the dark quiet of the large, marble-floored foyer. Something felt strange.

On the dark marble floor, right in front of the base of the dinosaur exhibit, was a blue silk pump. A single left shoe.

I looked up.

Draped over the giant fossilized head of the triceratops skeleton looming above was a woman. From the sag of her body, she didn't appear to be conscious.

My thoughts were shooting off a mile a minute, obsessing over the least important details.

Nothing can fix this now.

The wedding is ruined.

JERRILYN FARMER

Killer Wedding

A MADELINE BEAN
CATERING MYSTERY

For Christine,

Jerrilyn Farmer

AVON BOOKS
An Imprint of HarperCollinsPublishers

This is a work of fiction. Names, characters, places, and incidents are products of the author's imagination or are used fictitiously and are not to be construed as real. Any resemblance to actual events, locales, organizations, or persons, living or dead, is entirely coincidental.

AVON BOOKS
An Imprint of HarperCollins*Publishers*
10 East 53rd Street
New York, New York 10022-5299

Copyright © 2000 by Jerrilyn Farmer
Inside cover author photo by Ronna Kovner
Library of Congress Catalog Card Number: 99-96774
ISBN: 0-380-79598-1
www.avonbooks.com

First Avon Books printing: March 2000

Avon Trademark Reg. U.S. Pat. Off. and in Other Countries, Marca Registrada, Hecho en U.S.A.
HarperCollins® is a trademark of HarperCollins Publishers Inc.

Printed in the U.S.A.

10 9 8 7 6 5 4 3

For Dad Bob
the artist at the easel in the den
with love

ACKNOWLEDGMENTS

Annoyed that I hadn't planned better, I booked the only vacant hotel room in all Tucson, Arizona. A family celebration brought us to that beautiful city on the sold-out weekend of the International Gems & Minerals Show. Somewhere, thirty miles from Jonathan Kobritz's bar mitzvah festivities, my family gamely settled into our brand new "all-suite" shoebox. I can still recall the feeling of dismay at trying to squeeze into an overflowing "breakfast" room that first morning, as dozens of "all-suite" guests vied for not-entirely-fresh pastries. When, finally, the children had eaten and gone to play, I returned to our little table, cardboard teacup in hand, to spend a brief respite with my husband. I was not entirely cordial, it might be understated, when a tall, dark stranger with longish hair began to settle at our table.

I smile, now, at how close I came to missing one of the most mesmerizing personal stories I have ever heard, modestly told by this unexpectedly charming new aquaintance. To protect his privacy I will not mention here this gentleman's name. To prevent spoiling this book's tale I will not mention here details of his true-life adventures and daring youthful career. But acknowledge him I must. With a commemorative paper cup of hot tea, I would like to salute a passing stranger's wild and reckless past and his willingness to speak openly about it to one who—finally awake—warmed up quickly, full of questions.

As always, I want to thank Evan Marshall, wonderful

friend and gifted literary agent, and also Lyssa Keusch, wonderful friend and brilliant editor. I must also thank sweet providence for bringing that particular fascinating stranger over to that particular faux-granite Formica table in that particular breakfast room. And I must thank my beloved Chris for making all things possible, including, as only one of a million examples, not allowing me to shoo that particular treasure away on that particular morning.

PROLOGUE

*D*eath—my own—was the furthest thing from my mind as I tooled around Beverly Hills. Leaving behind the congestion on Rodeo Drive, where predatory Jaguars and Cobras stalked nonexistent curbside parking, I swung my big old Jeep up an alley behind a row of exclusive shops. Here, delivery vans did their blue-collar best to slip in and out of the exalted suburb without being noticed, preserving the mystique of fully stocked stores without the malodor of labor.

Here, amid the quiet bustle of behind-the-scenes commerce, the scrubbed alleys of B.H. witnessed the subtle, brutal drama of social wars won and lost. Behind each shop, a few precious parking spaces were reserved for those whom favor or a sharp-eyed shop owner smiled upon. It was to one such spot that I was headed. Darius Boyer, proprietor and star of Darius Floral Design, had invited me to "just park in the rear"—a mark of high favor in a neighborhood where parking privilege equaled social status.

I was behind the wheel of my old black Grand Wagoneer. It's a classic, one of those metal monsters, basically a tank adorned with woody panels. I pulled into the one open spot, snugly nestling it next to Darius's own gold Mercedes wagon.

It was nearly 4:00 P.M., and I was running late. Again. The cell phone seems to have been invented for people like me. I hate being late, making people wait. I dialed the number to my house. After two rings, Holly Nichols picked up.

"Mad Bean Events." She gave the standard business opening.

"Say 'Madeline,' " I tried correcting. "Madeline Bean Events."

"Too long." My assistant was unimpressed by my tone, which was not unprecedented. We are more friends than employer/employee. And in our newest venture, a catering and events-planning firm, she was the one who kept us all on track.

"I'm late again, Holly. I just pulled in behind Darius's. And this is not a quick stop."

"He likes to talk."

"I like to talk to him, too. That's why I'm here, actually. So I'm afraid I won't be home early enough to do dinner." I nibbled a cuticle.

"Can *we* do it?" she asked, her voice picking up an edge of eagerness, but dampened as if she didn't want me to notice, get pissed off, and say no.

Another decision I didn't want to have to make. I thought it over.

I love to shop and I love to cook. Half the fun of picking out perfectly fresh ingredients, like a fragrant and dewy bunch of purple-veined basil, or a basket of the sweetest Oxnard strawberries, was the anticipation of turning them into a new dish, creating a new recipe. But today it would have to be someone else's pleasure to cook up the dinner. That someone was Holly and my partner, Wesley Westcott.

"Fine." I suppose I didn't sound totally generous, if one was listening carefully. Late afternoons, I react to low blood sugar and get primal cravings for caffeine.

"You're a peach," Holly said, dryly. But I knew she was pleased. Wesley was giving Holly secret cooking lessons and she didn't think I knew about it. Perhaps she had decided to get more serious about her cooking and was waiting to surprise me with the news.

"I'll see you later, then." I punched the off button and flipped my phone closed. And then, without another thought, really, I opened my car door.

You see, it's minute events such as this—the timing of them, the serendipity of where you park or how long a phone call lasts, the habit of them, the routine—which can change one's entire life. But of course, we're so focused on the big stuff, we miss the point. We're busy obsessing on The Big Questions: Should I marry him? Should I have children? Do I believe in God? Who, quite frankly, knows?

But the tiny decisions are the ones that get you. Do I turn right? Should I go left? Balls set in motion that will have consequences far in the future. Or sometimes not so far.

Perhaps it's just as well that we aren't accompanied by corny movie soundtracks that play DUN-DUN-DUUN, menacingly, as we casually open our car doors on sunny blue-sky afternoons in affluent neighborhoods. After all, life is life, and with or without warning, what-cha gonna do?

Chapter 1

"**Y**ou ... look ... so ... thin!" Darius's dramatic voice spoke each word with its own staccato punch.

"Please."

"You ... look ... so ... thin!" Darius always knew the right thing to say to each of his friends and clients. And *that* was always the right thing to say.

"Oh, stop," I answered, pleased anyway.

"Protein power?" Darius guessed, as his hands flew, lacing more white roses into the charming flower arrangement on the counter between us. Darius knew each and every diet that every one of his clients was on. As a matter of fact, so did I. That's part of the job description when you cater in this community.

"I'm more into a tasting diet," I joked. "I end up having a taste of everything I prepare. The hard part is convincing myself that's enough."

"Mmm hmm," he said, a rose in his mouth, as he spun the flower arrangement around, looking for bald spots. Deftly, he found the spot and worked the stem in. "But I hear you are *not* working, these days. True or false?"

"Well ..." Rumors spread so fast. I had only just been hit with the lawsuit that week. I shook my head. "It's a long story. The people who bought my catering company need to get straightened out. That's all." I took a deep breath of cool, slightly moist air, appreciating the spicy sweet aroma of so many blooms at their peak.

"So-o-o," Darius asked, eyes agleam, "do you have a good lawyer?" I was sure he had several names he wanted to recommend.

"My buddy, Paul, is taking care of it. Don't worry, okay? We just have a little down time now. Why shouldn't we take a rest?"

"So-o-o," he said, tsking, "they slapped you with an injunction."

"We'll be fine." I smiled, in a fine way.

Darius looked around his empty shop and said, "Word is . . ."

I braced myself. I could tell we were in for some serious gossip.

". . . Vivian Duncan is looking for you!" And then he went on to explain why the most notorious wedding consultant in Beverly Hills had decided she wanted me to buy out her fabulously successful business.

I let him have his say. Darius's elegant shop contained the most sought-after blossoms in the world. The rarest tulips and specialty orchids were flown in from around the world, filling his cool shop with mystery and beauty. The walls were painted the color of dark moss, the better to show off each precious floral jewel. I loved to visit him there, to catch a few glimpses of the wonderful new arrangements he kept inventing for his picky clientele, and to hear the latest gossip circulating through our tight little world of party planners. I wasn't expecting today's central topic, however, to be me.

Darius fixed his green eyes on the project at hand and removed one single stem from the profusion of blooms in the vase. "Now then, what was I saying?"

"I'm not sure. But what *I'm* saying is I am not interested in buying someone else's business. Ever since I came into some money . . ."

"A *shitload* of money," Darius interrupted, smiling.

"Well, we were lucky. We sold my old catering company to a foolish buyer. That's true. But now every restaurant in town is after me to invest in their expansion.

Or there's a guy who wants me to be a silent partner in his chef's supply store. I mean really."

"But Vivian's the best wedding consultant there is," Darius said. "Frankly, everyone is simply shocked she'd consider leaving the business at all. What is she? Sixty? I don't know—she's been lifted so many times. But here she is offering you a once in a lifetime opportunity."

"Weddings make me nervous," I said, joking.

"Oh, ha-ha-ha," Darius said, with only the heaviest hint of sarcasm. "You refuse to settle down just to drive all the straight men in Los Angeles wild."

"Yes," I said, straight-faced, "that's my plan."

I looked at the flowers he was almost finished working on and sighed. "You . . . are . . . such . . . a . . . genius!"

He smiled. Yes, I knew what to say to my suppliers, too.

Just then a young couple entered the shop. Darius was the trendiest florist in Beverly Hills, and he had not managed to stay at the top of the heap by scaring away affluent couples, especially when the female half of the couple sported an engagement ring featuring an emerald the size of a cocktail onion.

"Hello, darlings," Darius called to them, full of professional charm. "I will be with you momentarily. Please look around." His eyes twinkled at them and then he turned back to finish his work. One of his trademark floral creations was nearly complete. In a round crystal bowl, a low arrangement had been made of two dozen tightly packed, burstingly large white roses. The exuberance of so many luxurious, velvet rose petals was only part of Darius's magic with flowers. His trademark creative stroke was found just below the waterline. The clear round bowl was packed to the brim with several dozen submerged fresh lemons, hiding and supporting the rose stems in one delightful masterstroke.

"Here you are," Darius said, as he made one more quick adjustment to my arrangement. I watched his elf-like features, deep in concentration now, his blond hair brushed down onto his forehead in bangs.

"Just one last word of advice to you, my pet," he added as he wrote up the receipt. "Be careful if you mean to take on Vivian Duncan." His voice dipped to *sotto voce* when he spoke the famous wedding planner's name.

"I'm not taking anyone on."

Vivian Duncan, the doyenne of this city's wedding consultants, was a daunting figure in our little pond. She captained an elegantly tight ship and had the power and resources to float quite a few other friendly boats as well. Her favored florists sailed high. Her select bandleaders were booked for years in advance. Her flotilla of favorite caterers found their own bookings equally buoyant.

"Are you sure you're prepared for that war, honey?"

"It's only business," I said.

"Maddie, Maddie, Maddie." Darius tsked about ten times. "She doesn't like people who tell her no. And you, my sweet, are a twenty-something, neatly packaged, bundle of 'no.' "

I love it when people underestimate my age.

"Why must there be any hard feelings?" I asked.

"Madeline, sweetie, look at yourself. *Mirror time!* You look bored to death."

"I do?"

"Thin," he amended, "and bored senseless. What other parties do you have booked? Huh? Why not—at the very least—listen to Vivian's proposal?"

I was, in fact, getting itchy to work. Since my partner, Wesley Westcott, and I had sold off Madeline Bean Catering, it had been rather slow going. After eight frantically busy, terribly fun years, we'd slowed to a crawl. And now, there was this ridiculous litigation going on at the moment, about whether Wes and I were legally allowed to work. Our sales contract contained a standard noncompetition clause, which prevented us from opening any new catering firm soon, but now the new owners were getting testy about us doing any major events-planning work as well. It was maddening.

"I'm just saying, think it over before you dis Vivian

Duncan." Darius added my purchase to my running tab.

I knew perfectly well how that one single woman had dominated elegant L.A. weddings. Vivian Duncan had done almost every celebrity wedding practically since Eddie Fisher had married Connie Stevens. Or was it Liz Taylor? Well, anyway, she had a way of protecting her turf in such a manner that no other name had emerged to challenge her wedding planner domination in decades. There were stories, too. Ill-fated stories. Stephen King–style stories. She had a rep as a fierce businesswoman.

"She gets exactly what she wants." Darius's voice got low again.

I shrugged, amused. In truth, I find it much easier to shrug in amusement since I have recently come into this good deal of money. But then, I wonder if Sophocles would agree that shrugging in amusement, no matter how well-funded, might not be, in itself, a fatal character flaw of Greek tragic proportions.

"Oh, honey!" Darius said, elf eyes atwinkle. "She'll eat you alive." And before I could defend myself, before I could say anything remotely pithy and above-it-all and elegant, Darius handed me my beautiful bowl of roses and turned his twinkle back to the attractive couple who was standing a few feet away, waiting for attention.

Outside Darius's shop, it was another sunny cloudless Beverly Hills afternoon. I shifted my packages. A little thing? Yes. But weren't we talking about just such an insignificant thing as this, one which suddenly has the power to alter life and death? And this one small thing may have made all the difference.

I began switching the heavy vase of flowers to my left arm, while fishing in my shoulder bag, one-handed, for the keys to my car. So I slowed my pace.

Suddenly, startled, I heard the roar.

Before I could jump back, a big black Mercedes screamed down the narrow driveway, leaping out of the back alley, gunning its engine, cutting over the curb, practically striking me. In shock, I spun, losing grip of my keys, losing grip of my purse, and, no! The heavy 'glass vase I'd been holding began to slip. I tried clutching for it, tried to catch my balance, tried . . .

As if in slow motion, I heard a pedestrian shriek. I heard the crashing tinkle of smashed glass. My legs were suddenly drenched, a wave soaking my jeans. I saw in a blur a skyrocket burst of broken crystal, chaotic careening lemons, wildly strewn roses, and then, too close, the alarm of red taillights and a flash of a California license plate.

A vanity plate. It wouldn't be hard to remember. The plate read: I DO.

Chapter 2

*T*ires screeched. Car horns bleated and blared. Amid the chaos, the deadly Mercedes sped down Rodeo. I was stunned, bombarded by a kaleidoscope of color and movement: the massacred centerpiece spread out on the sidewalk, the pavement now a puddle, the roses possibly salvageable, the lemons still rolling into the gutter. Sunlight winked off the shards of glass, crunching below my boots as I took a step back.

"Careful," said a woman, hurrying on. Her hands, I noticed, were clutched up at her mouth.

Looking down, I saw a flash of light glint off my jeans, then another. Tiny bits of broken glass had embedded in the denim. Great. I moved again and heard the tinkle and crunch as my boot ground more glass into the sidewalk. Luckily, I wasn't cut. I bent down and carefully picked up my keys. Shit! What a mess!

Still shocked, I thought I noticed a voice in the background, someone calling. The faint sound came from the direction of the driveway and the back alley parking lot beyond.

"Please . . ."

I stood still, listening hard.

"Help me . . ."

Heedless, now, of the mess, sidestepping one bruised lemon in my path, I quickly rounded the corner, afraid of what I'd find. Shit! Had that lunatic run someone down?

I jogged down the row of parked cars. About one-third of the way down the row, I slowed to a stop. I could hear nothing over the sound of my heart pounding hard. I took a deep breath to slow myself down. No one was there. And then I heard a faint sound. Someone talking.

"Yes, that's right, darling . . ." came the disembodied woman's voice, now speaking quite calmly.

Startled, I walked on behind the parked cars ahead. As I cleared a white Lexus, I now heard more distinctly the sound of low conversation. I looked down.

There, on the asphalt, in a rare empty parking space, a woman in a pink Chanel suit sat splay-legged. Holding a cell phone to one ear, she was talking with an unlit cigarette dangling from her lips.

"Just call and reschedule my five o'clock, Whisper, and don't mother-hen me," she was saying, and then she looked up.

"Thank God," she exhaled, looking me up and down, and then told the cell phone, "Someone's here now. Do what I said, dear," and punched a button to disconnect. To me she said, "Got a goddamn match?"

"Sure," I said, opening my purse, as I took in the unexpected sight of a woman, age fifty-plus, with that hair-matches-the-bag-matches-the-nails look, sitting on the pavement a foot or so away from a rare Beverly Hills oil spot.

"Hell of a day to quit smoking," she said, voice gravelly.

I bent down to hand her a book of matches. "Are you all right? Just a minute ago there was this big Mercedes . . . were you hit?"

The woman took the matches and expertly lit her cigarette, giving me a wink from a surprisingly wrinkle-free eye. "I know you, don't I?" she asked.

"I'm Madeline Bean. I cater parties. Perhaps we've met at one of . . ."

"Of course. Mad Bean Events. Well," she said, "what a coincidence. If you believe in them. I don't. I've met your partner, Wesley." She sat there, puffing on the cigarette. "You don't know who I am at all, do you?"

I looked at her carefully. She was small and a little too tan. On her ears were very expensive jewels. As she withdrew the cigarette from her lips, I noticed it was now stained with that shade of bright magenta pink that had been briefly in fashion in the seventies.

"Vivian Duncan?" I asked, annoyed that I hadn't put it all together at once. I'd seen Vivian in black and white several times. Her photo was often in the *Times*. But now I was rattled. The car. The accident. I was a half-beat off.

Vivian Duncan, I thought, trying hard to get back up to speed. Had Darius known she would be here this afternoon? Is that why he kept me in his shop a little longer? Was I being ambushed?

Vivian stretched a bony hand covered in gemstones at me. "Help me up, dear."

I reached for her hand and pulled gently. She tried to rise, but then I heard her groan and sink back down to the pavement.

"You're injured," I said, still not really understanding what was going on.

"No fussing now, understand? I'm not hurt. Well, not badly. Bruised, most likely. I just need to rest a minute."

"Should I call someone? An ambulance?"

"Of course not. I said no fuss."

"But that car. Did it hit you?"

"Not . . . exactly," Vivian said, her raspy voice an octave lower than mine.

I was struck by a stunning set of impressions. Fine one moment, I now flashed back to a few minutes before. I had almost died. Had that car swerved a few inches closer, it would have certainly torn into me, ripped me open, crushed me.

"That car . . ." I said, trying to regain my composure.

"That car," Vivian spoke up, "was mine."

"It's yours?"

"I had just parked." She looked at me to see if I was going to get hysterical.

I wasn't. "You had just parked?"

She nodded, patting the blacktop upon which she was still semisprawled. "Here."

"You were . . ." I closed my eyes and wondered why my brain, usually a rather speedy processor, had gone blinkish. If I hadn't stopped back there on the sidewalk, just for a brief moment, stopped so I could find my car keys, I would certainly have been run down.

I opened my eyes and stared at Vivian Duncan. ". . . mugged?"

"Car-jacked, I think they call it, don't they? The bastard pushed me so hard I can still feel his filthy hand on me." She felt the smooth pink fabric of her Chanel jacket over her chest and winced.

"We'd better call the police." I reached again to open my purse, but Vivian Duncan cut me off.

"Don't bother, honey." She waved her cell phone. "I've already taken care of it."

"Can I help you stand?"

She exhaled a gust of smoke. "Why the hell not?"

I bent down, trying to support her light frame, holding her behind her shoulders. She didn't weigh much. Soon as I got her on her feet, she stepped away from my arms, righting herself elegantly.

"There, that's not too bad," she said, feeling along her hip, but trying to cover the move with an attempt to lightly pat her skirt clean.

A couple was just approaching their parked car a few yards away and noticed our little scene. My jeans were still rather damp and Vivian was probably the only woman they'd ever seen wearing a soiled designer suit.

"Look. My car is parked just down there. You can have some privacy."

Vivian thought it over and then nodded her delicate, lineless chin. But when she began to move I saw her wince. I slowed down and tried to hold her arm, but she just swore like a sailor, sped up her rocky gait, and threw away her burnt-down cigarette stub.

I unlocked my Grand Wagoneer. But when I walked around the back to help her, Vivian quickly hopped up into the passenger seat before I could reach her.

"Would you like me to stay with you until the police come? Or can I . . . ?"

She lit a new cigarette and pushed the button to roll down her window. On the first exhale, she said, "I have a tabletop demonstration at Darius Floral Design . . ." She checked her gold Van Cleef watch, "Shit! . . . Ten minutes ago. You must know Darius."

"Yes. I was just there. In fact . . ."

"Are you going to listen or are you going to talk?" she asked. "There's a young couple—Sara Silver is the bride. Lovely, lovely girl. I've known her family for years. They're getting married in three weeks and this is the only time they have to make their final choices."

She felt along the edge of her skirt, fingers stopping at a tiny snag. "Ruined. I'm not presentable. I'd like you to go in there and make some excuse."

"Sure. Okay."

"Some excuse that makes me look good, dear. Not some lame 'she was car-jacked' nonsense. You know brides. She's nervous. She's self-obsessed, God love her. And she has every right to be. She's one of *my* brides, and Viv Duncan's brides do not worry about me. I worry about them."

Well, I thought, how nice for them.

"Just do me this favor, Madeline. Just take down Sara's choices. Her groom is Brent Bell. A nobody from nowhere, but a good-looking boy and he makes Sara happy."

I checked my watch. "So you'd like me to take over your tabletop demo. Okay. I can do that."

"Yes, dear, yes." Vivian sighed, her lineless face looking almost pleased with me. "You'll do. Now, run along quickly or they'll never forgive me. I've kept them waiting far too long already. And you know what happens when you leave the bride and groom waiting too long, don't you dear?"

"They start making out?"

"No, dear. They fight. And then, of course, they think having a wedding is not such a marvelous idea after all."

She handed me her fuchsia leather Gucci briefcase, quite an amazing number, and said, "Here's everything you'll need."

I was not quite ready to accuse Vivian Duncan of masterminding this entire hit-and-run production in order to lure me into some business scheme she had running, but then I couldn't exactly ignore the possibility either. I looked into her eyes, hoping to read the truth.

"Run along, Madeline, I'll be fine here. And save my bride."

Chapter 3

A blonde holding a shih tzu was standing at the counter while Darius was on the phone saying, "My, my, my . . ." He gave me a strange look as I reentered the shop. "Yes, Vivian, that *is* most remarkable. She's here now, so don't you worry."

Hanging up, he turned to me and asked, astonished, "What the . . . ? Now you're taking over Vivian Duncan's tabletop?"

In the latest trend among those who plan the city's most expensive weddings, nothing is left to chance. Wedding cakes may be tasted at L.A.'s finest bakeries, caterers hold seasonal tasting dates where clients are served several sample menus, and a day is set aside at the florist for a tabletop demonstration to allow the bride and groom to actually see all their décor choices, from centerpieces to table linens to china and candles.

I held up a pink leather portfolio, the one Vivian had handed me, upon which V.D. was engraved in gold.

"Charming initials," Darius said, with a wink, and gestured to the back of the shop. "The happy couple are waiting in the bridal room."

The blonde, having shifted her weight more than once, ignored me completely as she resumed her conversation with Darius, "So you don't think it would be too pretentious to do orchids?" while I slowly walked to the small room at the back of the flower shop. The tiny space had padded walls, upholstered in white moiré silk, and featured a small, round table set with three white iron dining chairs.

The couple I had seen earlier was occupying two of the chairs. The groom, who seemed to be in his early twenties, was very good looking—tall and fair, with thick curly hair. He wore a black polo shirt tucked into a pair of jeans. Next to him sat his fiancée, Sara Silver, a dark tiny bird of a young woman dressed in designer casual. Neither was smiling.

"Hi. Sorry you've been waiting so long. I'm Madeline Bean."

"Where's Vivian?" asked Sara, not sounding happy.

"Not here, I'm afraid. And you are Sara Silver, the bride?"

"Yes."

"Well, it's a pleasure to meet you. Vivian told me to treat you like royalty this afternoon. You know Vivian. She thinks of you as 'her' bride, and she says her brides should never worry."

"Vivian can be such a fuss," Sara said, starting to thaw.

"She insisted that you have your tabletop demonstration right now, just as you wanted it. Everything must be just as you want, of course, for your big day."

"Oh. Well. But what happened? Why . . . ?"

"Vivian would never complain, of course," I said, lowering my voice a bit, "but, regrettably, it is something that is rather . . . personal."

I took a quick peek at the groom as I settled myself down at the table. When women lower their tone of voice and dart a glance at any males in the room, it's sisterly code for "female problems." The proper response is to quickly drop the subject. I had Sara checkmated and she was kind enough to give me a knowing look and simply say, "Oh."

"Shall we get started?" I opened Vivian's pink portfolio and saw the heading, "Silver-Bell Wedding." Now, really. To cover my amusement, I turned to the cute young guy. "And you are . . ."

"Brent. Brent Bell," said Sara before Brent had a chance to say a word himself.

"Alright, it seems you have made some excellent choices. Your linens . . ." I murmured, looking quickly down the list of specifications for their wedding dinner.

For a moment, my eyes blurred and I felt as if I were looking at myself, at all of us, from a distance. If I hadn't slowed down on the sidewalk, if I'd taken only one more step, what then? I'd be in an ambulance right now, or in a hospital, or in a morgue. Instead, I was talking to a couple of strangers about the color of their napkins. I had been so lucky, I thought to myself. I had been so, so lucky.

". . . don't you think?" Sara was asking when I snapped back to the here and now. Fortunately, she was asking her fiancé. He bit his lower lip.

I looked down at the table between us, which had been swathed in one of the custom tablecloths Vivian had ordered. The fabric was a white hand-beaded tulle from India, it said in the notes. The tiny white beads formed dozens of majestic African elephants and gleamed and sparkled from the luxurious floor-length cloth. The beadwork was shown off as the large, white gauzy square sat over an underskirt of khaki linen.

"It's too bumpy," the bride said, smoothing her hand over the cloth.

I looked at the napkins. What had Vivian been thinking? How were you to wipe your mouth on tissue-weight fabric sprinkled with beads?

"These are the most amazing tablecloths I've ever seen. But if you object to the feel of the napkins, let's see the effect we get with plain damask." I busied myself, pulling a selection of linen options from the case provided by the rental supply company, and proceeded to conduct the meeting with only part of my brain. The other part kept wandering back to the miracle of being alive.

Looking down the list I noticed the couple had invitations out to 225, with 188 RSVP's in, and were to be married on June tenth, in three weeks time, with the ceremony and reception held at L.A.'s Museum of Nature. That alone caught my eye. Of all the venues available for rental for private parties, the museum was one of the most magnificent and most costly.

"So, are you satisfied with all of these choices?" I asked, finally, after we'd gone down the list of china and crystal and Darius had brought in several mock-ups of the floral centerpieces he could create.

Once again, Sara turned to her groom and asked, "Is this okay, Brent?" Darius, who was hanging around just outside the tiny room, and I also looked at Brent, who had remained passively silent throughout the display.

"Well?" asked Sara, sounding exasperated. "This is your wedding, too. Don't you have anything to say?"

"Whatever you like, Sara," he finally said. "If this makes you happy, I'm happy. I'm happy, even if it did cost your grandfather four thousand bucks for those beaded napkins you just threw away. It's not a problem."

Uh oh.

"If it's not a problem, then why did you bring it up?" she asked, her dark eyes getting quickly wet.

"Because you pushed me to say something, Sar."

"I pushed you? I *pushed* you? Do you think I'm pushing you into this wedding? How dare you say such a horrible, nasty thing in front of all these people?"

I believe she meant us, and at that moment I sincerely wished I could excuse myself from the claustrophobic space.

Darius, the rat, piped up a soft, "Excuse me," and vanished back to the front of his shop, leaving me with the happy couple.

"Maybe you're just not ready," Sara said, tears threatening. "Two years we've been together, college is out next week. But maybe you're not sure yet."

Brent Bell did not look at Sara and this seemed to work her up to a more anxious level of alarm.

"Oh my God!" she said, with a trace of a sob. "Do you want to call this wedding off?"

"Of course not," Brent said, mildly.

"I think you do!" she yelled, standing. She was very beautiful, in an exotic dusky way. And as she worked herself up, her black hair bounced. "Here you are, and it's just days before our wedding, and you humiliate me in front of all these people. How am I supposed to feel?" She turned to me. "He stopped talking about the wedding weeks ago. He just turned off. We went to taste wedding cake and that was the last time he said boo about our plans."

Can there be any doubt in anyone's mind why I am simply not cut out to counsel young brides?

Brent spoke up. "Sar, you don't want my advice. Okay? You just want to drag me along. That's fine. Here I am. Only don't suggest you are going to listen to me, okay?"

She didn't answer him but directed her comments to me, getting worked up with each word. "He wanted chocolate! For the wedding cake! Great idea, huh? Well, I'm *allergic* to chocolate and he knows it. So what does that say about how he feels about me?" Her nose began to drip as she cried.

"Then why do you ask me?" Brent started getting steamed. "It's my wedding too, right? And I happen to like chocolate. Aren't I supposed to have anything I like?"

She needed a tissue, and I didn't have one nearby, so I held out the white damask napkin. She took it and wiped her face.

"I'm going to give you folks a little privacy to iron out your plans," I said, taking my only opening to get the hell out of there.

"No! Wait. I think this wedding is canceled," Sara said, her eyes on Brent.

"Is that what you really want?" he asked her, hurt but subdued.

"What *I* want? Of course not! I love you. I want to

marry you. But you don't want to marry me, do you? *Do you*?"

"You think I don't want to marry you?" he asked, finally getting a little heated up. "Then why do you think I'm going through all this?"

"You're impossible!" Sara yelled. " 'Going *through all this*?' *This* is our wedding! You're supposed to *love* going through all this!" She turned to me, "Isn't he?"

"Sara. Brent. I don't know the two of you. I don't know if you have been happy together or miserable. I don't know if you have family troubles or career troubles or money troubles or health troubles."

They both looked at me, listening. I can't imagine why. Having a big eight years on them, I must have looked like an older and wiser soul. Or maybe they were both ready for someone, anyone, to talk them back down. With my recent brush with death, I was full of things to say.

"What I do know is that we have only got this instant in time. There are no guarantees that any of us will have months and years and decades ahead of us to make mistakes and fix them and learn from them. We might, any of us, be hit by a car walking out of this shop." Okay, so you knew that one was coming. Hey, I was freaked.

"So what are you going to do? Are you going to drive yourselves crazy? Or are you going to take what life offers and make it sweet?

"I'm a party planner, but believe me when I tell you, *parties do not matter*. So don't wig out, okay? This whole wedding thing should really be about, well, love."

Like I really know, I thought, as I stood back up. I was shaking a little, I can't imagine why. This cursed wedding-consulting business was so over-the-top emotional!

"I *do* love you, Sar," Brent said, putting an arm around her.

"Oh, Brent, honey," Sara said, clinging.

I quickly left them to sort it all out.

"Is it off?" Darius asked when I came up to the counter.

"Don't know. But I am not cut out for the wedding planner game. What do I know about it? I don't know if those two ought to be getting married!"

"So-o-o," Darius said, smiling, "Now tell me what *really* happened with Vivian Duncan."

"Why don't *you* tell me? Little coincidence, huh, Vivian showing up at your shop right when I'm here, and you talking to me so tenderly about me taking over her business?"

"Oh, Maddie. She did ask me to invite you over here this afternoon. She was planning to get here a little earlier and ask you to consider joining her team or whatever. But what went on there, outside, with that horrible car and whatever? I have no idea!"

"Maybe just a freak accident," I said, wondering what to believe. "Or maybe . . ."

At that moment we were approached by what might or might not be the Silver-Bell wedding couple.

"Madeline, please excuse us," Sara said, smiling. Brent hung back but seemed more relaxed. "We've decided you are right. We are going ahead with our plans. Hey, who says things should be perfect?"

"Well, actually, Maddie usually does," piped in Darius.

"Now, now," I said, trying to avoid any more doubts. "I've got an idea that is very exciting, very current, and it might help heal the wedding cake blues. The latest thing is to have the bakery make each layer of the wedding cake out of different kinds of cake, but still covered with the same frosting. Like a secret. Might that work for you, Sara?"

"How cute!" she said, turning to Brent. "You could have your chocolate cake."

"Yeah," he said, looking at me with a smile.

"Fine, I'll let Vivian know and she'll contact the bakery."

Ms. Silver and Mr. Bell walked out, arm in arm, and

Darius let out a low whistle. "Watch out, Vivian Duncan, a powerhouse of new age wisdom and the latest cake trends is among us! Is there anything, my dear, you cannot do?" With that he reached over the counter and presented me with a fabulous gift—a duplicate of the flower arrangement I'd earlier lost grip of, only this time done in the palest lavender roses above a bubble vase filled with limes.

"It's fantastic," I said. "The colors are amazing. Better than the last one, even."

"Cut flowers," Darius said, looking at the lavender blooms. "In the sixteenth-century Flemish paintings, they represented the transitory nature of life. You know, cut down in its bloom. Beautiful one moment and dead and rotting the next."

"Darius," I said, shaking my head. "You . . . are . . . so . . . damn . . . *up!*"

Chapter 4

At the end of a charming cul-de-sac, in the historic Whitley Heights section of the Hollywood Hills, amid a dozen pale stucco houses designed in the early thirties when residential architecture had real style, sits my little abode. Smack next to a retaining wall. Smack next to the 101 Freeway. In Hollywood Hills real estate, charm was either very expensive or extremely noisy.

Climbing up my front steps, the mighty river of rushing cars can be heard if not seen. But inside, door shut, the roar of traffic becomes instantly muffled. Darling though it is, this is not a house in which one may carelessly throw open a window. True.

Yet, I love the place. Adorable and affordable, my Spanish charmer has a pedigree that goes back to its original owner, a silent film comedian who was famed for his googly eyes.

"Holly? Wes?" I called.

The lower level of my house has been converted to suit my business, with offices where the original living and dining rooms were, and a largely remodeled kitchen, which can withstand the industrial-sized cooking assignments we love. Upstairs, I've converted the space into my private quarters.

I checked my watch as I walked through the empty entry hall, past Holly's deserted desk and computer. Six-fifty. I just couldn't wait to tell them about meeting Vivian Duncan. They'd die.

"Anybody home?"

As I turned on a light in my office, I detected the excellent aromas of frying olive oil and perhaps ham, wafting from the direction of the kitchen. Dropping my purse and Vivian's pink portfolio onto my desk, I heard Wes's voice calling. I hefted the bowl of lavender roses and headed toward the voice.

In the kitchen, I felt at once relaxed and restored. The bright lights gleamed off all the shiny white tiles, the brushed aluminum appliances, and the worn butcher-block countertops. My two friends were here, huddled at the large, marble-topped island in the center of the room.

"We didn't know *when* you would be home," Holly said, looking up, a cup of coffee in her hand. "Ooh, great flowers!" She pushed her stick-straight bangs back off her forehead and looked a bit anxious. "We started to make dinner, hope you don't freak."

"Moi? Freak?" How well they knew me.

Holly grinned. Standing with one hand on top of her head, white-blond hair pulled back off her forehead, this beanpole of a young woman was stretched to her fullest height, a height that was formidable enough even without the three-inch open-toed wedgies she was wearing at the moment.

"Anything left for me to do?" I asked, trying for nonchalant rather than freaky. I love to roll my sleeves up and become consumed in the, okay, I know it's hokey, the joy of cooking.

"Of course," Wes said, sticking his head up from the magazine he'd been consulting. "We were just doing *Bon Appetit* roulette. Why don't you take the main course, sweetie?"

I keep an enormous stack of cooking magazines, back issues for years. Sometimes, we just close our eyes and open the page and make whatever we land on. Apparently Holly had just gotten back from the market.

"Great," I said, looking at the recipe Wes was reading. "Great." I gave him a little hug.

Wesley Westcott is my right hand. Or perhaps I should say I'm his. We met just after I finished studying at the Culinary Institute in San Francisco about nine years ago, and have stuck like glue to each other ever since. I was working as the lowest sous chef at a celebrated foodie haunt up in Berkeley, paying my dues, and loving it. Wes was finishing up his Ph.D. in comparative intelligences, or something obscure, and he talked me into moving down to L.A. to see if we could start our own firm, catering big Hollywood parties and even working at the studios, catering meals for the stars.

I thought it was a radical idea. I'd been very wrapped up in my own bitter love life at the time. In fact, I'd been dumped by a chef. And a major move southward was the perfect escape. In this way, a new career was born, and Wes and I have been together to this day. I vowed never again to let romance enter into the picture when I was cooking, and with Wesley Westcott, I'd been able to develop the best relationship I've ever had with a man.

"What's this? *Paella*?" I asked, reading from the page they had marked. "Oh, the *pungent* taste of *saffron*!" I did a rather good Julia Child impersonation.

"But," Wes insisted, as I read through the recipe, "we're not putting in that many onions."

"I'm making the salad," Holly said, bending down to whisper in my ear. "Mad, honey, I think Wesley's taste buds are getting totally ghetto."

"As in . . . ?" I had gotten lost. Holly Nichols needed to come with her own glossary. Updated daily.

"Oh," Wes said, airily, "skateboarder talk. She's dissin' me. Thinks I can't hack the stronger spices." Wes retied the white chef's apron he wore over his denim shirt and dungarees. "Use however many onions you want to, board girl." He picked up another magazine and flipped the page, reading. "I'll do the cake."

The fun of cooking is enhanced, I think, when you

can do it with friends. And as I poured good olive oil into the heavy enameled pan, I began to gather my ingredients. First thing to do was finish sautéing the hot Cajun sausages. I loved the aroma and hiss of it all. While they were losing their inner pink, I lined up a dozen chicken thighs and a few dozen large shrimp, and began cleaning and chopping an onion (who needs two?) and peeling the dozen garlic cloves I'd use later.

"What took you so long?" Wes asked, always needing details. He turned the bowl of pale lavender roses around, checking them with his discerning eye. "You made it to Beverly Hills and got the full Darius treatment. And then . . . ?"

"What a weird afternoon," I said, as I removed the sausage and added the chicken, skin side down, to the hot pan. Holly handed me the lid and I covered the thighs to let them cook gently through.

"I met Vivian Duncan."

"No shit!"

Holly was standing next to me at the industrial eight-burner range, sprinkling oregano over a mixture of baguette cubes and coarsely chopped prosciutto. When she thought I wasn't looking, she swiped a few peeled cloves of garlic and tossed them into her pan.

"Hey!"

"So you met Vivian Duncan," Wes said, eyes gleaming. "Was blood drawn?"

"It's a pretty strange story. She had her car stolen in broad daylight right from the alley behind the shops on Rodeo. Right near Darius. She was so shook up she asked me to take over a client meeting for her. Isn't that odd? I mean, we work in this town for all these years and I've never ever run into her, and then all of a sudden there she was, sitting on the pavement with a huge run in her pantyhose."

"She was car-jacked?" Holly asked. "I give up. I mean, you hear about those things happening," she said, shaking her white-blond wisps, "but when old broads can't get a manicure in B.H. without getting mugged, it's too much. We should move."

"Away from L.A.?" I moved in for a surreptitious taste of Holly's *migas,* the Spanish starter of ham fried with garlicky breadcrumbs she'd been stirring up. She caught me and shooed me off.

"Well, we can't leave town yet," Wes said, diffidently, as he buttered his third cake pan and began mincing orange peel. "We've been invited to a wedding."

"What?" I spun and looked at him.

"My, what a coincidence," he said, chuckling. "While you were out, we got a phone call from that man who works with Vivian Duncan. Ted Pettibone."

"You're kidding," I said.

"What do they all call him?" Holly asked. In the small world of caterers and party planners and restauranteurs, the gossip factor was appallingly high, and I had to admit, Holly was responsible for a fair share of it.

"Whisper," Wes said. "Those who know him well call him Whisper Pettibone, although I don't know why. He spoke in a perfectly civil tone on the phone."

"Maybe he whispers sweet nothings in Vivian's ear," chuckled Holly, as she washed the arugula and romaine.

"Not even a possibility," Wes said, enjoying his fair share of gossip, too. "Vivian's married to that handsome man who doesn't do anything. Doesn't really work, I mean. And they have a grown daughter, don't they? But anyway, no matter what Vivian might be up to, Whisper is a, well, a *confirmed bachelor.*"

"Oh," said Holly.

"Oh," I said.

I added the cooked chicken to the bowl of cooked sausage, and began sautéing the chopped onion and garlic cloves. Recalling the recent garlic theft, I quickly peeled and chopped two more cloves.

"Did Whisper Pettibone invite us to the Silver-Bell wedding?" I asked, intrigued.

"The what?" Holly asked.

"June tenth at the Museum of Nature," Wes confirmed, as he moved to the food processor to mix together his dry ingredients—flour, baking powder, salt, and a cup of almonds.

"Sara Silver and Brent Bell. That's the couple I met with today," I explained to Holly. "Isn't it sweet that they wanted to invite us to their wedding?"

"Where in the museum are they getting married?" Holly asked. "Not in the Hall of Dinosaurs! That is so nug!"

"Nug?" I looked to Wes for translation but he only shrugged.

"Man, I love fossils," Holly said, excited. "The *Triceratops* was a plant-eater, did you know that?"

"Is that so?" Wes commented dryly. "Well, there will be no *paella* for that, uh, *bad boy*."

"I've always wanted to do a big event at the Museum of Nature." I added freshly sliced tomatoes and a couple of bay leaves to the cooking vegetables. "It is awfully cool."

"It is awfully expensive," Wes noted, as he continued to whir various sweet ingredients into his batter. "Didn't we look into renting that place for a wrap party one time, Mad?"

"Right. It's over ten grand just to get in the door, plus thousands for each additional room you need. It's fabulous but it's a hassle. They have a gazillion restrictions and rules and fire codes. Anyway, this couple, Sara Silver and Brent Bell, were going through a bit of a crisis today. Actually, I'm glad to hear they're over it."

I added a sliced red bell pepper to the pan and heard the delightful crackle as cold veggie hit sizzling oil. Heaven.

I quickly stirred arborio rice into the cooked tomato and peppers, while I turned down the heat under a pot of chicken broth simmering with paprika and saffron.

Wesley came over to lend a hand.

Holly sliced the sausage into nice thick diagonals, and tossed them in, and Wes began adding the cooked chicken to the rice mixture. I topped it by carefully pouring the hot chicken broth over all. With a tight twist of heavy-duty aluminum foil to seal in the steam and juices, Wesley lifted the heavy pan into the oven. Wes and Holly each went back to their own workstations, jobs still to do, but I was ready for a break.

"So it's going to be a fabulous wedding," Holly prompted, trying to pick up the thread of our conversation.

My refrigerator is never without a stash of Diet Coke and I poured myself a glass and got back to the tale of my day. "I hope so. They seemed like a very nice couple. And they have no discernable problem spending money."

Holly put her salad greens in the refrigerator to crisp up and said, dreamily, "I love that in a man."

"Well, then, I think you'd have a crush on the bride's grandfather. Apparently he's paying for it all."

Forty minutes passed while the savory *paella* simmered in the oven, spreading its marvelous scent of the Mediterranean. I stirred rich chocolate icing as Wesley finished up baking his orange-almond cake, and Holly happily filled us in on all the latest news she'd unearthed in her amazingly stealthy way.

The phone rang just as I was adding the garlic-marinated shrimp to my nicely cooking *paella*, so Holly answered.

"Mad," she said, "it's for you. *Whisper* Pettibone."

Wes put the cakes on the cooling racks and turned to listen.

Wiping my hands and placing the *paella* back into the oven, I took the receiver.

"Hello."

"Is this Madeline Bean?"

"Yes."

"We've never met, but I know you were with Vivian this afternoon. I hope you don't mind that I am calling."

"Why, no."

"I work with Vivian and of course she called me this afternoon, right after she ruined her wonderful suit. And, as I'm sure you know, replacing this season's Chanel suit in a size four is simply impossible. But we'll get over it. She told me the angels had sent you from heaven to take over her tabletop."

I doubted the angels in heaven were too worried about Vivian's party-planning schedule, but I thought it rude to make any such comment.

"The point is, Vivian stopped back for a moment to change clothes, naturally, but now she's off again. And she is not answering her phone. I'm simply desperate to find her."

"I beg your pardon?"

"Sorry. Is she with you?"

"Sorry," I said, imitating his precise way of speaking without thinking. "No."

"Oh. I see. Terribly sorry to burden you. Don't give it another thought." And then the man hung up.

"Vivian is missing?" Wes asked, a furrow creasing his normally smooth brow. Wesley was as thin as they come, and had that thick brown hair that stuck out with a little prompting and the right sort of gel.

"Apparently. And I'm getting a bad feeling. Suddenly, Vivian Duncan is all over my life. She even wants us to buy her wedding business."

Wes shot me an everyone-has-a-good-idea-what-we-should-do-with-our-windfall look.

"I know, but with all the ruckus, and then that poor woman looking pretty bruised, well, I never got it settled that we weren't interested. Don't worry. I will."

"First someone steals her car, then she gets lost. That woman is having a terrible, no good, very bad day," Holly said. Then she put the final touches on her salad, tossing the greens with marinated artichoke hearts and vinegar, adding fresh goat cheese, and topping it all with the *migas*. I had to admit, it looked spectacular.

"Let's eat," I said, pulling my *paella* out of the oven and peeling back the foil. A heady steam of saffron scented shrimp arose from the pan.

I looked up to Wes for some approval, but he seemed

lost in some other thought. A little tic played around his eyes. In the past, Wesley could always sense trouble. He had that exact look about him.

But, it was almost nine. I was hungry. And, let's be real. Who wanted to stop to think out what kind of trouble might be coming tomorrow when such a lovely meal awaited us tonight?

Chapter 5

*T*hree weeks squirmed by. I was not amused by the idleness of being out of work, and the only diversion from the monotony seemed to be the occasional phone calls from attorney Paul giving updates on the lawsuit that was crawling along. It appeared that Five Star Studios wanted to go to court. While they had no interest in the food business, their lawyers showed a litigious zest for keeping me from competing with my former, and now defunct, company. At least that's what I think Paul said.

When Wesley and I had taken Five Star's money for my old, and at the time, very much out-of-favor catering company, we'd agreed not to start a new company that would compete in the same field. It had seemed reasonable at the time. They'd given us nearly three million dollars for a business that was sinking.

But Wes and I had never intended to retire. We'd always dreamed of going beyond cooking alone, so we focused our energy on a new firm that allowed us to create entire events. We began Mad Bean Events a few months ago. Our kickoff extravaganza was a sit-down breakfast for thousands in honor of the pope's visit to Los Angeles. Of course, we did that one for free.

In our, well, enthusiasm, shall we say, we dismissed any thought of Five Star. In our minds, at least, we were no longer "caterers." After all, we weren't actually cooking. Instead, we subcontracted a caterer for the event. And besides all that, Five Star had never had any intention of operating a catering business. It's a long, strange story, but they had been "negotiated" into buying us out.

In the year since, they never so much as opened an office or hired a staff. Madeline Bean Catering was now only a name on their books to them. And a fond memory to us.

And, hell. We figured they'd never notice.

It seems, however, that Five Star Studios had not built up a three-floor legal department simply to intimidate their producers and their distributors. On the odd day when business was slow, they felt perfectly happy to use their lawyers to harass Wes and me, too. Hence, the nasty slump in Mad Bean Events after the heady triumph of entertaining the pope.

After that very high profile success, our phones were ringing. We were approached by several of L.A.'s leading celebrity fundraisers. In one week, we'd been moved from nowhere to the "A" list. Million dollar events that only last year we hadn't been able to bid on as caterers, we were now being invited to run. And at the height of this explosive launch of our new, improved, events-planning firm, entered the angry giant. Five Star Studios appeared waving lawsuits and announced we had already breached our contract when we put on the lavish party for the pontiff.

"Who was that?" Wes asked, looking up as I cradled the phone. We were in our office, an airy room with French doors out to the courtyard that used to be my home's dining room. We sat facing each other at a huge double-sized old partner's desk. Such antique charm costs an arm and a leg—the very same arm and leg that was currently being fought over by lawyers.

"Money," I muttered.

"Yes?"

"You know," I said, rubbing one finger along the edge of the desk, appreciating the warm, expensive patina. This large noble desk had been our one splurge, and it had only been ours for a few weeks. "Root of all evil."

"The lawsuit. No progress?" Wes asked, taking an easy guess at the state of things in lawyer-land.

"Seems Five Star is feeling generous. They're leaning towards forgiving our historic reception for the pope."

"Forgive us? Could they have possibly been influenced by the fact that they don't have a frigging leg to stand on? We didn't cook. We didn't charge a fee. We . . ."

"Yes. They have been told. And for the moment they are not threatening to press for damages on that *one party*."

Wes looked at me across the desk with a pained expression. "So they are beginning to be reasonable?"

"You know better than that," I said, daring him to smile. "Actually, my friend Brother Xavier called a friend of his at the Vatican, and he arranged . . ."

"What? To have all the nasty Five Star executives excommunicated!"

". . . *he arranged*," I said with emphasis, ignoring the interruption, "for Mrs. President of Five Star Studios to take a VIP tour of the Vatican Museum."

"I can't believe this. We were saved by art."

"Something like that. However," I continued, rubbing my scalp, "Wesley, they aren't going to drop their main lawsuit. They're hung up on the fact that we blatantly started a competing business. And even though they are wrong, they have so much money and so many lawyers on their payroll, they don't have to drop it. Paul says they can drag this on for years, even if they end up being proved dead wrong."

"Yeah, but why jump all over little guys like us? There's got to be a reason they won't let go. What do they want?" Wes asked, resigned.

"Their three million dollars back, probably."

Wes swallowed. "Oh, boy." He looked around, taking in the photo of the two of us standing with the pope, each of us holding a crystal glass containing strawberry smoothies. That was some breakfast bash.

"But we don't have all that money anymore."

I nodded. We had spent a lot on the pope's party, all donated to the cause. In addition, I had paid off my home's mortgage, part of which was a business expense. We'd bought a few pieces of furniture, as a treat.

"And," Wes continued, "we can't go out and earn back the money unless they give us permission to work."

We had been over this road more than a few times. It was always more or less gruesome.

"Our only option is to buy an existing company with the money we have left and build it up," Wes said, not for the first time.

I may have groaned. For months, I had been getting calls from every barely break-even food service company in L.A., and I was not interested. With the rumors floating around town of our new fortune, we were being pecked to death by a flock of hungry business owners wanting out. Under these circumstances, it was not surprising that Vivian Duncan, a woman who had never spoken to me in the past, was courting me big time.

"Please, Wes, don't say we have to become wedding planners. I don't think I could face many more jittery brides."

"No, dear." He smiled at me. Wesley has a very handsome chin, and the rest of his face wasn't bad either. His thick dark hair was currently cut like a brush, which I find slightly GI, but on him it worked. As always, he was immaculately dressed. Today, he wore a simple light denim shirt and khakis, but on his tall thin frame it looked elegant.

"We are not about to pay over two million dollars for a business that would give you hives."

"Well, thank God for that, at least."

"You ever hear where Vivian disappeared to that night Whisper called?"

"Not my business. Actually, I've been avoiding giving her the big N-O."

"You ever gonna tell her?"

I took a deep breath. "I hate to disappoint people. I

end up getting so worked up that when I finally talk to them, I blow it."

"Mad," Wes said, looking at me kindly. "Just say no."

"I've got to tell her tonight."

"Whoa, whoa, whoa! Tonight? You're going to confront Vivian Duncan with the news that we will not buy her business at the humungoid wedding of the century? You really think that's going to be the best moment to give her a pass?"

In Hollywood, we avoid mentioning words that sound too much like rejection. Series are not cancelled, anymore. They are "rotated out of the schedule." A T.V. project is not "turned down"; it's "passed" on. Almost sounds like a compliment.

"I've been trying to get my nerve up to tell her for weeks," I said, "but we keep missing each other on the phone. I'll just have to tell her tonight. If I can get her alone."

A slow smile spread across Wesley's face. "You got the guts?"

"Please," I said.

Wes regarded me but let it slide. Instead he said, "Holly will be happy. She's never seen a Vivian Duncan wedding spectacular in person."

"We can't disappoint our Holly," I said, standing.

"Is this my cue to leave?" Wes looked at his watch.

I looked at mine. Three-thirty. "I better get ready. We have to be at the Museum of Nature at six."

"I know. Holly is taking this thing pretty seriously. She's actually gone to the Brandon Hoskins Salon for a Day of Beauty."

That stopped me. Our hip-hop assistant was spending a day being manicured and pedicured and, in all likelihood, getting various parts of her body seaweed-wrapped. I almost pitied the poor salon.

Laughing for maybe the first time all afternoon, I felt some of the heavy pressure lift. "This wedding could be fun."

Chapter 6

I don't care what your mother taught you. If you are ever invited to a California wedding, wear black. Everyone does. Black is now equally appropriate for attending weddings or funerals and, frankly, for all occasions to which you must look five pounds thinner in between. Black is so cool, so classic, so slenderizing, that more and more brides are selecting gowns in basic black for their bridesmaids. Go ahead, pack a rose-colored dress if you must, but wear the black. You'll thank me for it.

The L.A. Museum of Nature is located near USC, set back on a public square. It's in a part of south central Los Angeles to which most of Sara Silver's wedding guests rarely venture after dark. It was past the museum's closing time. The vast adjacent parking lots were empty. But all things considered, no thoughtful bride would expect her friends and relatives to walk the lonely half-block from the parking lot to the museum entrance. Not wearing their finest jewelry. Not at night. Not in that neighborhood.

Wesley pulled smoothly up to the curb where a platoon of parking attendants, wearing crisp white shirts, stood ready for our arrival.

"I'm starving," Holly said.

"Down, Holly," Wes said. "They're valets, not hors d'ouvres."

As we stepped out of Wes's car, Holly and I took a

quick moment to straighten out our attire. Holly wore a long, black, strapless tube dress that glittered in the streetlights. Its metallic threads of elastic quilting molded the dress to her tall, slender form. The hors d'oevr . . . the valet parkers noticed.

Wes came around to check us out.

"Subdued," he commented to Holly, noting her bright red lipstick. She is the one among us who likes to take the occasional fashion leap. Then he turned to me, checking out the severe black silk dress, scooped low in front, that had cost me a fortune.

"I think," Wes pronounced in a whisper, "you may single-handedly bring back cleavage as an art form."

Holly, tottering on extremely high-heeled sandals, turned away from our discussion of my chest with hunting-dog-on-a-scent alert.

"Maddie! Was that Brad Pitt?" She strained to see the dimly lit form of a young man walking far ahead of us, as he disappeared into the giant entryway of the Museum of Nature.

"I'm *dying!* Brad Pitt! Is he a guest?" Holly pulled at her short, blond, spiky bangs.

We followed Holly, who had picked up her pace to a trot, veering around the spotlit and dramatic bronze replica of the museum's most famous artifact that had recently been installed out in front of the entrance. The statue showed dinosaurs, under attack. At night, the aggressive forms looked beautiful, the bronze gleaming in the indirect lighting.

I scanned past the building ahead of us, but not for celebrities. Wes stopped next to me and said, "The tent must be out back."

"Yes. Behind the far wing," I agreed. As caterers, we were both intrigued by the logistics of setting up a temporary kitchen large enough to serve dinner to 200 demanding guests. The museum is a star location, but its kitchen facilities are not available for private functions.

Up ahead, Holly stopped just past the sculpture and turned to us, impatient. "*Guys!*"

"I guess we'll check out the catering setup later," Wes suggested.

"Possible Pitt sighting," I agreed.

Holly had already walked up to the sixteen-foot-tall pavilion door and entered the three-story domed marble foyer. Two private security guards stood at the door, checking invitations against the guest list. I thought again of the expense of leasing this magnificent space for a private party.

Once in the grand foyer, I was stunned by the success of the decoration.

"Awesome," Holly whispered.

Several huge potted trees had been brought in for the party, each ablaze with hundreds of tiny twinkling white lights, glimmering in the semidark hall.

Instead of using the museum's fluorescent overheads, a lighting designer had been brought in to create a custom look for the event. Baby spotlights picked out the gold leaf detail in the forty-foot-tall rotunda ceiling. A hammered-silver bar had been set up at the far side of the foyer, lit with covered lamps, making each bottle of gin look like a glowing jewel, each row of glassware a sparkling necklace. In a further corner, an African drum band was playing an exotic rhythm, lit up on their low riser by perfect stage lighting.

Several dozen guests had already arrived, and, as Holly scanned the crush of tuxedoed men for a tousled blond head, even more new arrivals flowed past us. Each wedding guest appeared mesmerized by the brilliant effect; the light and dark shadows played against the breathtaking architecture. Surely most had visited during daylight hours. Struggling with maps and nephews and crowds, had any of us really noticed the beauty of the place, the spectacular columns, the inlaid marble mosaics on the floor?

Of course, the one sight I did remember quite clearly from prior daytime sightseeing was the centerpiece of the foyer. With the sound of tribal African music rendered by fine musicians on drums and reed flutes in the background, I turned to gaze at the museum's most famous display. Mimicking the new bronze sculpture in the courtyard were the fossilized bones of an enormous *Triceratops* rearing back, arranged in a fearful pose. Roaring over this beast was a skeletal *T-rex* positioned in vicious attack, its six-foot jaws open, its huge fangs like daggers.

The entire installation rose over twenty feet high on a black marble base. In the semidarkness of the room, spotlights threw fierce shadows onto the floor.

"Maddie," Wes said, catching my attention. I moved from the dinosaur display and joined him at a white-skirted table not far away. "Unusual location for a romantic ceremony. Very original. Who's the bride, again? A *Jurassic Park* fan?"

"Her family are big benefactors of the museum," I said.

"Ah, yes." He nodded. "Money talks."

Wes was standing at a table skirted in mosquito netting which held an awesome display of genuine Beanie Babies. A few hundred miniature beanbag leopards sat at the ready, each with a card tied around his neck with black satin ribbon.

"Are these the escort cards?" I asked, reaching out to the Beanie Baby Wesley was holding up to me.

"They're a special limited edition," Wes said, checking another one out.

"Amazing." A calligrapher had written the names of each guest and their table assignment on the cards tied to the necks of these collectible treasures.

Holly appeared, looking disappointed. "It wasn't Brad Pitt." She made a face. "I think it was Kato Kaelin."

"It's going to be a long night," I advised my star-struck assistant. "Hang in there."

Wes handed her a seven-inch leopard from the table. "Cheer up. Look at this."

"Holy shit! I can't believe it. This is a Beanie I've never seen before." She checked out its tiny label. "And it's for real!"

"Charming touch, aren't they?"

We all looked up to see Vivian Duncan, smiling broadly at us. She looked better than the last time I'd seen her. More upright.

Vivian explained, "Those were made for us and only us by the Ty company. Sara wanted to have something extra-special for all her guests to enjoy. Nice, eh? I tell you Madeline, you're going to love working with my clientele. They have so much to offer you."

"Vivian," I said. "I know you're busy right now, but I've been . . ."

"Darling girl," Vivian said, grabbing my arm warmly in her tight grip, "introduce me to your friends. Wesley I know." She smiled a dazzling faux smile in the direction of Wes and then focused on Holly.

"Holly Nichols," I said.

Holly, trying to do the right thing, held out her hand.

At that moment, Vivian disengaged herself from clutching my arm and swiftly turned toward a waiter who had just passed.

"Marco?" she said in an unpleasantly tense voice, her gravelly whisper almost coming out a hiss.

She caught herself and turned back to our group once more.

Holly said, "Miss Duncan, I'm . . ."

"Must run," Vivian said brightly to me, flashing me a tight smile. "See you later, Madeline. We must have our attorneys get together. Soon, okay?" And she turned quickly towards Marco's retreating back, leaving without so much as looking again at Holly or Wes.

I turned to Wes, almost smiling. "*Must run?*"

"*Must* drink." Wes pointed us towards the bar in the corner.

"*Must* barf," commented Holly, hiking up her strapless tube dress.

"*Must* drop the bomb," I added, trying to catch up with the pair making a beeline for the booze.

Ahead, at the bar, I noticed an unhappy-looking man, his thinning hair combed straight back from his tall, tan forehead. Wire-rimmed glasses winked in the subdued lighting, and as we approached he seemed to clear his throat. I looked at him and got the feeling he expected me to recognize him.

"Miss Bean, isn't it?" he asked in a low, smooth voice. I recognized the voice.

"Mr. Pettibone." So this was Vivian's aide-de-camp.

"At last we meet," he said, with a smile. It was meant, I think, to be charming, but came off as sinister.

"This is my friend and partner, Wesley Westcott," I introduced, as Holly began to order our drinks from the bartender. "And that's Holly Nichols. What a wonderful party."

"Yes," Pettibone said, not making eye contact with either of my friends. "So." He smiled again, and then whispered, "Do you actually imagine you could handle such a magnificent wedding as this one on your own?"

Wes was helping Holly get the drinks, and I realized I was the only one who could hear Pettibone's remark.

I turned to face him. "Ex*cuse* me?" This bozo was taking me on.

"Doubtful," he said softly, smile intact, and moved closer to my ear. "But, perhaps you are smart enough not even to try it."

"How rare it is these days to find open hostility. And you do it quite well, I must add."

"Why, thank you," Ted "Whisper" Pettibone replied pleasantly.

" 'Thank you' for what?" Holly asked as she rejoined us. Then she announced, "Shampoo!" and handed me a crystal flute of bubbly.

"Miss Bean thinks a lot of herself. I wish her luck. Is she courageous? Or simply foolish?" Pettibone's eyes darted away and then he murmured, "Vivian needs me. I'm sure we'll talk again, later," and quickly left.

"What was that?" Holly asked, sipping her "shampoo."

"Territorial bullshit." Wes appeared annoyed.

"He does not seem like a happy camper," I agreed. "I wonder how much Vivian has told him?"

By now, most of the guests had arrived in the grand foyer—a swirl of tuxedoed men and thin women in black designer dresses. The insistent, sexy drumbeat of tribal Africa swelled in the background beneath the happy, chattering roar. Glasses tinkled, relatives laughed, waiters sweated, future in-laws air-kissed, bachelors drank, Beanie Babies were snatched up, and teenage girls giggled, while the movements of the occasional semicelebrity punctuated the scene, followed more or less discreetly by so many pairs of eyes.

One group of movers and shakers I recognized included a man who owned a Cadillac dealership, a man who owned a bank, and a man who owned a football team and a lot of real estate south of Los Angeles. But the business community held no interest for Holly. Just as I was worrying that she might trail George Hamilton into the men's room, I caught sight of Vivian sending Whisper Pettibone away on some errand. This might be the best time to get to the woman. The wedding ceremony would start in another fifteen minutes. If I caught her now I could finally tell her Wes and I were not buying any wedding consultant firm—including hers.

Pushing through the crowd, I tried to follow Vivian's movements halfway across the foyer. With knots of wedding guests moving between us, I momentarily lost sight of her slight figure dressed in pale blue. I reached the other end of the foyer, puzzled. I had somehow lost her again.

"Looking for Vivian?"

Deep voice. British accent. I turned. There stood one of the most striking men I'd ever seen. Staring at my cleavage.

"Yes, actually."

His heavy, dark mustache drooped around a very sexy mouth. His large, brown eyes seemed focused about twelve inches below my chin. I suddenly felt flushed, and wondered if my one sip of alcohol on an empty stomach was entirely responsible.

"Back there," he said, pointing down a corridor, his gaze meeting mine.

"Thanks," I said. Witty.

"Not at all." He touched his hair, pushing it behind his ear.

Out of things to say, I turned down the corridor he had indicated to find Vivian.

Almost at once I heard her voice, and as I turned the corner, I saw her. Vivian Duncan was speaking on her cell phone. I slowed down, not wanting to intrude on her privacy. She smiled and waved me over as she continued to speak into the phone.

". . . in a matter of minutes. That's exactly what I'm saying, you idiot. It's their honeymoon, for Christ's sake. Get those tickets and get your ass down here!" Her tone was sharp, but she still managed to give me a friendly wink. Honestly.

"No, no. I said no, dammit!" she continued into the phone. "I am not carrying you on this one, dollface! I expect you to keep your word. This lovely couple is about to get married and I should think even a moron would know they need to have their tickets tonight. Good. That's settled, then. Get here immediately!" At that, she hit the disconnect button on her tiny digital phone and gave me a big, glossy smile.

"Details!" she said, tossing the phone into her tiny beaded bag. "But that's why they pay us so much, isn't it? How do you like this setup, honey?" She began walking me back toward the main foyer. I could hear the sounds of the crowd getting louder and had to stop her. This was my chance.

"Vivian, before we go back to the party, I thought I'd better get something . . ."

"Mother!"

I looked up to see a tall, thirty-something woman approach us, and sighed. What was I thinking? I should have known how difficult it would be to talk to a party planner just before an event. I'd have to wait until the wedding was over to get Vivian alone. I noticed that Vivian's daughter did not look a whole lot like her mom. Dark-haired, built on a heavier frame, she wore a deep gray pantsuit with no makeup or jewelry.

"Beryl, darling, I'd like you to meet the woman who is buying out your mother's business. Madeline Bean, please meet my daughter, Beryl."

"Nice to meet you," Beryl said, hardly looking over at me before plunging ahead. "Mother, I told you . . ."

"Before you 'tell me' anything, you know I've asked you to call me Vivian. It may not matter in front of dear Madeline, but in front of my clients I insist." She stood there looking at the tall young woman with disapproval. "Now, Beryl, if you don't intend to wear those lovely earrings I had made for you, then send them back to me."

"Vivian!" The young woman sounded strained. "Vivian, you must stop forcing my father to run your little errands. I just got a call from Dad . . ."

"Whining, I'm sure," Vivian said, with a throaty chuckle. She pulled a cigarette out of her evening bag and played with it. "I give him so much business and how does he repay me? By doing the most incompetent job he can possibly do."

"Mother!" Beryl's irritation was getting the best of her. "Vivian, he's your husband. Can you for once talk about something other than his ability to do business? You know he doesn't really care about any of that."

"Madeline," Vivian said, keeping her eyes on her upset daughter. "Wouldn't it be nice if we could all live a comfortable life and never have to think about business? Is that what your father tells you?" she said, with heat, forgetting to address her caustic comments my way. "Your father is not able to deliver the wedding couple's honeymoon plane tickets *before the goddamn honeymoon!* I have to send Whisper to the house because I doubt very seriously whether your father can find them and find his way down here. Pretty sad, Beryl. But what exactly was your point, dear? I'm in the middle of a marvelous wedding and," she consulted her exquisite jeweled wristwatch, "the ceremony is about to begin."

"Just forget it!" Beryl's voice had lost its thin veneer of patience, although no one back at the party was likely to overhear the row going on down this corridor.

I had already turned to escape when I saw Wes, coming to look for me.

"Did you tell her?"

"Impossible. My timing sucks."

We walked back to the main foyer, leaving the heated pair to their own family drama.

"Was that Beryl Duncan back in that hallway?" Wes asked as we gathered with the two hundred others to file into the Hall of Large Mammals where the wedding ceremony was to take place.

"She's Vivian's daughter. Do you know her?"

"I know Beryl Duncan slightly. Friends have used her. She's the meanest divorce attorney in Los Angeles."

"Between mother and daughter, they do seem to have all the bases covered."

Before Wes could comment, we entered the hall.

"Oh my God," I whispered.

Two long walls of the large museum hall were lined with glass-windowed exhibits. Each diorama showed a different natural habitat in which were displayed various large mammals, from snow leopards to grizzlies, a tribute to the lately underappreciated art of taxidermy. Eerily frozen enactments of nature glowed from the lit cases along the walls, while the rest of the hall was quite dark.

"Amazing," Wes said.

"Funky," I whispered.

Large potted ficus trees, atwinkle with tiny lights, formed a backdrop at the end of the long aisle which was flanked by two sections of chairs. Tall standing candelabra, in pairs, proceeded down the aisle at each row of seats. The white wax pillars flickered down the narrow aisle, giving the museum gallery the look of some surreal monastery. A full orchestra was set up at the side, playing a classical piece as the elegantly dressed wedding guests found seats.

Holly was already seated and she turned and gave us a small wave. We slid into a row about midway down the aisle and joined her.

"I went to the bathroom and you wouldn't believe the flowers they have in there."

"Darius," I murmured to Wes under my breath as Holly went on.

"And the buzz is that Spielberg will be here for the dinner." She took a moment to look over the crowd, now mostly in their seats.

Wes cleared his throat.

"What?" Holly looked down at us. "Oh." She settled back in her seat. "Was I standing? Jeesh."

"Don't worry about it," I said, smiling. "So, who'd you see?"

"Maddie. There's this amazing guy across the aisle and two rows back. He's been staring at you."

"Really?" Wes craned his neck as the twenty-four-piece string section began to play the theme from *Out of Africa.*

"Is he incredibly handsome?" I asked, dropping my voice.

Wes gave a quick look back and answered, "If you dig cops."

What? I turned my head impatiently, expecting to catch a quick glimpse of my dark, mustached Euro-stranger, and instead came eye to eye with a more familiar face. I was caught checking out Lieutenant Chuck Honnett of the LAPD.

"He saw you," Holly pointed out.

Bitch.

"Honnett?" I said, snapping my head back. "What's he doing here?"

"Friend of someone, probably," Holly suggested. "Are you going to dance with him later?"

Wes let a grin escape.

The two of them had decided that I was harboring a

secret thing for this cop. Which was nuts. I don't like authority, with the single exception of my own, and I especially don't like cops. Tell me this, who in their right mind would ever want to be a policeman? Someone who has to bully people and catch them doing things they shouldn't. A cop sees things in black and white and no matter how gray the world really is, a cop is happy to call it black and pull out his gun. In my opinion.

I'm not saying they don't have a place. Even vicious, brainless guard dogs have a place. But still, I wouldn't want to sleep with one.

"I doubt he'll ask me to dance," I answered. "I haven't heard from him. It's been a long time."

"Oh, he'll ask," Holly said, snorting. "He's hot for you. He can only see you from the back now, but just wait until he gets a load of your chest in that dress. His eyes will water."

The string section played on, and two six-year-old flower girls took their first steps down the long aisle. Each wore jungle-print velvet dresses with ivory satin bows and solemn expressions. I'd bet good money that mothers had strongly suggested this would not be the time to act goofy. The tiny ladies threw rose petals from little baskets as they moved up the aisle.

Turning to get a better look at the procession, I was free to check out Honnett, whose head was now turned back to watch the flower girls. In a classic tux, he looked almost, well, dashing. His rough, tanned, rugged face seemed softer. Yeah, he looked damn good in that tux.

I wondered if he could feel my eyes on him, but he didn't turn back my way. We'd met a little over a year ago under pretty bizarre circumstances. Police business. Not that I could imagine meeting an LAPD detective under any normal circumstance.

As I stared at Honnett, unnoticed in the sea of turned heads, I saw his mouth twitch into a wry smile as he watched the little darlings prance past on their floral task. I noticed, in the soft candlelight, his thick, brown hair was a touch more gray than I'd remembered.

Well, he was too old for me, anyway. Mid-forties, I'd guess. And even though we'd talked about getting together at one time, I'd since heard a rumor he was married. Or separated. Same thing to me. I quickly moved my eyes towards the back of the room, to catch the next bridal attendant, but not so quickly that I didn't scan the seat next to Honnett. A woman in her thirties, dressed in black of course. Very thin. Very long neck. More later.

"Honnett will catch you staring," Holly whispered, as we watched an adorable little boy come down the aisle carrying a ring on a cream satin pillow.

"Hush," I warned her. "I'm looking for some other guy."

"Who isn't?" she whispered. "Omigod!" she yelped, and clutched at my hand.

"What? Who?" I asked.

"Brad Pitt, seven o'clock," Wes offered calmly.

I swiveled my head to where I thought seven o'clock should have been and made eye contact. Not with Brad Pitt. With my British mystery man as he came walking down the aisle.

"I'm going to faint. It *is* Brad Pitt. I'm going to faint." Holly began to make slight fan-waving gestures at her pale face with her left hand.

Instead of watching the line of beautiful bridesmaids as they entered the procession, each on the arm of a groomsman, I turned to Wesley and whispered, "Coming down the aisle. See the guy with the longish black hair?"

We remained silent as they passed right by our row.

"What a body," Holly sighed. "Who is he?"

"Don't know."

"He's the best man," Wes said, softly. "Maybe the groom's brother."

"Too old. Too Euro," I answered.

But before we could go on, the violins and cellos began playing "Here Comes The Bride," and we all stood and turned our heads to watch Sara Silver make her grand entrance.

I had to admit, Vivian had done a stunning job with this wedding ceremony. In the semidark, amid hundreds of flickering candles, among the animals frozen in history, the bride made a striking entrance. Dressed in a slender sheath of white burn-out silk that I was positive must be a Vera Wang gown, Sara Silver was escorted down the aisle by a man too old to be her father. Deep Pockets Grandpa, I was guessing. And then I recognized Grandpa's face. I'll be damned. It was a face I recognized from old T.V. reruns.

I watched Sara pass, moving slowly to the lush music, like a virgin princess in a mystical jungle. At the head of the aisle she was met by Brent Bell, her husband to be. Together, they walked up to the clergyman who was officiating at the service.

At that moment, the darkened display case behind the bridal party suddenly lit up. The diorama that extended across the entire back wall of the Hall of Large Mammals could now be seen. In it, two African elephants were engaged in a primitive, animal act. A large bull with immense tusks was up on his two hind legs. The female looked resigned.

Love, I was reminded, could be ferocious.

Chapter 7

I crossed the deserted foyer and peeked through a pair of double-high doors. While the bride and groom were busy taking their vows, I had slipped out of the ceremony to take a look around. Weddings make me jumpy.

A few last-minute workmen were adjusting tall ficus trees around the impressive Hall of Small Mammals, a twin in size and shape to the one where the nuptials were now in progress across the way. Twenty-five tables, swathed in the finest beaded Indian organza, sparkled, their skirts refracting tiny gleams picked up from the diffuse lighting. The most amazing ice sculptures, perfect frozen replicas of a haunting list of endangered species, graced the center of each table.

Here, too, the dozen exhibit cases set into the walls provided the main source of illumination. In one, a family of beavers was at work on a dam. In the next, a porcupine stood alert beside a pond. Across the way, wolves stood on a winterscape knoll, snouts raised, mouths forming O's, suggesting eternally silent howls. Nature under glass—a mixture of creepy and curious, tacky and touching.

Tacky and touching. Well, that could also describe the state of my late relationship with my former boyfriend, Arlo Zar. The trouble with weddings was they made you introspective about the state of your own love life. How romantic they could be when you were sitting on the aisle holding hands with someone you cared about. How alienating when you were just getting over a man you thought would be around for a while longer.

I couldn't go back and face the wedding vows, and I was determined to find Vivian Duncan. Down one hallway, I discovered double fire doors held open with pegs. Beyond them, a large tented structure bustled with activity. Ah, the food. Stepping from the tomb-quiet museum into the noise and swirl of the cooking area brought with it the delicious aromas of simmering sauces and expensive spices.

"Madeline Bean!"

"Freddie Fox!"

The big man stood near a giant trough, its eighty gallons of water coming to the boil, his round face shiny from steam. Freddie, the chef/owner of Santa Monica's favorite restaurant, Fox on Main, was in charge of this dinner. His restaurant catered many of the hottest parties on the west side of town. Freddie was doing what I usually did in the middle of major catering jobs—tasting and laughing and joking around. I felt a pang of something like envy.

"So you brought out your boiler for the crawfish?"

"But of course," he said, smiling. "We are doing my famous *étoufée*, darlin'. "

Freddie kissed my cheek, and then stood back, holding me out at arm's length. "You are not dressed for cooking tonight, baby. You are dressed to kill."

"Tonight I'm a civilian. But tell me . . ." I peered into one of the large tubs behind the boiling station. Live crawfish for days! "How many pounds total? A thousand?"

"A thousand pounds, live. On the dot. How do you do that?" Freddie asked, smiling widely. "Flown in a few hours ago."

I could barely hear Freddie. Not far off, a droning roar like the unmuffled scream of a dirt bike engine whined from beyond the far end of the tent. I looked up, startled. Through an opening at the back, I could see a powerfully built man, shirtless, wielding a chainsaw. He was standing in the loading dock carving a five-foot-high ice sculpture of a rhino. Each time the jittering saw blade bit into the 300-pound block of ice, the pitch of the aggressive buzz changed.

I stood watching. The quivering blade kissed ice once more, gouging out the area under one perfectly formed tusk, and then the man looked up. The dark, intense eyes of a power chainsaw freak met mine.

"He's Ethiopian," Freddie Fox commented. "Or South African. Anyway, he's a brother." He smiled.

The iceman, muscled chest wet with sweat, stood out in the night under a lamp, breathing hard. He pulled his saw from the sculpture in progress and let it rev noisily in the air, his gaze still on me.

"He's wild," I said.

Freddie snorted. "We're all wild in here, take a look."

Three men, young and Hispanic, moved closer and began to lift the first large tub teaming with seafood. Their joking Spanish stopped for a moment as they heaved the tub up and began to tip nearly 200 pounds of crawfish into the boiling water in the trough. There was practically no backsplash. Pros.

"So," Freddie said, leading me to a quieter corner. "Are you here to look us over? From what I hear, you'll be running Vivian's business pretty soon."

"Is that right? And when will I be elected Queen of the May?"

"Just give me a call and I'll set up a demo dinner for you," Freddie continued. "We'll have fun. Now that you're giving up catering, we can work together on weddings. Cool, huh?" My former competitor's eyes gleamed.

Cool? I was about to answer when a shout from the back of the tent called Freddie away to make some critical decision about the balsamic vinegar and whether or not it was the same brand he had ordered.

"Gotta get this," he said, turning to take over that debate. "Call me."

"Where is Vivian, do you know?" I had my own crisis to solve.

"I saw her about ten minutes ago with her old man," Freddie said, happy to pass on one last comment. "Whoeee. Man, she was brutal." He put his hand up and rubbed his short, black hair under a navy Negro League baseball cap. "Now I know Vivian is loaded, but no man should take that abuse. Know what I'm saying?"

I stopped backing out of the room. "Vivian is what?"

Freddie chuckled. "She's worth millions, they say. Shit, she don't have to do any of these damn wedding gigs. But, shi-i-it . . ." He walked back to me, lowering his voice, forgetting his balsamic worries for a second, "I would sooner be kicked in the groin than be married to the woman."

"Freddie." I laughed.

He gave me a peck on the cheek and hurried off to his vinegar debate.

Back in the semidark hallway of the museum, taking the first turn quickly, I jumped. Someone had been standing there, just outside the kitchen door. Waiting. Silently.

Startled, I collided with dark flesh—smack into the warm, hard, damp body of the mad dog, chainsaw-toting ice sculptor.

Chapter 8

"**W**ho was that guy?" Holly lifted a flute of Taittinger to her lips, taking a tiny sip of the pricey champagne, branding the crystal with a curve of her bright red lipstick.

"It's that dress," Wes observed, checking out my exposed assets. "It's effective."

I began to feel self-conscious. At most parties, you'd find me in my high-buttoned white chef's tunic. I was, frankly, more comfortable cooking the meat than *being* the meat.

"You know, being a guest is stressful."

Holly drained her slender champagne flute. As soon as her arm lowered, a waiter magically appeared, offering a tray for her empty glass. Holly stared after him. "How do they do that?"

"They have a huge number of waiters," I said. "The service is mega."

I surveyed the crowd of wedding attendees, postceremony, as they milled about in the giant foyer, clustering in groups around the twenty-foot-high pile of dinosaur bones exhibited in the center. Now, awaiting dinner, the noise level had ratcheted up a few notches. More drinking does that. The bride and groom were still inside with the photographer and would be out to greet guests in a few minutes. It would be another half an hour, at least, before dinner would be served.

"Yo! Mad!" Holly waved to get my attention. "Finish the story. Who was the amazing half-naked black dude, for God's sake?"

Before I could answer, she spotted a circulating champagne server and made eye contact. The obliging young woman delivered fresh drinks to our group and moved on.

"They are good. They are very good." In the noise of several hundred conversations, I was ignored.

Wesley, who had been carefully scoping out the rest of the crowd, said, "I don't see any half-naked men. Don't tell me I missed them."

"The ice sculptor guy," I said. "He was wild. He works without a shirt, although you would think that might not be the safest policy. I don't know, maybe the clothing gets in the way of his chainsaw."

"You," Wes said, considering the deep plunge of my new dress, "attract an odd sort of man. I've noticed that before."

We all sipped our champagne. What's true is true.

"Say what you will about Vivian Duncan," Wes acknowledged, "but she does put on a hot event."

Holly's eyes roamed for celeb sightings as she sipped. "This place rocks. Did you see all those beady little eyes staring at us during the vows?"

Wes asked, "Is she talking about the taxidermy or the groom's family, I wonder?" And then, as we laughed, he lowered his voice a notch. "You must admit, this is a bizarre site for a wedding. What's the bride's deal, again? Doesn't she write sitcoms?"

"No. Sara's the granddaughter of the guy who produced that famous old wildlife T.V. series. Do you remember *Exotic Kingdom* from the sixties? I think I still see it rerunning on cable."

"*Exotic Kingdom*." Wes smiled. "Why is all this use of dead puma in the décor suddenly making sense?"

"*Exotic Kingdom*?" Holly asked. "Wow. I've caught it on TBS."

"It was one of the earliest nature shows. Big Jack

Gantree went out on safari and did the narration," Wes said. "So, that's who Sara's grandfather is! He's so old now, I hardly recognized him."

"I hear he gives *beaucoup* bucks to this museum," I said.

"Big Jack Gantree. I wanted to *be* him when I grew up," Wes said.

I took Wesley by the shoulders and repositioned him a half-turn.

"Well, there's your hero. Right over there," I said.

Directly beneath the *Triceratops* under attack stood an elderly man with a rugged tan and a hardy crop of white hair.

"Right, right, right," Wes said. "So Big Jack is alive."

"Just barely," Holly noticed.

Wes chuckled. "I knew that old guy giving the bride away looked familiar. Man, he's changed."

"He started doing *Exotic Kingdom* before I was born," I said. "He paid for this whole wedding. I gather Gantree took over raising Sara when she was a baby. I'm not sure what happened to Jack's daughter but I think she died. And Sara's father left or something. So Big Jack Gantree raised his granddaughter in the deep bush country of Beverly Hills."

"Sometimes," Holly said, "I drive around B.H. just looking at the houses. All those big, giant houses, you know? And I figure each big old house is worth like two or three million dollars. Maybe more. There they are. Block after block. Up and down the streets of Beverly Hills, there are like *thousands* of them . . ."

Wes shot me a look, which I interpreted to mean: we had better prevent Holly from making eye contact with any more champagne servers.

"So!" Holly seemed to be making rather a zigzag line toward, one could only now hope, her final point. "I just drive around B.H. and think, 'Who are all these rich people?' You know? Like how could *so many* people I never even heard of have made *so goddamn much money*?"

"Well," I said, "there are a lot of affluent families in Los Angeles . . ."

"No, no, no, no, no . . ." Holly interrupted. "I mean, *yes* that's true. But I mean, like *who* are they? And I always think they must be people who made truckloads of money back in the old days of Hollywood. Way, way back, so no one would ever know who they are now. See? Like this old dude Jack Gantree. That's all I'm saying."

As Wes and I considered the two main points Holly had made—(1) Who are all these rich people who can afford homes in Beverly Hills? and (2) How could anyone, inebriated or not, call "the sixties" the "old days of Hollywood"?—I spotted Vivian across the foyer, speaking with this evening's host.

Gathering my resolve, I stepped away from Wes as he began to wax lyrical to Hol about his favorite *Exotic Kingdom* episode—the one where Big Jack and the team took a foray into the protected game reserves of Rhodesia—and approached Vivian and Gantree.

"Hello, Madeline, dear," Vivian said. "Have you met our host this evening? Jack Gantree meet Madeline Bean. I believe if I can be persuaded to retire someday, Madeline might just make a very nice wedding planner. We'll see."

"Vivian," I said, evenly, ignoring her pointed comment until I could pay my respects to our host. Like any culture, L.A. has its rituals. "Hello, Mr. Gantree. I'm such a fan of your television career. My friends were just reminiscing about our favorite memories of *Exotic Kingdom*."

"Was it the one with the bull elephants?" he asked, excited now, a gleam in his eye. "That stampede was real, you know. You couldn't fake it back in those days. My God, the cameraman was almost killed in that shot, but he stood there like a man. Was it the elephants? Or was it the chimps? The young ladies," Gantree explained to Vivian, "just adored the chimpanzees. My daughter was with us when we shot that show and she wanted to dress the chimps up in clothes. What nonsense! But the children who watched the show loved that episode."

While his body had grown frail compared to his robust "Big Jack" image from T.V.'s past, his spirit seemed quite vigorous.

I smiled. In Hollywood, it was considered polite to allow elderly producers to relive their favorite shots from their glory days. As well as good business.

"What a beautiful wedding you've made for your granddaughter. I hope you are having a good time."

"Marvelous," said Gantree, giving my hand a squeeze. "Viv throws the best parties in the world. This retirement talk of hers is ridiculous!" Gantree gave Vivian a disbelieving look.

"Now, Jack. I think I deserve a break, don't you?" Vivian asked, her throaty voice laughing a staccato ha-ha-ha. "And Madeline is making me an offer I simply can't refuse."

"Actually Vivian, no. I'm not . . ."

Jack Gantree smiled.

Vivian's smile, on the other hand, vanished.

"I could never do justice to the empire you have built," I finished, hoping to strike a gracious note.

"Here, here," Jack said, raising a champagne flute to Vivian. "We old-timers have a lot of life left in us yet!"

"But we were all set," Vivian said, a disturbing note of gravel edging into her party voice. "And I'm sure we can teach you . . ."

"In any event, my lawyers tell me I will soon have no money," I said with finality.

"Lawyers!" Jack Gantree said, his ruddy face darkening. "They're like niggers! Don't you trust them."

"Jack!" Vivian said, coloring a little. "Now I'm sure you don't mean that."

I was shocked. "I . . . I try very hard to fight prejudice, Mr. Gantree. I try not to lump every . . . every lawyer, or any other type of human being, into one heap. I believe every . . . *lawyer* should be judged as an individual. Wouldn't you agree?"

I noticed that Vivian was trembling a little, whether from the fact that I'd turned down her business offer or that I was telling off the host at his own party, I couldn't say. I continued, quickly, as no one said a word. "Why, I just learned tonight that Vivian's daughter is an attorney."

Gantree lowered his glass and looked at me. "I stand corrected. On behalf of all the . . . *lawyers* in the world," he smiled at our little game, "will you accept my apology?"

Damn. I'd really gone too far. Diplomat Bean. Vivian put her hand on my arm, grabbing tightly.

"Excuse us, Jack," she said, with a wink and a smile, "Madeline and I need to discuss business. Negotiations can be so unattractive, and we don't want to spoil your granddaughter's big night."

"Not at all," he said, smiling back at Vivian, but leaving me out of the gesture.

"Dinner's coming," she promised, and then led me off to one side, literally in the shadow of the towering *Tyrannosaurus rex*.

"Don't you *ever* make a scene at one of my weddings again," Vivian scolded.

"I'm leaving now, Vivian." I was furious. "Get a grip and just back the hell off."

In that instant, Vivian shifted gears and gave a good impersonation of an impish smile. "How wonderful! Looks like the dinner is being served. Go on ahead, Madeline. Sit down with your friends and enjoy. We can discuss silly old business details another time. You're absolutely right."

I thought I glimpsed Honnett in the crowd that had begun moving toward the side hall.

"And don't worry," Vivian was saying. "I'll give you the name of my attorney, dollface. Believe me, he can get you out of any legal mess you've gotten yourself into. He's a savior. But for now," she opened her arm expansively, "have a lovely evening, okay? You know my promise? I pledge that each and every Vivian Duncan wedding is a night to remember!"

Before I could adjust to the sudden change in her tactics, she moved off. And in the crush of guests, I noticed the beautiful man with the thick mustache and the deep brown eyes—the most appropriately titled "best man" at the wedding. He was talking, earnestly, with a group of men about his own age. They all appeared affluent and attractive in their dark suits and dinner jackets. But the man I was drawn to had a leaner, more sensual look. Maybe it was the long hair. Something about him intrigued me.

"Holly could use some food," Wes said, approaching from another direction. "Shall we go in to dinner? I'm dying to finally see the setup."

Holly teetered just behind Wesley, stepping for a moment directly in front of the spotlights that illuminated the *T-rex*. Her short, white-blond hair became a halo.

"I saw you talking to Vivian," Wes said, concerned. "You didn't tell her here."

"Oh, yeah. I told her." We merged with the gathering crowd of guests heading towards the open doors of the Hall of Small Mammals. Just a human herd going to feed.

"Vivian is taking my firm 'No!' as an opening gambit. I'm quite the little negotiator, Wesley."

He put his arm around me, concerned. "How about that."

"Maybe we should leave."

"Now?" Holly wailed. "*Now?*"

We had entered the grand hall, where two hundred and someodd guests were finding their assigned tables and getting settled amid the glitter of potted trees with twinkle lights. Everywhere, guests were tossing their beanbag leopard place cards on tables to hold their spots, having fun. A new dance band was playing *Baby Elephant Walk* from *Hatari!*

Standing there at the back of the giant hall, we analyzed.

"Ice sculptures are so seventies bar mitzvah," Wes said, commenting on the décor. "But check it out! With all these kitsch embalmed mammals, the ice thing works."

"They're fabulous," Holly agreed. "Real kooky."

I had to agree. The room was spectacular, and now, brought to life with so many happy guests, there was finally that missing note of warmth and animation that the static dioramas had lacked.

"Did you get a contact number on the naked ice guy?" Wes asked, ever the networking caterer.

I held up a small, white business card. Wes smiled. In truth, I was every ounce the networking caterer as my partner.

Holly drifted over to the table to which we'd been assigned. Sitting there, beside an unclaimed open seat, was a star of stage, screen, and T.V.—Dick Van Dyke.

"Jeez, you guys. Did you see our table? I'm sitting next to the guy from *Chitty Chitty Bang Bang*!"

How quickly these decisions are thrust upon us! How innocent they seem at the time. If we stayed, Holly could talk to a star. If we stayed, Wes could sample Freddie Fox's cuisine. I considered our party clothes and began to soften. And then, Holly whispered something in my ear. I turned and saw Chuck Honnett at a nearby table. He caught my eye and waved. Who, I wondered again, was that skinny woman seated beside him?

So I gave in and said, "Let's just stay for dinner." Just like that. Leaving would be such a hassle, I reasoned. Staying had so many attractions. I was hungry and food was here. A primitive reaction, I know, surrounded by so many pairs of small mammal eyes.

Chapter 9

*T*he waiters were clearing the dessert plates which held scant traces of the masterpieces—miniature zebras made of white chocolate mousse drizzled with bittersweet chocolate icing. I turned to Wesley. "These servers . . ."

"I know. The best."

Among top caterers, the actual food and the way it was prepared and presented were always exceptional. That was a given. But having on tap really well-trained serving staff was the critical difference, the mark of the elite and expensive best.

I pushed out from the table, preparing to make a run to the ladies, and turned to see if Holly cared to join me. Her mouth was open, her arms thrown wide, as she appeared to be singing a line from the song "Truly Scrumptious" to Mr. Van Dyke. In the bustle and swell of so many diners, she couldn't really be heard for more than a few tables and I had to admit, Mr. Van Dyke didn't seem to be particularly annoyed. I guess he'd had to put up with worse fan encounters than a giddy blonde in a tube top reliving her recent youth. Don't think celebrities have it easy. Even at private parties, everyone knows all the words to their songs.

I edged my way between a couple of tables, when a man's hand on my shoulder stopped me. Honnett. I hadn't realized he was heading for the door before the cake was cut as well.

"Madeline," he said, smiling down at me. His tough-jawed face looked particularly good set off by his tuxedo. I knew if I mentioned it, it would embarrass the hell out of him.

"Don't you look good all dressed up," I said.

"Yeah, well. Shit." He smiled again. "You know I'd feel more comfortable out of this thing." He shrugged large shoulders in his black jacket. "I figured it was cheaper to rent this rig than to buy a whole new suit."

"How . . . practical." I love to see a man off-balance. And in my past dealings with Lt. Chuck Honnett, I'd rarely had that opportunity. "So she's a rental? Neat. I like that whole wide lapel thing you're trying to bring back."

"Shut up, Bean."

"So how does a police detective wind up at such a trendy wedding? Who do you know here anyway?" I turned to ask my question since he was walking a bit behind me, following my snaking path between tables on the way out of the hall.

"I went to school with Brent Bell's dad. Some of the guys from that group were invited. I didn't expect to run into you. Is this one of your parties?"

"No. Actually, I was invited too. By the . . ."

We had just come out of the Hall of Small Mammals, leaving behind the roar of the crowded dining area, into the dark quiet of the large, marble-floored foyer. Something felt strange. The round room was deserted, naturally. The African music ensemble were long gone, as were the servers, since all the action was now back at the formal sit-down dinner in the hall we had just left.

"Restrooms are back down that hallway," Honnett said. Then he stopped walking too. "What?" He looked at me.

On the dark marble floor, right in front of the base of the dinosaur exhibit, was a blue silk pump. A single left shoe.

I looked up.

Draped over the giant fossilized head of the *Tricera-*

tops skeleton looming above was the body of a woman. Her face was concealed. From where we stood, I could easily make out the light blue dress that Vivian Duncan had been wearing that night. From the sag of her body, she didn't appear to be conscious.

"Jesus!" Honnett said. "I don't fucking believe this!"

"Is she dead?" I whispered, backing up.

"She's not sightseeing. How the hell did her body end up . . . ?"

"I don't know. I can't imagine." I felt like I was going into shock. My thoughts seemed disconnected. "There's scaffolding," I pointed out, "over in the corner."

Despite my growing numbness, I could distinctly hear my voice, sounding calm and rational, as if it were coming from someone else, while my thoughts were shooting off a mile a minute, obsessing over the least important details. Nothing can fix things now, I thought. This wedding is ruined.

I moved to the side to get a better viewpoint, while Honnett jumped over the railing and put his hands on the base of the exhibit, pulling himself up to stand on the black marble pedestal. The lowest part of the body, the shoeless foot encased in pale hose, was hanging about ten feet above Honnett's head.

Vivian had plunged right on top of the skeleton of the *Triceratops*. The news guys were going to be brutal. DINOSAUR KILLS BEVERLY HILLS BUSINESSWOMAN AT WEDDING. Film at eleven. Just like that, this party had become a nightmare. And Jeez, what about the bride? Poor Sara.

"Poor Sara." I must have said it aloud, as my worry and shock ping-ponged to the young woman whose wedding fantasy would forever be connected to this bizarre and violent accident. Vivian never wants her brides to worry about a thing. Shit.

Honnett came back over to me. "Doesn't look like she's breathing. I can't touch her anyway. Not until the medics get here." He looked up. "And I don't think those old bones could hold me. I'd probably wind up owing the city a couple million bucks for destroying their relics."

"What? Were you thinking of climbing all the way up there? Up the spine of the *T-rex*?"

"Well, sure. If I thought I could help her," Honnett said. "But she's not breathing."

I shook my head, stunned at how quickly the evening had gone south. "How could this have happened to Vivian? Was she pushed?"

"Vivian? Vivian *who*?"

I looked up at Honnett, reassessing. Maybe I knew more about the people and events of this evening than the detective. "She's the wedding planner, Vivian Duncan."

He gave me an odd look, but I was quickly overcome by a resolve to help. It's funny how we react to a crisis. Chuck Honnett's first impulse was to get physical—to climb all the way up a twenty-foot-high pile of bones, if he had to, to help someone in trouble. I was the analytical type. The kind who insisted on reading the instruction manual before I installed a new microwave.

My mind began racing. I had a desperate impulse to set down the events of the party. Maybe I should sit right down and make a list of all the people Vivian had been quarreling with during the evening. Lucky I had brought my purse with me. I always carry a pen. The little gold one that Arlo had given me for a . . .

"You hanging in there?" Honnett looked at me, hard.

It's funny. I really don't remember sitting down in my tight black dress, but there I was down on the floor, searching through my evening bag. Honnett was pulling out his cell phone, making a call, as I tried to remember the name of Vivian's husband. She'd talked to him on the phone earlier, I remembered. Yes, I was being very clear and methodical.

"D-U-N-C-A-N," Honnett was saying into his phone. "Yeah, that's it. I'll be here."

I began to feel very bad. What were the five stages of grief, anyway?

"You sure it's her?"

"Vivian Duncan was wearing a dress that color," I explained. Honnett had his little pad out and was writing down notes, too. He looked at me, sitting on the floor with my own small notebook, and his expression softened.

Next thing I knew, Honnett was taking off his jacket and placing it over my shoulders. He was also talking in that quiet voice cowboys use when they talk to a spooked horse. He kneeled down next to me, looking more thoughtful than I usually see him.

"You going to be okay?"

I nodded, annoyed.

"So do you think you can tell me about this woman, Vivian Duncan? Any reason I should have heard of her?"

"No reason." I blinked and my lashes suddenly felt wet. "Isn't that sad? She was the biggest wedding consultant on the West Side. Everyone used Vivian for their weddings. Everyone. She was . . . well . . . very powerful in party-planning circles."

"Uh huh," Honnett said.

"I know that must mean nothing to you. But she was important."

I stopped trying to explain. Even though Vivian Duncan had been a sometimes-shrewish presence on the party circuit, she had built up an impressive reputation as a businesswoman. She'd had a family. Not that I knew a lot about her personal life, but still I cared. I cared that another human being, one who had been so full of plans and energy, was now quite dead.

I looked up at Honnett, still hunched over his notepad, biting his pencil. I began to realize how little any of this personal stuff meant to a policeman whose job brought him into contact with too many lives and too many deaths. How could he ever truly care about each poor soul? I felt a fresh emotion.

I pitied Honnett that he had what it took to be a cop. That toughness. That cool. The distance he needed to do his job had robbed him of his ability to feel. Or had he perhaps always lacked sensitivity, and that led him to be so well-suited to this work?

He was motivated by the disturbance, by rules being broken, I thought, while I was motivated by the person whose human frailty had somehow propelled her to die among million-year-old bones.

Honnett handed me a tissue. While I was thinking how hard his soul was, he was probably thinking what a wuss I was. Perfect.

"She was in charge of this party, you know."

"Awkward," Honnett said.

"You think she could still be alive?"

"The paramedics are on the way. But I don't see how."

"Could it have been an accident?"

Just then, the outer doors to the museum were pushed open by a pair of running emergency workers. The uniformed men stopped, heads thrown back at the sight of the dinosaurs. Silhouetted in the dim light, the medics stood with mouths agape as they took in the awful sight of a well-dressed woman's body hanging down from above in a deathlike, broken droop.

At the very same time, a woman dressed in white came out from the dinner. It was, of course, the bride. She was smiling widely, holding a bottle of champagne, most likely looking for the john, but spying the paramedics and us first.

It was only a matter of time before she looked up.

That was the last quiet moment I remember. I jumped up to find a towel to clean up all the broken glass and spilled Taittinger.

Chapter 10

*I*n hindsight, Monday morning was not the best choice for an all-company meeting. And to make matters worse, my favorite attorney, Paul Epstein, was late.

I was still upstairs getting ready while the whole crew was gathering down in the kitchen. Where else?

I stared into the full-length bathroom mirror for the third time and finally focused on what was there. Too much hair. Too little makeup.

Pulling a brush through my hair took a strong grip and a stronger scalp. I managed to urge most of it into a low ponytail and, with a flip of the wrist, I'd bound it all up in a hairband. Done. Then, a few swipes of blusher, wherever the hell that was.

Downstairs, I heard a low rumble of voices and the scuffle of shoes as seven people traversed the entry hall on their way to our living room.

There was no use putting it off. I had to head downstairs and face them. These were my friends, my co-workers, who had been waiting for word on the fate of Mad Bean Events. Were we still in business? Or should they be scrambling for new jobs? Enquiring minds . . .

Down the stairs, I took a quick detour into the kitchen myself. A Diet Coke was in order. Ten A.M. and I was already on the caffeine. I'd have to watch it.

I checked the window again. No Paul. Oh, well. I could guess what his advice was going to be.

Slowly, sipping from the can, I walked back to the living room. I could hear their voices from down the hall.

". . . must have gone ballistic. Man!"

"She was cool." I heard Wesley's calm voice as I approached.

"Another dead body. She must have wigged!"

"Well, she is kind of getting used to it, isn't she?" That last voice belonged to a young woman who did the most fabulous desserts in L.A., Lisa Lee.

I had been the center of conversation. And why not? I had discovered a body. Again.

"Ladies, gentlemen," I said, walking straight into the middle of the room. They turned to me. Lisa, Alan, Holly and Wes, my trusty Alba, and a few other fine teammates. Amid the general hubbub, Ray Jackson, boyish in baggy jeans, with a shirt that could have fit over a camel billowing over his wiry frame, flashed me a grin.

"Yo, Mad. How do you do it?"

"Get mixed up in crap?" I smiled at Ray. "It's a talent."

I threw my portfolio onto the coffee table, and with a few more adjustments, our informal business gathering came to order.

Sitting or standing or leaning on the furniture was the cadre of our steadiest employees.

"So where is Mr. Paul?" Alba asked. "He no coming today?"

Alba had been working for me ever since I moved to Los Angeles. Ageless and built on a sturdy frame, she'd begun as my one-day-a-week housekeeper and moved from there to a full-time lifesaver.

"We'll see. But I'm glad," I said, plunging on, "we could get together today. Before I get into the purpose of this meeting . . ." I looked around at the small group of hopeful faces. My friends and fellow workers.

"Which is to see if we all still work here, right?"

"Yes, Ray. I just wanted to say a few words about last night. As you have all heard, there was a death. It was Vivian Duncan. At the moment they are treating it as a *possible* homicide. Okay? We'll just have to wait until we hear more."

"You mean they're still holding out some slim possibility that the old lady offed herself by taking a nose-dive into prehistory?" Alan, one of my head waiters, was nothing if not direct.

"Okay. *Probable* homicide." I cleared my throat. "Now, as regards our other pain-in-the-butt matter, we seem to be having more trouble with Five Star."

Holly looked beat. I wondered if she'd ever gotten to sleep.

Around the room there were murmurs of disappointment.

"I knew it." Ray turned to Lisa Lee, the young pastry chef next to him on the sofa. "Those big studio bastards." Ray was around twenty, the youngest of the group. He'd been filling in as our part-time runner for about two years as he worked on his business major at UCLA. He was about the only person I had working for me who didn't secretly hope to be an actor. How he'd managed to make the seven-mile trek from Watts to Westwood was enough of a miracle.

"That's it, see? It's those fucking lawyers, man. They are the lowest. They are scum. You know the joke. What's the difference between a dead dog in the road and a dead lawyer in the road?"

"There are skid marks in front of the dog" came the rapid-fire answer from behind us. "Sorry I'm late."

We all looked up.

"Hi, Paul." Wesley and I watched our favorite attorney make his way across the living room. He pulled up a straight-backed chair next to the white loveseat and settled down.

"Hello, children," he said, deadpan as always. "Have I got news for you."

Paul Epstein is one of the good guys. At least to me. He adopted me, so to speak, a few weeks after Wes and I had moved to L.A. from Berkeley. Our goal, of course, was to start our own catering firm. But in order to make some money, I had introductions and references to a few SoCal chefs from my culinary school up north. Paul had been a regular at Café Bel Air, the bistro where I first landed.

With tousled, graying, sandy hair, a bit of a gut, and a wardrobe straight out of J.C. Penney, he was not the buttoned-down type. Paul Epstein wasn't easy to peg as a lawyer in a town filled with blow-dried sharks. And for eight years, he had steadfastly refused to accept a fee on the work he did for me. He kept saying, "Wait until you make a profit. Don't worry. I'll get paid."

It was a matter of great celebration, a year ago, when I cooked a grand meal for Paul and handed him a sealed envelope. With the buyout cash from Five Star, I had finally been able to pay Paul back for his faith.

"So give it up, man. Good news or bad news?" Ray fidgeted on the sofa, bouncing a loose-jointed ankle across one knee.

"Well, Ray," Paul said, face straight as always, "when has a lawyer ever had good news?"

The only way you'd guess Paul had a sense of humor was that after he said something he considered humorous, he'd give you a three-beat grin. I'd learned to look closely at his doughy, expressionless face. This time there was not even a half-second of smile. Shit.

"Here's the thing," Paul said, his low voice a monotone rumble. "I got a call from Stevenson, Craig and Munsen. Very depressing guys."

When Five Star served us with their injunction to cease business activities, Paul had consulted with some law school cronies, lawyers from a big downtown firm who owed him poker money. *L.A. Law*–style creeps.

"Sorry, folks. They strongly urge Mad Bean Events to shut down. So," he looked around the disheartened group, "keep the faith. And Madeline will get in touch as soon as we get this bugger resolved."

It was like we figured. Wesley gave my hand a squeeze.

"Just for the time being, folks," Paul was saying as they began to stand up, moving toward the door.

"Miss Madeline?" Alba had walked over to pick up the empty can of Diet Coke I'd left on the table.

"Thanks, Alba." I stood up. "Wait a second, guys. I have some checks." I pulled open my portfolio and withdrew several envelopes. "It's for a month. Let's hope we've gotten this thing settled by then."

The group surrounded me, thanking me for their money, wishing me well.

Ray stayed behind. "Since you paid me and all," Ray said, quietly. "Why don't I come on over and help you with stuff?"

"Thanks, Ray. I don't think I'm allowed to be in the party business, so there won't be any work."

"I can always find something to keep me busy," he said, smiling.

When they were gone, Wes and Holly and I sat back down with Paul. Alba had bustled off into the kitchen.

"Well, that's that." I kicked off one red clog and watched it skid across the hardwood floor.

"Wait until you hear this, Maddie."

I looked at Paul. He was more animated than I had ever seen him. Wes noticed it as well.

"The reason I was late? There's a rumor going around that Five Star may be bought."

"Someone's buying out the studio?"

"They say that food company, Sammy Foods, is looking them over pretty good. And it's no coincidence that I get a call this morning that maybe Five Star would consider an out-of-court settlement after all."

"You're kidding?" I looked at Paul.

"Maybe they need to clear their books of ongoing cases, whatever. I need to get back to them. But don't you worry. This thing is far from over. Buck up there, kiddo."

"Thanks, Paul. Hey, would you like something to drink?"

"Can't stay, pal. I'm supposed to be moving tonight,

but my office is a mess. I gotta get packing." He smiled at me. "Anyway, you've gotten yourself mixed up with the police again, haven't you? Better watch yourself. Next thing you know you'll be in their computers."

"What can I do?" I asked, smiling at him.

"It's the computers that get you. They start tracking you, baby, and that's all she wrote. Keep below their radar, Maddie. That's the way."

Paul was a major conspiracy theorist. We all have our hobbies.

Holly looked at me. "Maddie, maybe I could go over and help Paul. If you're not going to be needing me this morning, I mean."

"Great," I said.

"Yeah?" Paul raised his head, relieved. "Excellent."

"Okay," Holly said, standing, grabbing her enormous mesh shoulder bag. "I'll go catch Ray. See you tonight."

"I'm going out for dinner tonight, actually."

All eyes were suddenly on me.

"It's Honnett." I looked over at Paul. "He's this cop I know. From before."

"Right," he said, deadpan. "The one that's had the hots for you."

"Hots?"

"That's legalese," Wes explained.

"Listen. He asked me a lot of questions last night. Naturally. Poor Vivian Duncan is dead. I told him I'd get together as much information as I could and we decided to go over it at dinner."

They stared at me.

"What?"

"So is it a . . . ?" Holly looked at me, hesitant to use the word "date."

"Holly, get off of her case," Paul said gruffly. "Can't you see she's got a business meeting?"

"Right," I agreed.

But then, dammit! Paul hit us all with his three-beat grin.

*   *   *

It was just before lunch. Wes had gone out and I was
sitting alone in my office, brooding. I had been trying
to pull together all the papers I could find that related
to Vivian Duncan and her business. Since she had been
trying to woo us, her attorney had sent over a lot of
documents that made her look very good on paper. In
addition, she had also messengered over half a dozen
memory books, albums of photos filled with samples of
invitations and menus from many of her firm's most lavish weddings.

Just then, Alba came to my office, filling up the doorway, looking full of purpose. She called out in her high-
pitched voice, accented with Spanish, "Miss Madeline,
there is a young lady at the door for you. She said is
important." Then she moved aside.

Behind her I could see a woman's shape.

"Sara?"

Yesterday's bride walked on into my office and stood
there, silently. Alba took the cue to leave.

"You didn't go on your honeymoon." As if their entire wedding, and all their future memories of it, hadn't
been screwed up enough already!

She shook her head.

"Oh, Sara. Sit down. Is there anything . . ."

"He's gone." She stood in front of the large desk I
usually shared with Wesley and stared at it. "Brent is
gone."

"What do you mean?" I was suddenly alarmed.

"He just took off. I haven't seen him all night. We
were . . . we were supposed to leave on our honeymoon
this morning." She looked at her watch. "A few hours
ago, I guess it is."

"That's terrible."

"Grandfather was sending us on a photo safari, but
now those plans are ruined. They said we couldn't
leave." She shook her head at the harsh memory. "Even

Brent's dad's friends couldn't pull any strings. Let me tell you, my grandfather was furious!"

I imagined that Big Jack Gantree was on the phone with a U.S. senator even as we spoke.

"But I thought you said Brent was missing."

"It's the last straw! Last night, we were separated for a while. And then, later, I couldn't find him *anywhere*. He just disappeared."

"From the wedding?"

She nodded, and then all at once her lovely young face crumpled. Tears streamed down her cheeks and her nose began to run.

"I left the dinner. Just for a minute, I told him. And then . . ."

"That's when you came out and saw . . ."

Her tears kept coming. "Then the police wouldn't let me go back into the dinner. No one would let me back into my own . . . my own wedding."

I'm very fast on the Kleenex. I had a new box over to her in about two seconds.

"Thank you," she sniffed, pulling tissues from the box, one at a time, until she had a fistful.

"So you didn't see Brent," I said.

"No. When they finally, finally, *finally* . . ." She honked into the tissues and then wadded them up. "When they let me back into the hall, the tables were all moved around. My friends had already gone home. My grandfather was beside himself by then to let everyone go. They were old, some of my great-aunts, you know? But Brent . . . I just . . . He just was gone." She threw the wad of Kleenex onto the desk, bursting into fresh tears.

"Great wedding, huh? Great memories. This wasn't the way it was supposed to turn out." She attacked the box of tissues again. One by one, her fingers grabbed them into a ball.

"Sara, honey, you have no idea where Brent might be? Did you call his family?"

"Of course I did. He never came home. I called everyone, even his relatives, the ones that came to town for the wedding." She sniffed. "Nobody's seen him."

"He's probably just upset."

"*He's* upset?" She looked at me, aghast, her point of a chin quivering. "*I'm* upset! And I don't want to tell the police he's missing," Sara whined on, before blowing her nose in the handful of tissues.

Why, I wondered, had she come to tell me all this?

"My grandfather says," Sara dabbed at her eyes, carefully, "that you are friends with Chuck Honnett."

That's right. Lt. Honnett, the old school buddy of the missing bridegroom's father, should be told about this.

"If we go to him, he'll have to make a report. Make it official. But Grandfather thought that you . . . well, could you ask him to find Brentie for me? Sort of off the record?"

"Sara. They don't do that. You need to make an official . . ."

"*No*. I will not go to the police and tell them my new husband hasn't had the balls to come home on his own wedding night!"

Chapter 11

*I*t was turning out to be one of those days.

"Don't expect me to cry."

Vivian Duncan's daughter, Beryl, with her short brown hair, and her fierce gray eyes, and her navy Brooks Brothers suit, appeared calm.

"Okay," I said, folding a kitchen towel.

Beryl had insisted it was imperative that we meet about her mother's business, right away. When I tried to talk her out of it, she insisted on coming over. I felt myself sinking another inch deeper into wedding consultant quicksand.

Wes says people like to bounce things off of me. I make people comfy. It's my curse. Holly thinks it's less complicated than that. She said people hang around because of the food. I wondered, looking at Beryl: succor or sugar?

"Here's the irony," Beryl was saying. "Now that my mother is dead, everybody feels so sorry for me." Her voice trailed down low. "Which is really funny. You'd have to know my family to get it. Vivian was not the traditional mother. She had very high standards. Extremely high. I never . . ." Beryl took a deep breath and plunged on. "I was a disappointment. When she found the time to notice me. Now that Vivian is dead, I'm finding it hard to feel very sad. She was not a nice woman."

It might surprise you, but listening to Beryl Duncan trash her dead mother didn't strike me as shocking. It all depends on what you expect from people. What I expect is: people are weird. This viewpoint has always worked for me. It allows for a lot of, frankly, odd behavior to cross my path without need for constant judgement.

My feeling is, no one can know what's going on with another human being, no matter how many daytime talk shows one might watch. I'm practical. Since I don't have the energy to be walking a mile in everyone else's bloody moccasins, I just give everybody *credit* for having suffered through lousy childhoods and leave it at that.

In fact, it's kind of a good guideline for living. Cut 'em some slack. Tread softly. Be careful how you judge. I figure you never know what hellacious pain the average jerk is in, so be kind. Come to think of it, this attitude of mine may explain why people I hardly know keep turning up. And like Beryl, they tend to unload.

"Do you think I might have a taste of that?" Beryl was checking out the large bucket of homemade ice cream on the counter.

Or, then again, maybe Holly was right about the food thing.

I'd been working on a new ice cream recipe with my brand new toy when Beryl had insisted on a visit.

"It's almost ready." I went to a drawer and pulled out a silver teaspoon.

"Vivian was not cut out to be a mother," Beryl continued, perching on the edge of a stool, resting her plain hands on the marble countertop. She didn't wear any rings, I noticed, and her nails were short and unpolished. "It was all about her. Always. The rest of us didn't exist. Or, no—we existed as *accessories*. When I was very young, she used to order her hairstylist to bleach my hair, too, so Vivian's blond would seem real. I was only four. She was embarrassed at the preschool mothers' day luncheon or something. She thought I was throwing off her image, I guess. And I was so young, what did I know? I thought mommy hated me."

See what I mean? Everybody has had a lousy childhood. Even if they weren't beaten, there are still scars.

Beryl ran her hand though her cropped brown hair. "And do you want to know what's really pathetic? I just stopped coloring it. Years of therapy, let me tell you, just to free myself from peroxide."

I pushed a spatula into the ice cream. Firm to hardish. Nice. Not that I wasn't sympathetic to Beryl and her "issues," exactly, but then I couldn't let my pet project melt, either. In any case, it didn't seem to matter. She just kept on talking.

"I realize the woman is dead now, but Vivian was an unhappy woman. She was a hollow, miserable, self-centered, ego-driven . . ."

Beryl needed to get it all out. When she took another breath, I fully expected her to speak even more ill of the dead. Instead, she seemed to run out of venom. "What flavor is that?"

"It's experimental. I call it Deep, Dark Brown Sugar."

"Really." Beryl picked up a silver teaspoon and fiddled with it.

Although it was not quite lunch hour, was there ever really a wrong time for ice cream?

"By the way," Beryl said, "if I can ask . . . why did you tell all those stories to the police?"

I looked up at her, drawing a blank.

"Last night," she said. "You really slammed my father."

"They get pretty pissed if you don't answer direct questions," I said. "I've found this out through past experience."

"So who cares what the police think?" Beryl had the typical lawyer's viewpoint.

"Sorry, Beryl. Your dad was fighting with your mother last night. Other people may have heard them. I don't think the police will necessarily . . ."

Lest I forget, in her everyday life Beryl was a tough

lawyer, and by the tone of her comments, I was getting a dose of her lawyer style. Beryl's look of intense, oh-give-me-a-break-ness stopped me cold.

"Can we cut the crap? Someone broke Vivian's neck. They say she couldn't have jumped. They don't think she fell. So what does that make it? Cops don't have much imagination. Naturally, they figure my father murdered Vivian."

"Did they arrest him?"

"Not yet."

"Then there may be other suspects."

She met my gaze. "I have a lovely alibi for the time after I left my mother at the museum."

"Oh."

"Ah, you're surprised. As it happens, I was a guest on an Internet chat show for the full hour between eight and nine last night. My sources at Parker Center tell me Vivian was killed sometime after eight-fifteen. So I'm in the clear. But my poor father isn't so lucky."

I couldn't help myself. I started wondering who else might have wanted to see Vivian Duncan dead. And just because one is typing away on an Internet chat, is there really no way to get another person to continue typing for you while you slip away? Or . . .

"So why are you doing that?" she asked, swerving the topic back to ice cream. By now, I was on subject-shift alert and took it in stride.

I had scooped mounds of the fresh Deep, Dark Brown Sugar ice cream onto a tray. I was starting to squeeze and pat them, using plastic wrap to protect my hands, into perfectly sculpted palm-sized balls.

"After I mold them into works of art," I explained, with just the right touch of modesty, "they go into the freezer. Three hours. Then we'll roll them . . ."

"Roll them?"

"In toppings. Like shredded coconut or bittersweet shavings or chopped nuts and cinnamon or mini white chocolate chips. Each one different. They should look nice piled up on a platter."

I've often found myself settling down, destressing, by the simple steps and movements necessary in working with food. As Vivian's mixed-up daughter sat there watching my hands go about their swift work, the rhythm of ice cream molding seemed to have a settling effect on Beryl Duncan as well. A little more thoughtfully, then, she introduced yet another subject.

"Aren't you a little curious why I'm here?"

"Curious?" I looked up at her and smiled. "Beryl, I'm curious about everything. Trust me. It's one of my most endearing weaknesses. Or so my friends keep telling me."

"Then why haven't you asked?"

"I figured you would tell me when you were ready. I imagine your mother's death is a terrible shock."

For a split second I caught sight of an expression that might resemble sadness, but it was quickly replaced by her usual disapproving facade. "Well, it's about her wretched business. Who is going to take over Mother's work? She's got weddings scheduled for two years solid."

I stopped patting my ice cream balls. All those poor future brides, I thought. Now here were young women who were probably weeping over the loss of Vivian Duncan.

"Mother told me you were buying her company. Well, actually, that's not quite true. Vivian never told me anything. Whisper told me. But now, Vivian is dead and she's left a terrible mess. Anyway, the point is, the reason I rushed over here today is, I think you should do the weddings."

I had just spent the better part of last night trying to disentangle myself from Vivian's clawish dreams. But here I was again, just like in one of those unalterable recurring nightmares, sinking deeper and deeper, unable to wriggle out from the death grasp of Vivian's determination.

"Beryl, it was all a mistake. I never wanted Vivian's

company. Besides, I'm in no position to buy it. It was all something Vivian was dreaming up."

"Don't tell me that. I can't cope with that!"

"Why don't you have some ice cream?" I suggested. "We'll figure something out." I pulled down two pink bowls from my Metlox collection.

"Deep, Dark Brown Sugar," she said, after a thoughtful spoonful. "It's brilliant. But what's that other flavor that makes it seem so intense?"

It always came. They always want to know the secret ingredient.

"My secret," I said conspiratorially, like a magician revealing his trick, "is sour cream."

"Wow."

"You have to add it just before the ice cream begins to set."

Beryl regarded me. "So will you help me?" She had finished her ice cream. "Let's leave buying the business out of it. Will you help me?"

"Why not Whisper Pettibone? Isn't he the best choice?"

"Yes. Whisper has the master planner in his office and he should be doing all of this work! But who knows where that man is? I've been trying to call him all night and all morning, but I can't find him. He won't pick up his cell phone. And he's not answering my pages, either." She sighed. "He was very close to Vivian. He's probably a mess."

"I'm sure he'll turn up." I *hoped* he'd turn up. And soon. I couldn't help but notice the sucking sound as the quicksand rose over my ankles.

"Look, please, could you just do me this favor? The master planner sits on Whisper's desk. Just go down there and get the schedule, so we can start making calls. I'm late for a meeting as it is. I'm getting a good defense attorney for my dad. Just in case."

She placed a small key ring, which contained two keys, on the island counter between us.

"I'd like to help you. Just so you understand that I

will not be taking on any weddings, okay? As long as . . ."

"Thanks! You're great," she cut me off. "When you get the date book, if you'd call all the brides, that would be a start."

"You want *me* to call?"

Beryl looked at me from under plain eyelids that had probably never held a dab of eyeshadow. "I've never been married, okay? I specialize in divorce. I don't know how to talk to those women. Can't you *smooze* them or something?"

"Schmooze," I corrected.

"You're perfect. Look, Madeline. I've had you checked out. You are smarter than you look."

I glanced up at her.

"I mean, for a caterer."

"Hmm. Thanks."

"You know what I mean. You know a little more than just how to add sour cream to bring out the flavor. I think," she continued looking straight at me, "that you're interested in what happened to Vivian. You told me yourself, you're curious. And you're a natural detective. One of your clients was killed last year and the word was you were responsible for finding the killer. Isn't that right?"

"Well . . ."

Okay, I couldn't help myself. I *was* curious. Why had young bridegroom Brent and slimy old Whisper Pettibone both disappeared? Had they, I thrilled, slipped away together? On the young man's wedding night? And, really, there were so many other questions bubbling to the surface.

"I think you could help me, and not just by calling a few brides. I think you could probably save my poor dad a whole lot of grief," she said, standing and handing me the key to Whisper's office, "if you would kindly help figure out who killed my mother."

Chapter 12

*T*he 400 block of South Melwood Drive offered a jumble of retail establishments located in gracious two-story buildings that dated from the forties. Gourmet delis and upscale pooch groomers sat side-by-side with specialty dry cleaners and French bakeries. Here, several blocks of shops and cafés vied for neighborhood customers across wide Wilshire Boulevard from the city's chicest boutiques. For Beverly Hills, south of Wilshire passed for low-rent.

Above these shops, up on the second floors, various anonymous offices went almost unnoticed by the foot traffic on the street below. These were the types of businesses for whom appointments were discreet, and services could be contracted with a minimum of publicity.

Between the storefront belonging to Hilda, European Tailoring and Alterations at 409 South Melwood, and Melwood Fine Wines at 411, a stairway led up one flight and ended at a landing where two doors faced each other. On one dark, heavy, paneled door was a small brass plaque announcing VIVIAN DUNCAN WEDDINGS, BY APPOINTMENT ONLY. Across the landing, stood a matching door. On it, was simply the word PRIVATE marked in small brass letters. Apparently, for the past twenty-four years, Vivian had turned right at the top of the stairs, while her devoted assistant, Ted "Whisper" Pettibone, had turned left.

I climbed the granite stairs, leaving the bustle of noonday traffic down below as the street level door closed slowly behind me. So I wasn't really sure if I heard a strange noise coming from the floor up above.

I stopped, midway up the staircase, hyperalert, listening hard. No further noise was audible.

And anyway, why shouldn't there be noise? Just because I was approaching the offices of a woman who had died, that didn't mean there couldn't be someone about. Where, after all, was Whisper? Party planners have a very finely tuned sense of duty. No matter the emergency, the party must go on. And that went double for weddings.

Wait. I *did* hear something this time.

I pulled out my cell phone and hit the speed dial button. A few moments later I heard Wesley answer the phone.

"Yes?"

"Wesley? It's me. I'm over on South Melwood."

"I got your note. So you're going to take over Vivian's wedding clients now?"

"No."

"Good."

"Well, not unless it's absolutely necessary." I waited a beat, then added, "So do you want to kill me?" I leaned against the cool wall, still halfway up the narrow staircase between 409 and 411 South.

"You know, for a tough chick, you sure seem to let people push you around."

"I know. I'm working on it. But here's the thing. I told Beryl Duncan that I'd find her mother's wedding files. I'm just about at Whisper's office, and ..."

"Yes?"

"I thought I heard a noise," I mumbled, feeling terribly idiotic.

"You wimpin' out?"

"It's spooky inside this staircase. Very otherworldish. But now that I have you talking in my ear, I am ready to rock."

"We are quite a team."

"Aren't we? So now I'm going to go up the stairs. Hey, where are you anyway?"

"Driving over Mulholland. I'm going to help Paul move some of his books. You know, I kind of promised him awhile back."

In addition to his lawyerly skills, Paul Epstein was a man of many outstanding and often odd qualities. Like a mad genius. His résumé, if he would ever commit anything about himself to paper, would be amazing. He played seven instruments beautifully. He'd been a Marine in Nam. He couldn't part with a single book he'd ever read, and I believe he read just about every book published. And, due to his passionate belief that conspiracy theorists were the only clear-headed thinkers in the country, he had designed a stealth lifestyle, always underground, always on the move, never at one address for longer than nine months.

I reached the landing, faced the door marked PRIVATE, and knocked. After a few seconds, I pulled out the key ring Beryl had given me.

"So, what gives?" Wes asked. "Are you . . . vmmph . . . mphet?"

"Wesley?" The phone just spat out static. Great. Wes must have been driving through one of the many annoying dead zones in L.A.'s cellular grid. In the hills, that wasn't so unusual.

"So what's happening?" Wes asked, perfectly clearly.

"I'm trying the keys. The first one doesn't work." As I slipped the second key into the lock, I hitched up my shoulder to hold the tiny cell phone up to my ear. Using both hands, the second key turned easily in the lock and, twisting the doorknob, I felt the door opening.

Then, bam! All hell broke loose. Somehow, the tiny upper landing was instantly filled with men. Big men. Shouting men. Men with guns drawn and pointed at me. Large hands shoved my back, flattening me against the door jamb as the doorknob to Whisper Pettibone's office flew out of my hands, and the door slammed wide open.

"Wes!" I shrieked, trying to grab my cell phone before it fell.

Static on the other end. Dead zone. Shit.

"Wes!"

"SHADDAP! NOW!"

A man's hand grabbed my wrist and jerked it behind me. With my faced pressed into the wall, I couldn't see anything. But I felt my cell phone slip and go crashing down the stairs as I felt the rush of several massive men push past me, entering the office I'd just unlocked.

"Who the hell are you?" I yelled, feeling an adrenal rush of clarity replace the fear. I tried to make sense of it. Where had they come from?

Hell! They'd been in Vivian's office all along. So, they were either the guys who had killed Vivian. Looking for something. Or . . .

"Are you *cops*?" I yelled, as I heard the sound of men scuffling

"LAPD! Let's see some I.D. Now!"

Holy shit! I'd walked right into the middle of some police ambush. Dehumanized in under five seconds.

"Madeline Bean," I said, trying to dig through my bag for my driver's license. I took it out and handed it to the man. "Vivian Duncan's daughter sent me here."

"Cuff her," one of the cops said.

"What? You can't do that!"

I felt cold, hard metal as my wrists were cuffed. Strong hands grabbed my shoulder, a little less brutally, and turned me around to face a tall, black cop. Beyond him, in the open doorway to Whisper's office, the floor was covered with dumped files and ripped photos.

I turned to look into Vivian's office. The door now stood wide open. The same landslide of papers could be seen. A chair was knocked over. A silver candy dish stood empty on a desk littered with ripped notebooks.

"Oh my God."

A young, good-looking officer, wearing an LAPD windbreaker, came back to the hallway. "It's just like the other one, sergeant. The whole office is destroyed."

"You mean they were ransacked?" I asked, feeling a little sick at the sight of the aftermath of all that fury.

Another officer came to the entry landing and made his report. "The computer is history. Just like the other one."

"Smashed up?" the sergeant asked.

"Something like that."

And then he looked back at me. "So you claim you had nothing to do with any of this? Is that what we're supposed to believe?" He looked down at my license. "What did you say your name was? Bean?"

"Madeline Bean. I'm a caterer."

The first officer disappeared back into the offices of Whisper Pettibone. I heard him say to his buddy, from deep inside where I'm sure he didn't think he would be overheard, "Glad we got her in cuffs. Wouldn't want an unauthorized caterer running loose in Beverly Hills."

"We had this place staked out," the sergeant said. "Where'd you get that key?"

"Sergeant . . . ?" I tried to read his name from the pin on his shirt. So I could have Paul sue the city and cite the name of the correct asshole.

"Leeland."

The door from the street opened and several more police officers climbed the stairs. I could see some of their uniforms. Beverly Hills cops. And behind them, it looked like some guys in street clothes. One was carrying a camera case. It was getting to be a regular law enforcement convention.

"You're in a lot of trouble, Miss Bean. Better tell me about the key," Leeland said.

"*I'm* in a lot of trouble? Get my lawyer, you dip!"

"You don't get a lawyer. You haven't been arrested. Just shut up with your big threats and answer the question. We know there were three keys. One was Mrs. Duncan's, which we have. The other belonged to the assistant, Pettibone. A third one is supposed to be for Mrs. Duncan's husband and you're not him. So explain how you got a duplicate key."

I tried to calm down. "I told you. Vivian Duncan's daughter gave it to me. Maybe it came from her father, I don't know. She couldn't find Whisper Pettibone and she asked if I could do her a favor and help with some of the wedding work."

Behind the trio of BHPD uniforms and the police photographer, a plain-clothes detective arrived on the scene. He reached us at the top of the stairs and looked us over. Me in my khaki shorts and black tank top, handcuffed, amidst several bulky, sweating cops.

"Found her entering private premises with an illegally obtained key, sir. Under questioning, she admitted the key did not belong to her. Says she's a caterer."

"You need her in cuffs?" he asked.

"I'm pretty dangerous," I suggested.

Keeping his expression stoic, Sergeant Leeland set me loose under the watchful eye of the new top man at the scene, Detective Chuck Honnett.

"Sorry, ma'am," Leeland muttered. "You were in the wrong place at the . . ."

"Thanks, Lloyd. I've got it from here."

I rubbed my wrists. Not because they hurt. Just to emphasize the point that I'd been handcuffed. Me. A law-abiding citizen. A favor-doer. An unarmed caterer, for God's sake. What could be less threatening?

"You okay?" Detective Honnett took my hand gently and turned it over, checking out my wrist.

The guilt thing worked like a charm on Honnett. It was one of his more endearing qualities. "Have a seat," he offered, indicating the top step. I sank down and he joined me. Behind us, the commotion of various and sundry investigators filled the small, enclosed space. As I sat there with Honnett, more criminalists joined the investigation.

"So who tore up Vivian's and Whisper's offices? The same people who killed Vivian?" I asked.

"We'll see," Honnett said. "We're just getting started on this one."

In the stairwell, the walls around us strobed from the

reflected flashes coming from inside the open office door.

"So, where'd you get the key?"

"Beryl Duncan came to my house. Vivian's daughter. She pretty much bulldozed me. She demanded that I help her get the wedding plans so she could notify brides about her mother's death."

"And that's all you know about any of this?"

"Sort of." I liked to bug him. Sitting next to Honnett on the stairs was rather nice.

"Don't screw with me, Bean," he said, weary.

"Excuse me, Detective Honnett," the young handsome officer said. Honnett looked up. "There's a closet in the back room that's locked. It's the room with the copier machine, so maybe it's just a locked supply closet. Leeland wants to know if we should break it down."

I suddenly thought of the key ring, still hanging in the door lock.

"Honnett. I've got another key. There."

The young cop pulled the key out of the door and walked back into Whisper's office.

Just then, downstairs, the door to the street opened once more.

"Maddie?"

"Wesley!"

Wes bounded up the stairs, two at a time, his lanky frame hiding the strength of a long distance runner.

"Damn it, Madeline, you had me frantic! I called 9-bloody-1-1 and they said there were already six officers out at this address. I thought you were dead!"

"Hey! Honnett!" We heard the shout coming from deep inside Whisper's office. "Get in here quick!"

We followed on Honnett's heels, charging back through the torn-up office, moving past the entry room and down a hallway. One room, larger than the rest, I pegged as Whisper's own office; several others were used to store files. All were in a shambles. The back room held office equipment. Leeland and several men stood outside this room. Wes and I tried to follow Honnett as he made his way back, but we were stopped at the door.

"Look at this," Leeland was saying.

"Son of a bitch," I heard Honnett respond.

Then I turned sideways and slid past the beefy cop blocking my view.

At the back of the equipment room, next to the copier, the closet door was open. Inside, shelves held boxes and cartons, each ripped open, revealing the office's extra supplies of coffee sweetener, Hershey's Kisses, and tea bags. On the floor, half inside the closet and half out, stretched the body of Ted "Whisper" Pettibone.

Chapter 13

*S*itting at a booth at Kate Mantellini's, the table in front of me was covered with the office-in-a-purse effluvia that normally got toted around just in case. Spread among the loose business cards and Mayfair Market receipts was my personal datebook, several pens, and my pager. I slapped through the clutter on the tabletop, palmed the card I'd been looking for, and began dialing the number on my cell phone.

"Hello," I spoke into the phone, watching a perky waitress arrive with a large Diet Coke, and careful not to disturb my essentials, set it down. "You just saved a life," I said to her, *sotto voce*, and then got back to business on the phone. "It's Madeline Bean at two-thirty. I'm afraid your mom's business files were trashed, along with about everything else in both offices on Melwood. Also, that police detective wants to talk to you. Just a warning."

Wesley looked up at me from behind the huge Kate Mantellini's menu in which he'd been engrossed.

"Machine," I explained, and then turned back to the phone and spoke quickly. "So you're going to have to track down Vivian's upcoming brides yourself. Try her answering service. Nervous brides tend to call their wedding consultants and leave frantic messages. Oh, by the way, Whisper Pettibone turned up. It's a long story, but, cut to the chase, they've taken him to Cedars. Ciao."

"Nice message." Wes watched me gulp down half a glass of soda.

In the catering and events-planning business, much of our work involves communication. From contacting the guy with the best rentable cotton-candy–making equipment to rescheduling the Cal Arts instructor who performs custom temporary tattoo art at bar mitzvahs, it was necessary for me to make a thousand calls. So leaving an effective message was a skill I'd had a zillion opportunities to perfect.

As I drained my glass, my other hand was busy punching in the number to the hospital, which I do with just one thumb, ladies and gentlemen! If my speed record was down a tad, it was just that I was having a little difficulty reading the correct numbers off the note I'd scribbled earlier on the back of someone's business card.

"Checking on Pettibone?" Wes asked, handing me a menu. Subtle. The man was hungry.

Of course, when you dial into a large institution like Cedars-Sinai Medical Center in West Hollywood, you don't actually get to talk to a human. Instead, there's a gauntlet of challenges awaiting you, requiring precise listening and number-selecting skills, which may or may not get you to where you need to go. I tried to listen, but found myself tempted by the enormous list of California chic, designer diner food on the menu. I don't know if it was my sudden interest in reading the details of Kate Mantellini's disturbingly perfect meatloaf, but soon, I was lost in an audio no man's land, where a surreal voice read off an unending list of extensions, none of which made a whit of sense to me. I touched the OFF button, annoyed.

"Ready?" The bright-eyed waitress had reappeared. I wondered if the wait staff at West Side restaurants have perfected the art of showing up at tables the moment they spy a cell phone being disconnected. Just one subtle finger movement and they swoop, before their window of opportunity evaporates.

"Shall I?" Wes asked, hopefully. I usually let Wesley

order for me at restaurants. One reason is I can take an excruciatingly long time to determine whatever it is I think would be the perfect thing to eat at that exact moment in the foodie universe. For another, Wes does a masterful job of selecting the best combinations of food.

As Wes quizzed the waitress on ingredients, I again picked up my phone, but this time I looked up Det. Chuck Honnett's cell phone in my tiny phone directory and dialed. By the time Wesley had satisfied his culinary pickiness with the perfect late lunch order, I was back off the phone.

"That was Honnett. Pettibone is okay. Hit hard on the head, they're saying. Unconscious for several hours. But he's awake now. Last night he was sent by Vivian to go pick up some documents at her home. I think that must have been the honeymoon plane tickets, actually," I said, putting two and two together as I explained everything to Wes. "But when Whisper got to Vivian's, no one was home. He figured her husband must have decided to come and deliver them after all."

"So when did Whisper get back to the wedding?"

"Apparently, never. He told the cops he made a quick stop at his office on Melwood before returning. That's when he was attacked. He thinks it was only one man, but he was jumped from behind and never saw much of anything."

"He's lucky to be alive. It sure seems to leave him out of the running for who killed Vivian."

"Hmm." I looked around for Bright-Eyes. I had forgotten to ask for another Diet Coke. "I'm not sure I trust Whisper Pettibone," I said, slowly. "Who's to say he's telling the truth? So far, it's only his word that he never made it back to the wedding. For that matter, who even says he was really mugged? Maybe he faked the break-in. Let me think. I was standing there in the landing this morning . . ."

"That would have been *before* you were a victim of an overzealous police action?" Wes almost never panicked, and preferred understatement to almost any other type of statement in the universe.

"Exactly," I agreed, equitably. "I'm talking preassault, here. And I remember clearly, the doors showed no signs of damage. Those locks hadn't been jimmied, that's for sure. So I'm just saying . . ."

"Oh ho." Wesley's eyes twinkled. "What kind of random burglar comes equipped with a full set of keys to the offices? So you're not buying Whisper's story. This is so you, Maddie."

"What?"

"The person with the best alibi so far immediately gets your suspicions up. Interesting."

I smiled. "I'm only pointing out that Whisper Pettibone has not yet proven he's in the clear. You know, he did have a pretty annoyed look on his face at the wedding last night. He was bugged that Vivian wanted to sell her business to me."

"Uh huh," Wes said, nodding. "Annoyed and unconscious. Deadly combo."

The food arrived and we took a moment to get settled, me furiously sweeping all the receipts and pens and sunglasses into my shoulder bag, clearing the decks as it were, while our waitress set down steaming hot food beautifully presented on overlarge white plates before us. To top things off, she had, just for the heck of it, brought along a fresh glass of Diet Coke. Ah, that woman's tip had just enjoyed a mental merit increase.

"Anything else from Honnett?" Wes asked over a forkful of pasta primavera. "You two still on for tonight?"

"I think so. He's going to call me. He says we need to talk."

"Talk." Wes put down his fork. "Has this thing maybe made a subtle transition from a dinner date to interrogation?"

"That would be my guess." I sipped my drink. "The press is already at Cedars. I'll bet the Pettibone thing is the lead story on the four o'clock news."

Wes smiled. "That is, if they can't dig up some late-breaking medical news on the safety of silicone breast implants."

True. There was always an implant story on the L.A. news. I was philosophical. "News is news. Whisper Pettibone is but one man. In this city, silicone news touches everyone."

Wes raised one eyebrow.

"Except me," I added, smiling. "Of course."

"Well, Honnett owes you, Maddie. After his police goons jumped you, you could very easily sue the city."

"Come on. I'm over it. And, if *every* innocent citizen who was assaulted by the LAPD sued . . ."

"Paul would love it! Seriously. It's his greatest fantasy to wreak havoc on the establishment."

"Let's not give him any ideas, all right?" I was not inclined to take anyone to court. Paul considered this my one true flaw. I was antilitigious. And he lived for the thrill of out-tricking the enemy in court.

As I jiggled my straw, adjusting the ice cubes in the tall glass so I could get one last swig of Diet Coke, I remembered the business card I'd used to jot down the hospital number. I went searching through the mess in my leather bag and retrieved it.

"Hospital?" Wes was finishing his primavera, looking satisfied.

"No." I turned over the card and read the name and address engraved on the front:

VERDUGO WOODLANDS COUNTRY CLUB
3000 Fairway Drive
Glendale, California 91207
Chef Jose Reynoso, Executive Chef

"It's from the guy I met last night who did those astonishing ice sculptures. He gave me this card." I handed it to Wes.

"Jose Reynoso. Is that the ice sculptor?"

On my way to the loo, I moved around to Wesley's

side of the booth, standing over his shoulder.

"No. See, written in pencil in the corner? It's Albert Nbutu. This chef at Verdugo Woodlands Country Club knows how to get him. Say, would you mind calling Reynoso? Ask for a direct number or address where we can reach Albert Nbutu, okay?"

"Sure."

When I returned a few minutes later, I was a hundred times more presentable. My unruly hair was freshly twisted into a large knot, the stray tendrils for the moment in captivity, and an application of lipstick renewed my feeling of having it all together. Wes, I noticed, had already paid the bill.

"It was my turn."

"Yeah, catch me next time." That is what Wesley Westcott always said. He was a dear, generous man, but I was going to have to be quicker on the draw if I expected to keep our friendship on an equitable basis.

Before I could protest, he continued. "Guess what? That number for Albert Nbutu was bogus."

"What?" I thought back to the previous night. After walking right into him, I'd apologized and introduced myself. I'd asked for his card. He had pulled one from the back pocket of his jeans. His professional contact, he'd told me.

I was concerned. "You mean there was no Chef Reynoso at Verdugo Woodlands?"

"Oh, yes. He's a real character. Very nice, in fact. It's this Albert Nbutu person who seems not to exist. Chef Reynoso never heard of him or anyone who fit his description."

"Odd."

"Yes."

"Disturbing, even."

"Agreed. But, if I may ask, since we aren't planning any parties just now, what would you be needing with an ice sculptor anyway?"

I couldn't explain it. Something about the way Vivian's and Whisper's offices had been destroyed. Something about the jagged rips across everything from the furniture to the computers to the dozens of dumped manila folders had made me suddenly very curious about the man I'd met briefly the night before.

And his chainsaw.

Chapter 14

*H*alfway across town, I changed my mind. I had an even better idea.

But perhaps I should tell you the first idea. As Wesley and I were awaiting delivery of our two separate vehicles from the Kate Mantellini valet parking attendants, Holly called, relaying an urgent message from Beryl Duncan.

Oh no, I'd said back to Holly, not her.

Beryl was waiting by the phone, apparently, for me to call her back. She was frantic. Her father was *a wreck*, she said. *Emotionally*. He couldn't take care of himself. He missed Vivian. Imagine that. I was quite sure a lot of this story was exaggeration, but the gist was that Ralph Duncan was so, well, *drugged to alleviate grief*, Beryl said, that he was incapable of taking care of the family pooch. He was out of control.

Beryl was out of control, if you asked me. Repressed grief, perhaps. I felt no hesitation at making such a snap diagnosis, as, like the rest of the country, I felt I had earned a psych degree watching *Oprah*, with a doctorate in *Sally Jessy Raphael*.

Infuriating as she was, I still thought, "poor Beryl." I mean, trying to figure out if you love your parents more than you hate your parents is a full-time hangup for most of the people I know. And that wasn't even taking into account the emotional mess of having the hated/loved parent murdered directly after you last quarreled with her. So I tended to give Beryl some extra slack.

She begged me to go straight to her father's house and pick up the poor dog, for pity's sake. She, herself, was much too stressed busting her hump on her big-time celebrity divorce case. And, she pointed out, since I wasn't really working at the moment . . .

Well, heck.

Wes was standing right there when I disconnected with the overwrought Beryl. And, true friend and dog fanatic that he is, he suggested the best solution for Beryl, dog, and me might simply be for Wesley to rescue the mutt and bring him back to Chez Wes for a brief vacation from whacked-out, drugged-up, for-all-we-knew-homicidal Ralph Duncan.

So, while Wesley was driving over to B.H. to pick up Esmeralda, I was headed home. Or so I thought. But on my way, somehow the old Jeep got off track. In fact, if I was not mistaken, I seemed to be getting onto Forest Lawn Drive just before the turnoff to my own neighborhood of Whitley Heights.

Forest Lawn Drive takes a winding, peaceful path past the world famous cemetery to the stars. But aside from its questionable status as one of Hollywood's more morbid sightseeing destinations, it lay directly on a route that would be taking me to Glendale, home of a huge shopping mall, a modest community college, and Verdugo Woodlands Country Club. What a coincidence.

A quick check of the Thomas Bros. guide, ten more minutes of steering east and north, and I was approaching the tree-studded hillside neighborhood that surrounded the club. I pulled up to the valet and stepped out into the late afternoon sunshine. A doorman in uniform hesitated for a fraction of a second and then turned to open the front door for me.

It was then I realized that I was not exactly attired for a day at the country club. I smoothed my khaki shorts, but they were still about six inches shy of golf course code.

"Don't bother," I said. I gave him a cheerful smile.

"Can you point me to the service entrance?"

"Sure, miss," he said, his hand releasing the open door, and pointing left. "That way down past two doorways. Turn into that little driveway and you'll see it on your right."

I thanked him and moved on briskly, walking along the low, elegant clubhouse. It was an enormous, contemporary mission-style building of a very modern design. On my side was a long parking lot for club members and guests. On the far side I caught breathtaking glimpses of the lush green of a golf course. All was extremely quiet—the hush of privilege. Only wealthy birds were permitted to tweet. I counted doorways, turned up a service driveway, and tried the handle on the proper door.

Inside, the activity in the large industrial kitchen belied the serenity of the club's exterior. Four-fifteen on any afternoon, a banquet kitchen is usually jamming. After all, another night, another wedding. The show must go on.

I watched a group of young men doing prep work. They were speaking Spanish, which is not unusual for kitchen staff in Southern California, but I dismissed the idea that one of these men could be Chef Jose Reynoso. Instead, I looked around at other knots of white-coated staff, assessing. When I came to the back of a man's head, wearing a toque, I knew I'd spotted my quarry.

"Chef Reynoso?"

"Yes?" The executive chef turned and gave me a very large smile. All teeth. Well, all except the one on the top left. That one was gold.

"I hope I'm not disturbing you . . ."

"Not at all." His smile never wavered. This was a gentleman suited to a job where he must keep five hundred or so picky country club members happy. Short and powerfully built, Chef Jose Reynoso had a thick thatch of black hair beneath his tall chef's hat, and I could see a line of fine sweat across his brow from working over hot stoves all day.

"I wonder if there is someplace more private where we could talk?"

"But of course, miss," he said.

Just then, the ripping noise of a motorbike's engine whined loudly and close by. I spun around. A man in an adjacent room, wielding a chainsaw, stood over a solid block of ice.

It wasn't Nbutu.

"Too noisy here. Let's just go to my office. It's right this way." Chef Jose led me to a tiny cubicle next to the kitchen. In order to dampen the noise of the racing chainsaw blade, he semiclosed his office door when I was seated, and picked up a white towel to wipe his brow.

On his wall were many certificates of merit, framed, that spoke of the chef's prowess in constructing life-sized gingerbread houses, for baking towering wedding cakes, and at winning institutional ice-sculpting contests. My, my. Fancy that.

I was quite certain Chef Jose knew a good deal more about my ice sculptor friend, Albert Nbutu, than he had been willing to admit over the phone to a stranger like Wesley. But why had he clammed up?

"My office is a terrible mess, isn't it?"

"Not at all," I said, politely, sitting down on the only chair facing the small, cluttered desk.

"Well, miss, how can I help you?" Chef Jose beamed at me, gold tooth gleaming.

"My name is Madeline Bean. I wonder if you have heard of the International Society for Ice Artistry?"

"Why, no. Is it new?"

"Quite."

Chef Jose's eyes glistened and I do believe he smiled a little brighter. "Well then, I must join. Of course. Would you be kind enough to tell me of the registration fee?"

"Oh, no. I'm not here to collect dues, Chef Jose. I know you must belong to several ice-sculpting organizations." I looked quickly at the ashtray on his desk.

"The American Food Service, I know, holds wonderful competitions."

"Yes, of course. We have been very fortunate, you know, to win this year's top trophy. Best in our division, of course. But also Best in Show."

"Exactly, exactly," I said. "I apologize for just dropping in unannounced. Actually, I am friends with one of your club members. She was raving to me about your wonderful work."

"One of our members?"

"Yes. In fact, I was just over at her house." I looked down at my shorts. "Gardening."

"I see. What member is this?"

My eyes found a name on a work order on the chef's cluttered desk.

"Swanson."

"Swanson?"

"Yes. Mrs. Don Swanson."

"You are a friend of Mrs. Swanson?"

"You seem surprised," I said, lightly.

"Why, no. Of course not, miss. Then you must be coming to Mrs. Swanson's ninetieth birthday party next weekend."

"Of course! Anyway, Mrs. Swanson insisted I stop right by and interview you," I said, pulling a small notebook from my bag, along with a pen. "You bringing home the ice-sculpting trophy to Glendale and all. Which is why we at the ISI . . . A, um, ISIA, we call ourselves, why we would be so grateful for just a moment of your time. For our journal. You must help us out, Chef. You really are the man of the hour."

"Well, isn't this wonderful? I would love to oblige, but at the moment I'm preparing for a banquet. We have the annual club dinner honoring the president."

"The president." I looked at him, picking up my pen. "Of the United States?"

"Of Verdugo Woodlands Country Club."

"I wouldn't need more than a few minutes. For instance, where did you first learn to cut the ice?"

"You mean 'carve'?"

"Yes." How could I get through an interview if I had no idea what the lingo was? Terrific.

"Oh, I began many years ago. I was working for a resort in Arizona then, and the executive chef liked me. He offered to send me to Hawaii for a seminar in ice sculpture so we could improve on our Sunday brunch displays."

As he continued with his happy road to ice-sculpting fame, I took notice of the various framed awards and photos, hoping I might lift an appropriate catch-phrase or specific jargon that might keep me from blowing my own cover. He was just finishing up, talking about how he felt God had meant him to give back, and now he trained many young apprentices in the noble frozen art.

I was about to ask him about those he had trained, when my eye startled upon a framed photo among the clutter. It showed a team of four men in front of a mammoth ice sculpture of Gwyneth Paltrow. In drag.

"My, that's a marvelous work!" I said, when I realized he'd noticed me staring. "Was that an award winner? My readers would love to see a picture of one of your great pieces."

"No, that one was not for competition," he said, with a deprecating laugh. "No, just a private commission. That one was custom-ordered for the post-Oscars party for the movie *Shakespeare in Love*. Perhaps you've seen the movie?"

I nodded politely, but I couldn't take my eyes off of the photo on the desk. The man on the far right was Chef Jose Reynoso. The man next to him was Albert Nbutu.

"The work on . . . on Gwyneth's face is astonishing," I said, lifting the photo for a closer look. The ice sculpture was in the background. In the foreground, all four men in the picture were shirtless. From the hand of each man hung a chainsaw. And all but Nbutu were smiling big cheesecake smiles.

"I'd love to use a few of these photos." I waved

vaguely around the room. "They'd be perfect for my story. Might I borrow some to show my editor? I promise to return them as soon as possible in perfect condition." I picked up another, to make it look good. It was an elaborate banquet display for the American Uvula Association.

"My, what a marvelous . . ." I studied the five-foot-high ice sculpture on the dessert table in the photo. ". . . *uvula*! So real, you can't believe it's ice!"

"We had the devil of a time hanging that down over the table," Chef Jose said modestly.

"I'll get these right back to you," I said.

"Well, I would love to do you a favor, Miss Bean, but I'm not sure . . ." Chef Jose was not accustomed to having to say no to a request. I knew the feeling. We caterers and party chefs are in the "yes, we can" business, and only feel good when everyone is happy. It's a curse.

"Thank you so much. And, of course, I'd love to send our photographer out to do a shoot of your work. Perhaps I could call you to set up a time?"

"That's great. Maybe we can work up some special sculptures for your magazine. I'll start thinking of subjects we could do."

"Wonderful." I stood up. "I'm afraid I've taken up too much of your time."

As he walked me back into the main kitchen, I slipped the 8x10 of the uvula as well as the frozen Paltrow, frames and all, into my large shoulder bag. He did not object.

As the valet pulled my old Grand Wagoneer up to the curb outside the main entrance to the club, I took another look at my prize. Albert Nbutu's sleek, muscled torso stood out in dark contrast to the other men in the group. I wondered again why Reynoso had lied to Wes about knowing Nbutu. And then, in the bright sunlight, I caught a new detail I'd missed when scanning the photo inside. On Albert's right shoulder I could make out the faint markings of a tattoo. That's right. Now I remembered. When I had run into Albert in the dark hall, I had seen or more like sensed that tattoo. But now I was curious.

I realized the valet had been standing for some time beside the open door of my car. I passed him two bucks and hopped in. But before I pulled off, I took another careful look at the photo of Albert Nbutu's tattoo.

It looked like a design of some kind of faceted jewel—a diamond, perhaps. And there seemed to be a word inside the gem. It was impossible to be sure. After all, the dark lettering on ebony skin was a challenge. But as I stared I began picking out letters.

S-A-N-D . . . Slowly, I got the hang of the slanted script. It looked like the word was SANDMAN. No, there were too many letters. I scrunched my eyes and began again. SANDAWANA, or perhaps it was SANDAMAMA.

Sure. Fine. Excellent. Now what in the hell is SANDAMAMA?

Chapter 15

I stripped off the black tank top and let it fall to the floor, where it joined the shorts I'd just stepped out of along with various other items of discarded clothing. I noticed the little pile did a fair job of covering the tiny white hexagonal tiles on the bathroom floor. Sometime soon I'd gather up the laundry into the basket. Maybe July. Such are the minor luxuries of living alone.

Fingers under water, I checked the shower temperature. Old pipes take a minute. Out the bathroom window, the early evening sky was gray and cloudy. Like yesterday and the day before. June gloom. It passes for a season here in L.A. And a state of mind.

I was relieved to finally step under the hot needles. Water rushed over my head. The shampoo was found. And all the while, I kept wondering about this Vivian Duncan thing.

I squeezed conditioner over my thick tangles and combed my fingers through, turning the problem over more thoroughly in my mind. Maybe this Albert Nbutu had nothing to do with Vivian's death. But maybe he had seen something.

I spent the obligatory hour getting my hair dry and putting on fresh makeup, while thinking about how I might track him down. When I left the country club, I'd put in a call to Freddie Fox, but he was no help. He had hired Albert through Chef Reynoso and had no other contact information. Another dead end.

I selected a thin, gray V-neck sweater to wear over a silk camisole and a long black skirt. Back in the bathroom, stepping over the scattered fashion debris, I checked the big mirror. This first date business was tough.

The floor. Hmm. Did being newly single give one the freedom to be sloppy? Or, conversely, must one be hyperneat, so one's nest is in shape for any last-minute romantic possibilities? Ah, there was the rub.

I carefully straightened damp towels and scooped up scattered clothing. Walking to the hamper in my bedroom, I felt marvelously organized and virtuous and, well, open to whatever the heck might come.

Next to my bed, I keep a small wooden box with a sweet family history. This high school woodshop project had earned my brother, Reggie, an A$^+$ in ninth grade. Reggie's way with pine could not be denied. That boy had always had a talent for design, and his experimental use of dove joints had taken my young breath away.

I perched on the side of my bed and swung the lid of my brother's box back on its hinge. Ta-daa. The Madeline Bean jewelry collection. No big whoop. One watch, a four-thousand-dollar Tag Heuer knockoff. Wes loves to buy me $20 sidewalk specials from the Manhattan corner vendors when he's back east. One pearl and aquamarine ring from my parents on my thirteenth birthday. One good pair of small, heavy gold hoops. I put those on, removing the tiny diamond studs I often wear.

I had a fair amount of good silver from the time Wes and I catered a party in Rosarito Beach a few years back. It marked the end of all those ocean scenes they shot there for the movie *Titanic*. We spent a week setting up the party on the beach. We had thought of holding the party on deck of the mock ship they had constructed. But it turned out no one wanted to go back out on that ship again. *Ever*.

In between running all the food and water across the border from San Diego, I prowled the vendors in town. In one dusty antique shop, I discovered some very old silver pieces. By week's end, I'd worn the owner down with brilliant bilingual bargaining. I loved my prizes, but they were wrong for this evening.

I looked through my small holdings. How do other women manage to acquire all their expensive baubles and bangles? Perhaps, I reasoned it out, they withhold sex until after a suitor pays up with a ruby necklace or something. I smiled. No wonder I didn't have any fine jewels.

Which of course, brought to mind my former boyfriend, Arlo. We had had our moments. Many of them. We had, I thought with regret, been quite hot. At one time. I sighed, looking at myself in the small mirror in the jewelry box.

To give Arlo credit, he had tried to be generous. I had shut him down. He bought me the diamond stud earrings. And once, early in our relationship, he'd picked out an outrageous gift, a very expensive watch from Van Cleef. It was back at our first Christmas together. Naturally, I had insisted he return it. Too weird. I mean it practically cost as much as the balance on my mortgage. How, I wondered at the time, could anyone wear such an expensive item on her wrist? Now, I wondered how it might look sitting in my jewelry box. Older and wiser, that was me.

In a tiny black box was my favorite necklace. I picked out the long, thin gold chain that held a tiny cross, covered in *pavé* diamonds. This had been a gift from a previous boyfriend. I dangled it from my raised hand, watching the tiny diamonds glint off sparks. Again, too many memories. Perhaps this evening called for a necklace that did not come attached to the history of a former lover.

Of course. Wesley had given me a choker. Tiny gray pearls were spaced out between short lengths of gold

chain. Perfect. I raised it to my neck and reached around
to clasp it.

It was almost eight o'clock and I hadn't yet heard
from Honnett. Not that I was getting nervous. I checked
my answering machine and, sure enough, three messages
had appeared since I'd entered the shower.

*"Hello, Madeline. Beryl Duncan here. I heard from
my father that your friend managed to pick up Es-
mie . . ."*

Oh, right. The dog. Wesley was amazing, I thought,
as I fiddled with the strap to my watch.

*". . . What a relief. I am so swamped here at work,
and I expect you aren't busy, so please do make that
call to pick up Vivian's messages, would you? I'll be at
my office number all night, if you need to reach me."*

That woman had somehow leeched herself onto me,
and didn't show signs of letting go. If I weren't so terribly curious about what Vivian had been up to, just
before her last wedding, I would blow busy Beryl off.
But, damn it, I *was* curious. And concerned. And interested in everything. Always. My life and welcome to it.
The thought did drift through, just fleetingly, that if I
came up with anything interesting, I might offer it up to
Lt. Honnett.

What was I thinking?

Sad, I acknowledged, but true: even though Honnett
was a cop, even though, for all I knew, he was probably
married, even though he'd never made a serious move
on me, even though we had a history of botched dates,
I was attracted to the guy. I had better get a grip.

This is what came of too much leisure time and no
work. This is what came from loneliness and feeling
sorry for myself after breaking up with Arlo. This is
what came from having a little too much money and
getting comfortable. Ancestor Puritans I'd never before

realized I must have lurking in my gene pool, asserted their voices in subconscious protest. I needed to get back to work. Ah, well. I jotted down Vivian's message service number.

The truth was, I was missing that rat, Arlo. Maybe that was the root of my troubles. If only Arlo hadn't been so . . . well, Arlo. With his food fussiness and his quirky moods. If only he had been capable of more than joking around. But then, those jokes were part of the attraction. Not to mention, those jokes had won him an Emmy, earned him a fabulous salary, and made him a producing superstar on his sitcom, writing scripts. So changing Arlo wasn't the answer either.

The doorbell rang, interrupting my downward spiral of self-analysis, a pursuit which always leaves me with the bittersweet realization that while I may get the occasional clue as to what it is I really want in life, it's probably bad for me, anyway. Better, I figure, not to go there.

Down the stairs, I almost tripped trying to get to the door. Had Honnett decided to just drop by?

"Hey, Mad."

Nope.

Standing at my front door was the unannounced, uninvited Arlo Zar.

"Arlo. Hi."

"So, can I come in?" He moved up to me, slipping an arm around my waist. In my bare feet Arlo has maybe an inch on me. And I'm only five foot five. Arlo held me a little tighter than a friendly hug.

"I thought we weren't going to be dating anymore, Arlo."

"I know. We agreed. You're right. But I wasn't thinking of tonight as a date, so that's all right."

"Uh huh." I stood looking at the man I'd been seeing exclusively for the past four years. He was undoubtedly cute, in a wire-rimmed, curly-haired, great smile, really thin sort of way.

"What's up?" He must have noticed my outfit and my general state of fixed-upness.

"Here's the thing . . ." I let it hang there for a minute. God help me, but he looked really good. The rat.

"Am I interrupting something?" He tried to grab a look through one of the front windows. My house is up a full flight of stairs from the curb and, standing there at the doorway, he could look into the bay window of my downstairs living room. It was dark. "Look, Mad. I have things to say." He gave me his best puppy dog look. "But they sound much better, you know, like, *inside*."

"Maybe," I suggested, "we could get together for lunch some time. No patio seating, I promise." Arlo and I were trying to make this difficult transition from lovers to friends. I figured lunch was a "friend" kind of deal.

"Jesus, Maddie. You're killing me, here. Can't I come in for a minute? I mean what's the harm? Do you have a date tonight or something?"

It had been almost three months since we broke up. For real. And another two or three months before that, when we kept meaning to break up but kept drifting back. It had been hard to make that clean break. And yet, when we'd tried to work things out, nothing much changed. Holly said it was because I was evolving while Arlo was stagnating. Emotionally. Something like Arlo was from Mars and I was from Venus. I had to take her word for it. She kept up on the romantic state of the solar system.

The phone rang from inside the house.

I turned to look. "I better get that."

"Oh, yeah. Sure. Don't want to keep the new boyfriend waiting. Don't worry. I can let myself out. Oh!" He smacked his forehead. "That's right. I *am* out. Perfect."

"Call me first, next time," I said, and then closed the door on the last chapter in my romantic life. See? I can move on.

I got to the phone in my office a few seconds too late.

The call had already been picked up by my answering machine. I could hear Chuck Honnett's voice, coming from the speaker, leaving a message.

". . . was going to drop by, but I guess you aren't home. Maybe I'll try your other phone num . . ."

"Honnett?" I picked up the handset and interrupted his message.

"That you, Bean?"

"I just got in." Well, I had. "What's up?"

"I'm in the car. I just had dinner with a few of the other investigators working the Vivian Duncan murder, so I wondered if I could maybe swing past your place and . . ."

I waited. Was he going to say "ask a few questions," or "hang out and relax"?

". . . try to apologize for screwing up our evening."

Ah. Even better. He said he'd be by in half an hour. My, my, my! Ain't life a kick! My mood was 100% improved.

While I waited, I played back the remaining two messages. One was from Sara Silver, the abandoned bride. She was staying at her grandfather's house up above the Sunset Strip, and wondered if she could talk to me. She had questions about some wedding etiquette and Vivian was, well, gone.

I shook my head. Poor kid. If this was one of those questions like—if the wedding consultant takes a nose-dive into a dinosaur, and the bridegroom takes a hike, must the poor bride return all the lovely wedding gifts?—I was not quite experienced enough to guide her. I wrote down her grandfather's address and played the next message.

"Madeline? If you're there, pick up."

Wesley.

"It's almost seven and I'm figuring you are out for the night with that big lug, Honnett. Honey, behave!

*Holly and I are going out to eat, so call me if you need
me."*

I smiled. Those guys. I picked up the phone, but it
wasn't Wesley's number I dialed.

Sitting back, I found the number I'd written down and
called Vivian Duncan's phone mail account. Beryl had
left me her mother's private password, and after a few
more seconds I heard a mechanical voice saying, "You
have," long pause, "ten," another pause, "new messages."

I switched the phone to speaker and listened, taking
down names and numbers that meant almost nothing to
me. Most of the messages dated from the afternoon of
the Silver-Bell wedding, before Vivian had died. They
were mostly routine. But it was so sad—listening in on
the woman's private messages, knowing she'd never return any of these calls, hearing those voices speaking to
Vivian as if she were alive.

Whatever else Vivian Duncan had been, she had been
a strong and vital woman. What could have possibly
gone so wrong in her life that it had ended in murder?
I continued listening to the various unknown voices,
most of them so concerned about their own little dramas.

Some left little messages along with their names. One
woman wondered if the fruit from Paris had arrived?
Fruit from Paris? Another young woman left a long list
of questions about dentists and the timing for getting her
teeth bleached. One mother wanted to fly to New York
with Vivian to look at gowns—not wedding gowns, but
mother-of-the-bride gowns. I would have to call them
all back tomorrow. They must have heard about Vivian's
death, by now, but they wouldn't know where to turn
for their upcoming weddings.

I sighed. I would also have to visit Whisper tomorrow
and see if he was up to taking over. It really was Beryl's
responsibility, but as she was dumping on me, I figured
I could see it through. I continued taking notes until a
voice came through the speaker that sounded vaguely

familiar. It was a man's deep bass, with a hint of a European accent. British.

"Vivian, I know I'll see you shortly, but I want to make sure you bring the ruff. I'm counting on you, my dear. The sultan is not a very forgiving man."

I sat up, alert. Was that a threat? And what was he talking about? The *ruff*? The *rough*? The rough . . . *what*? I played the message back a few more times, but it became no clearer. I wrote down the hotel that he was staying at and his room number.

There was only one message left, and I played it out. This last one was from Vivian's husband, I gathered. I listened to it closely.

"Vi, I got your message. Well. I got several of your messages. Don't worry about a thing. I will get the tickets issued for that damn couple. Their final destination is Harare, right? I thought I had written it down. Well, anyway, if you get this message dear, please call me at home. Oh. I see by the clock that the wedding is probably already starting by now, isn't it? Oh, dear. Well, I'll try your mobile phone."

I wondered if that was the phone call that I'd walked in on, when I approached Vivian before the wedding ceremony. The one where she came unglued at her "dear" husband's irresponsibility. Had he been yelled at and humiliated one time too many?

I replayed his message and listened for the sound of seething, pent-up rage. It just didn't seem to be there. But how much could I tell from one short phone message?

I looked back at my pad and circled the hotel and room number I'd scribbled down. I picked up the phone and called The Four Seasons, asking for room 512.

"And may I ask the name of the party to whom you wish to speak?" The operator was brisk and friendly.

These luxury hotels were used to screening calls. Hell.

"I had a message from a gentleman, a British gentleman, and he only left his room number."

"Oh. I am sorry, but . . ."

Policy. Right.

I cut in. "I'm helping out a friend who owns . . . well, she was a wedding planner, actually. This gets a bit awkward as I can't actually ask her for more instructions."

"Omigod! Not the one who died on the dinosaur!"

"Well . . ." Of all the horrible things that can happen, you don't ever want to "die cute." Not in L.A. Trust me. "Well, yes, actually."

"Just a minute. I'll call the room and ask the guest if he can take your call. Who shall I say is calling?"

"Madeline Bean. Tell him I was working with Vivian Duncan."

"Of course. And I am so sorry," the voice said, thrilled, "for your loss, Miss Bean."

What can I say? We live in a city where celebrity is the ultimate clout and where murder made celebrities quicker than casting directors.

"Hello?" The familiar voice came through the line.

And then I had it! The one from the wedding, with the beautiful eyes and the black mustache and the long, sexy hair.

"Is this Miss Bean?"

"Madeline, yes. We've met, actually. Briefly. Before the wedding last night. You pointed me in Ms. Duncan's direction. I was wearing black." Now that was helpful. "But I'm sure you don't remember. I've got reddish-blond hair . . ."

"Why, of course. You are harder to forget than you give yourself credit. You wore a tiny cross, am I right? *Pavé.* Very chic."

"Thank you." Hot damn. I thought I'd caught him gazing at my chest. These designer dresses are simple but deadly.

"I must apologize," I said, "but I never got your name."

"I am Zeller Gentz. Terribly rude. I do beg your pardon. Please call me Zelli. All my friends do."

"I know you must be wondering why I'm calling. The family asked me to help with some of Vivian's business responsibilities at this difficult time. Just until others are able to take over, really. And I picked up a message you left at her office . . ."

Just then, my doorbell rang.

"I'm sorry, Zelli. Someone is at my door and I have to get it. I wonder if you would mind if I called you back? Perhaps tomorrow?"

"I have a better idea. Tomorrow is my last day in town. I'm going back to Zurich the day after. Why don't you join me for dinner?"

"Dinner?"

"Tomorrow at eight. Why not? Will you meet me here at the hotel? They have a very nice dining room. I would be very interested to talk to a friend of Vivian's."

"Really?" Well, well, well. "So would I."

"Yes? Good. Although, in point of fact, I haven't seen her in many years."

We rang off. In point of fact, I hardly knew Vivian. But this was too intriguing! A fabulous man. A killer English accent. An old crony of Vivian's with stories to tell about her past.

I ran to the door. There, at long last, was my date for the evening, Chuck Honnett.

"Hi."

He stood there, looking down at me, bemused and cool as a cuke. He was so tall I had to crane my neck to make contact with his royal blues.

"You ate dinner already, right?" he asked.

"Don't worry about me. Would you like to sit outside? I can make a fire."

"Sure." He followed me into the house.

I walked him through my office and out the double French doors that led to the courtyard. While Honnett settled down on the patio furniture, I started up the outdoor fireplace for warmth. I brought out a tray for sustenance: a plate of lemon/raspberry bars I'd baked earlier. A bottle of brandy, a pot of coffee, and the frosted bowl filled with scoops of homemade ice cream, fresh from the freezer, each crusted with a different luscious topping. I placed a couple of crystal dessert bowls on the table, along with spoons, and told Honnett to help himself. He smiled, quizzing me on what ice cream topping was what, and ended up serving himself three scoops.

"Look, Madeline. I got a call on the way over here. It looks like I'm needed back at the department."

"Right away?"

"You know how it is. I can't always predict when I'll be available. I'm sorry."

I began taking little stabs with my spoon at a scoop of the Deep, Dark Brown Sugar ice cream, studded with homemade mocha coffee chips.

"It's the Vivian Duncan case," Honnett said. "I know you were friends with her. So I'm sure you understand."

"Of course," I lied. Now why was it, again, that I had sent Arlo away?

"Man, this is fantastic." Honnett ate the ice cream with gusto. He poured a second cup of coffee. He ignored the brandy.

"So you're sure it was murder, then?"

"No question. Her neck was broken. Hit over the head, most likely. We're pretty sure she was killed somewhere else and then dragged up the stairs to that lighting rig and pushed off onto the dino exhibit."

"That's just so horrifying and, I don't know, kind of stupid. Why would someone go to all that trouble? Wouldn't they be seen?"

"Everyone had already gone to the dinner and the killer was goddamn lucky. Anyway, the coroner found smoke in her lungs. Cigarette smoke. His theory is that she was maybe taking a break, grabbing a smoke, and was jumped from behind. We checked around outside and found a few butts with her lipstick. Out back by the kitchen setup. But we are still looking around. By the position of the blow to her neck, it must have killed her instantly. M.E. thinks she . . . that's the Medical Examiner."

I nodded and took a taste of ice cream.

"He thinks with the smoke still in her lungs, she probably died before she could exhale."

I coughed, involuntarily. Naturally, I stopped eating.

Honnett looked into my eyes. "This isn't too graphic for you, is it?"

"Heck, no. Me? Strong like bull."

"This is all part of our ongoing investigation, so none of this information leaves this patio."

"Sure."

"It's nice here." Honnett looked around my small courtyard, at the wall fountain and the garden to the side. In the subdued lighting and the glow of the fire, he finally seemed to notice me.

"That reminds me," I said, "I was looking for that man who did the animal ice sculptures for the wedding. Do you cops know how to reach him?"

"The ice sculptor?" Honnett shot me a look, puzzled. "What does he have to do with anything?"

"I'm not sure. But I was thinking about Vivian's and Whisper's offices. They looked more than trashed. They looked . . . like . . . shredded. And ice sculptors use chainsaws. Do you think a chainsaw could have been what caused all that damage?"

Honnett thought it over, sipping his coffee. "Pretty unlikely. But I suppose it's possible. I'll mention it to the forensics team." He smiled at me and suggested, kindly, "Even if you are right, I'm sure you know that there are millions of chainsaws in this county, and not one of them is registered."

"There ought to be a law!" I smiled back, but didn't let go of my argument. "But why can't I locate this ice guy then? The country club he gave me as a reference denies they ever heard of him. And when I went to check it out for myself . . ."

"You . . . what?" Honnett interrupted me, looking more concerned.

"When I went out to the club I kinda looked around in the chef's office and I found a picture that showed the guy I'm looking for. So I just sort of took it."

"You say you went out to the suburbs, talked your way into some country club, did an unauthorized search, and stole personal property?"

"I think this is one of those glass is half empty, glass is half full things. What I did was visit a fellow chef. I was invited into his office. And, well, I was allowed to borrow the photo."

Honnett's serious face cracked, at the edges, where a smile broke loose. "What you're telling me is that you didn't break any laws, right?"

"Right."

Honnett relaxed.

"Not any I *know* of."

"Maybe I don't need to hear this story in its . . ." He stood up, preparing to leave. ". . . entirety."

So much for new romance.

"I can respect that. You are a rules guy. But don't you want to see the photo?" I stood up, too.

"You hang onto it. We may get to it later on in the investigation."

"You're shining me on, aren't you? You're not even going to check it out . . ."

"Look, Madeline. I'm sure you appreciate that I can't tell you everything that's going on. Right now, we're following up other leads. I can't say more than that."

So he'd been holding out on the hottest details in their case all along. It figured. He's a cop. What did I expect?

"What?" Honnett asked, standing with me at my door. "Did I say something wrong?"

"Oh, by the way . . ." I looked him squarely in the eye. "Who was that woman you were with at the wedding last night?"

"The what?"

"Skinny. Big hair. I don't believe I had the pleasure of meeting her."

He relaxed into a genuine smile. "I was with my cousin. Joan."

"Not your wife, then." I mean *really*. Who was he trying to kid? Who had a cousin Joan?

"My *wife*?" Honnett let out a low chuckle. "You are hunting in the wrong woods, partner." He took a step closer and put his hands on my shoulders, really looking at me for perhaps the first time all evening, "I loved it that you made all that dessert stuff for me. It was the best ice cream I've ever eaten. No lie."

"Um hmm."

"I'm not married, Madeline, if that's what you think. I have been. I've tried it. Twice. It's not that I didn't find the right women. It's just that maybe I'm not the right man."

"Not the right man. Uh huh. You can do better than that. How about parting with a few personal details?"

"About me?"

"About your availability. Or do you belong to the police department?"

"Well, I guess you might say I'm kind of stuck. I know I need someone, but who would have me? I've tried it alone. You know what that's like. That gets to be . . . Anyway, I'm way too old and grizzled for a beautiful young girl like you."

Hot dog! Date talk. "Young woman like me," I corrected, smiling at him.

"I can't even use the right words. I'm too old for a beautiful young woman like you."

"Well, let's see, old man, just how ancient are you?"

He laughed. "Old enough to know better." He pulled me a little closer. "Are you?"

"Hell, no."

We stood there looking at one another. And then he kissed me.

Chapter 16

I readjusted my laptop computer and snuggled into a more comfortable position on my sofa. What had happened to Vivian Duncan anyway? There was very little that made any sense. I began to make a list, which is how the organizer in me takes over.

On that first day I'd met her, in the alley parking lot behind Darius's flower shop, Vivian had just been attacked, and now I was getting a sick feeling it was somehow connected to her death. In fact, looking at the rash of incidents that had sprung up in the past several weeks, I wondered if a pattern might emerge. I quickly typed in all the bizarre crimes I could recall.

First, of course, I listed the car-jacking. Violent and shocking as I had found it, Vivian's reaction had been much more calm and in control than mine. I had just met her, of course, so I had no idea what sort of person she was. I had put her reaction down as that of a consummate professional who deals with crises every day. But now I wondered. Perhaps she had had some secret reason of her own to play it cool.

Hey, what did I know? I had assumed the car-jacking was random. I had assumed, like any urbanite, that driving a fancy car came with risks, such as having your fancy car stolen and chopped up for parts. I had assumed the indomitable Vivian Duncan was just not going to stand for playing the part of the victim. But now I wondered if she were, in fact, trying to cover something up.

Vivian had sent me a magnificent flower arrangement the next day, in thanks for my help. Her note mentioned she had gotten her Mercedes back and it was fine. Was that just a typically gracious Duncan gesture? Or had she an ulterior motive? I was caught. I had managed to construct a scenario in which the poor dead wedding planner was cast in the role of co-conspirator in some mysterious crime. I was really scum. And yet . . .

If these suspicions were true, there was more behind that assault on Vivian and her sedan than just a couple of punks looking for black market car parts for some Valley chop shop.

Tomorrow, I would visit Whisper Pettibone to turn over the business messages. I made a note to ask him about Vivian's car while I was there.

I moved on to make quick notes about other crimes and mysteries that might be somehow related. After all, Vivian's office had been broken into and destroyed, as had Whisper's. And Whisper had been assaulted as well. It certainly appeared that their business might be targeted for some reason, but why? What kind of records could a wedding consultant possess that would provoke someone to commit a murder?

As an afterthought, I typed in a note to ask Paul's opinion. He knew about business.

Paul, of course, believed the government was out to get everyone—one of his pet conspiracy theories. He had already found secret new digs and moved, always one step ahead of whatever ghosts pursue him. But he might know if Vivian's business seemed suspicious.

I added a few notes to my list regarding some of the other odd characters in the drama. Beryl Duncan, the daughter too hurt to grieve, and her father, who was reportedly so distraught he couldn't even be trusted to take care of Vivian's pet. And could any of this really be connected to the missing bridegroom, Brent Bell? Or, had he taken the weird opportunity fate had thrown him to take the escape clause from married life?

And that made me think again of the bride and her family. Sara Silver seemed emotional, and why not under the circumstances? But what about her scary old grandfather? T.V. icon or no T.V. icon. Come to think about it, Big Jack Gantree said that he and Vivian went way back. Cast now in the light of Vivian's murder, I was extremely curious how far back they went.

And how did the handsome Zelli Gentz fit into the picture? That, at least, I could try to find out at dinner tomorrow.

Looking over my list, I began to feel I had a plan. But all of those questions would have to wait until tomorrow, and I was still itching to find out what the hell it all meant. And then I remembered one more name to add to my list of odd characters.

Set up on the tiny pine coffee table were the photos I'd borrowed from Chef Reynoso.

Who are you, Albert Nbutu? I studied his image, trying to guess his age. Forty, maybe? Or fifty? He was in excellent shape, his arms sinewy, his stomach flat and hard. Perhaps he was thirty. But, no. Something around his eyes showed a sadness, or a weariness, or maybe it was more like a wariness. Older, I figured, and a hard life.

I thought back. The few words we'd exchanged the night before had been tinged with an accent. Not exactly Caribbean. But . . . something. Didn't Freddie Fox say Albert was from Ethiopia? Then I spent a few more minutes trying to decipher the word tattooed across his shoulder.

I logged onto the Internet and began searching on the word SANDMAN. Oh, brother. 73,000 matches. Dandy.

It was almost ten o'clock before I'd exhausted myself tracking down the top 200 websites that had popped up as a match. Trust me. What I couldn't now tell you about the Sandman project to study sleep biorhythms, or the dark hero of Neil Gaiman's cult classic comic books, or, for that matter, some professor of psychiatry named Carl Sandman at the University of California at Irvine, you truly do not want to know. I had even found a site that offered the original lyrics to the golden oldie "Mr. Sandman." I was getting nowhere. Slowly.

I raised a fresh strawberry to my lips and typed into the search field the word SANDAMAMA. The search engine chugged on the odd word. This time I would not be spending two hours following strange, fruitless leads. This time there were no matches. I brightened up and stretched.

It was getting late. And no, I wasn't thinking about Honnett. Or how disappointing it was that he had to leave. Or what a turn-on it is when a man is dedicated to his work, even creepy cop work. Or that he was trying to make like he wasn't controlled by his feelings. Like Honnett as Spock. But, come on! I'll bet . . .

SANDAWAMA drew a blank, too, so I typed in a few more words.

Where was I? Oh, yeah . . . I'll bet I can get him to care about someone . . .

Whoa! I stopped myself cold. Now that is a truly healthy reason to be attracted to a man. Why was it I always had my finger over the self-destruct button, ready for action?

Back to Nbutu, I studied the tattoo in the photo once more. I'd been coming up blank with several unheard of words, but kept at it. Next I tried the equally unlikely SANDAWANA.

To my surprise, 71 matches appeared. Who'd have thunk?

Using the fingerpad, I quickly pressed the first entry. This website displayed the recent winners of the Sandawana Cup, a prize for championship Staffordshire Bull Terriers. *CH. Magliam True Grit of Fonna, CH. Tenacious Juno Bedford Blossom of Millenium, KUSA National Dog 1989, CH. The Brown Bomber of Westmax.* I found my eyes blurring at the list of pedigree names.

And what could all these cute little bulldogs have to do with Nbutu?

"Madeline!"

I jumped and then realized it was Wesley's voice I heard calling from downstairs.

"Anybody here?"

He'd let himself in, as he often did, probably to pick up work he needed from his office.

"Hey, Wes! Come up," I called back down. "Save me."

"We thought you would be out on your big date with Chuck Honnett."

Ah, Wes was not alone. Holly's voice grew louder as she mounted the stairs and came into my little upstairs living room. Her purple top was cropped high above the hip-hugging black Capri pants, showing off a tiny tattoo of a holly berry just below her navel.

"We came bearing food," Wes said, entering right behind Holly.

His olive cargo pants were perfectly pressed. Naturally. But I was more impressed by the ample bag he held up. That looked promising. Doggie bag alert.

"Where'd you two have dinner?"

"Miyagi," Holly said. "That place is so hot! Everybody was there tonight. And we sat on the third level, which was rockin'."

Miyagi was a relatively new sushi club on Sunset built in three stories. Each level of loud, sushi bar madness was hipper than the next.

"Wow. You scored." I looked hopefully at the bag and gave a brilliant impression of a doggie whimper.

"Down, Spot. I'll just clear off this table for you." Wes moved a few magazines.

I smiled as I put down my notebook computer and gathered up the notes from my all-night project.

Inside the white bag was a container filled with an assortment of my favorites: spicy tuna roll, yellowtail, and Miyagi's specialty—caterpillar roll. It was kind of like a macho California roll with freshwater eel wrapped in rice and covered with avocado. I was in heaven.

Holly flopped down on her favorite chair, rubbing her long fingers in the soft sage-colored chenille fabric, but Wes seemed uneasy.

"What's up?" I looked at Wes with concern.

"It's Vivian's dog," he said, glancing out my window toward the back of the house. "I left her down in the courtyard with a bowl of water, but . . . She's really a dear."

"Wesley! Bring that poor gal up here."

Wes brightened and left.

"So it's you and me," I said to Holly, waiting for her to question the whereabouts of my date. Instead she was focused inward.

"I'm supposed to meet Donald after midnight. Man, he's been so busy lately, I've hardly seen the guy. We only have time for a quick jump and he's gotta go back to his place and work on his screenplay."

"Well, that's probably natural for writers, Hol."

"I mean, I told him to keep the lights on while we do it, or I won't even remember what he looks like anymore, you know?"

"Hol? Too much information."

"You wimp." She laughed. "So what happened to Honnett? You look like you never even went out."

"He was here. He showed up. Don't worry. He had to go back to work."

"Oh. So what is it with us? Why are we involved with these work geeks, anyway? What we need are some unemployed actors! Now, they have got time to boogie." She looked at me with dancing eyes. "Let's get us a whole stable of unemployed actors and it would be sex, sex, sex—morning, noon, and night! We would not be two chicks sitting alone getting way too excited over some lousy take-out sushi on a Monday night, mama!"

I cracked up. So pathetic and so nailed.

I heard the jingling of a dog collar accompanied by Wes's soothing voice coming up the stairs. And into the room walked one very odd-looking dog.

"Hi there, girl," I said, patting her proud but almost hairless nose. She was tall and quite thin, and she had an extremely short-haired golden brown coat, with a strange cowlick thingie along the top of her spine. I also noticed her dog collar had a hanging pendant with a very large square-shaped green stone, like a simulated emerald.

"She's Vivian's dog, all right. Check out those accessories." Holly reached over to scratch the calm dog's head. "I mean, who'd I have to hump for a choker like that?"

Wesley grimaced. "Ah, ah, ah . . . she heard that. I'd watch your leg, honey."

See, Holly and I have rather similar observations on life, only expressed a shade differently.

"Boy, she certainly is one calm, cool dog," I said. "So what is she? She looks very . . . uh . . ."

"Wacky," Holly suggested.

"Well, I can tell you for sure she's not a Staffordshire Bull Terrier," I said, with the superior attitude of a woman who has just looked at eight dozen photos of same.

"She's a Rhodesian Ridgeback, I believe," said the man who knew everything. "See this fur?" Wesley drew his hand across the dog's back, feeling the stubby fur cowlick that ran down the center. Imagine a shaved dog with a mini-Mohawk. "This is her ridge."

"Ah."

"Cool."

We all took turns feeling her ridge. It actually felt quite good. And the dog didn't mind a bit.

"Esmeralda, down." Wesley gave her a friendly command and the sweet-tempered dog behaved brilliantly, resting down on her haunches next to the sofa.

Wes sat down next to me and noticed the photos I'd been studying all night.

"Wow. You scored. How'd you get this picture of Albert Nbutu?"

"Long story. I decided to visit Verdugo Woodlands. Funny how this picture of Nbutu was on Reynoso's desk, eh? I had to make up a whole song and dance, but the chef was actually a lamb. Now, I wonder what was going on? Why did he pretend he didn't know this guy when you called, Wes?"

"Beats me. Maybe you showed him more leg than I did."

"To be fair, he didn't see your leg, Wes. I'm sure he would have appreciated it, given half a chance."

"Thanks, sweetie. So how'd you get him to talk?"

"I didn't want to spook Reynoso so I didn't mention Nbutu at all. He got the impression I was from some ice sculpture magazine."

"Good one." Wes was amused.

"Boy, people can get interested in some pretty weird stuff," opined the queen of weird herself, with a straight face.

"He let me borrow some photos and the great part was, he didn't look very closely at the ones I took. It was masterful, if I do say so myself. Only I've hit a major snag. I thought I would find some brilliant clue in this photo that would help me track Albert down in thirty minutes."

"And?"

"That was five hours ago."

Curious, Holly moved over to squeeze in on the sofa. "That's your ice sculptor guy? What a body." She traced his image over the glass with one long purple fingernail. "Cool tattoo."

"Can you read what it says?" I asked.

Holly took the frame and squinted close to the picture. "I think it says Sandman, maybe."

Wesley took the picture from her and studied it.

"Isn't that a jewel?"

"Yes. Like an outline of a diamond, I think."

"No," Wes said, still studying the photo. "It's square. Like an emerald."

Of course it was.

"Interesting, isn't it?" Wes asked us.

"Uh . . ." Holly didn't get it.

"There's an emerald on Albert Nbutu's shoulder, and there's a fake emerald on Miss Esmeralda's collar," I said, thinking.

"And, of course, Esmeralda is the Spanish word for emerald," Wes finished up.

Holly giggled. "You guys know too much."

"Wait a minute. Holy shit." I pulled my PC back into my lap. The screensaver, the floating words EAT DRINK SEX that Wes had long ago programmed into my computer, disappeared and the Champion Bull Terriers website blinked back on. I hit the back button and came, once again, upon the list of 71 matches for the word Sandawana. Scrolling down almost to the bottom of the page, I came back to a listing I'd just barely glanced at earlier. Sandawana showed a match on a website for something called the Mining News.

A few seconds later I was at the opening page that described various mining operations in several developing nations. I used the FIND function to get to the word I was looking for. It brought me directly down to the word Sandawana, as in the Sandawana Mine, as in a location in the interior of the country of Zimbabwe.

"This is a little freaky," I said, clicking on a few more buttons. Wes and Holly watched the screen flash through its silent progression of images. "Wasn't Zimbabwe formerly called Rhodesia?"

"Yes it was," Wes said. "Rhodesia became two countries—Zimbabwe and Zambia—back in the seventies."

All three of us pondered the fact that Vivian owned a dog whose country of origin contained a mine whose name, Sandawana, was tattooed on the shoulder of an African who was present at the occasion of her demise. Of course, it made absolutely no sense.

Wes looked at me and asked, "What exactly gets mined at Sandawana?"

"Wait! Don't tell me. Don't tell me," Holly said, excited.

I pushed a button and in a few seconds we would have our answer . . .

Holly jumped up, like a *Jeopardy!* contestant on uppers, and excitedly blurted out, "What are emeralds?"

. . . just before the image appeared on the screen.

Chapter 17

*T*he robber barons who run the parking structure at Cedars-Sinai Hospital engage in legalized extortion. Seriously. They charge an arm and a leg for every twenty minutes, and you're crazy to pay it. Better to park at the Beverly Center and walk. That way, either coming or going, you get to cruise the mall if you want. I usually want. But this morning, I was in a hurry.

I checked in at the visitors' desk and was directed to the proper bank of elevators. Up to the South Tower, fifth floor. Walking along the linoleum, smelling hospital smells, I began to feel some compassion for Whisper Pettibone. While maybe I had not formed the best impression of him, and maybe his manner was decidedly waspish, he certainly didn't deserve to end up in a hospital bed. I resolved to tread gently in our interview, to be my most nurturing self. Nurse Cherry Bean—kind, caring, sweet-tempered. A goddamn angel of mercy.

At the door to room 599 I stopped. What to do? For some reason—and really, I blame the HMOs—the hospital fails to provide doormen to announce you. And yet, what an intimate space is a sickroom—a bedroom, really—in which to have a casual stranger, such as myself, barge. I faltered, standing in the hallway. I would hardly have looked forward to visiting the acidic Mr. Pettibone when he was full of his usual vinegar, dressed to the teeth. To approach him while he was in bed, loosely wrapped in some hospital-issue gown complete with breezeway bottom, was a thrill I could have happily lived without.

Just then, a middle-aged nurse opened the door, startling me. She gave an exasperated "tsk-tsk-tsk" and walked off. Apparently, Whisper Pettibone was a charming patient this morning. Wonderful.

I stepped forward and looked into the room. Whisper was sitting with his bed half-inclined, staring at the wall opposite.

I knocked softly on the open door, hoping to get his attention.

"Excuse me. Mr. Pettibone? It's Madeline Bean. Do you feel up to a visitor?"

"I feel like bloody HELL," he said, turning to look me over. "I think I may die, but whether from the brilliance of my hospital treatment or of boredom I would hate to wager a bet." Whisper took a few labored breaths and said, "But why are you still standing out in the hall? Enter. Come in. I can't very well carry on a conversation with you if you insist on standing a mile away."

I entered the room. Whisper was hooked up to an IV line that led to a stand on wheels parked next to his bed. His head was bandaged and one arm was set in a cast. Several fabulous flower arrangements were in evidence, set side by side on the window seat. His skin, always a suspiciously deep tan, looked sunken on his prominent cheekbones, dark against the white linens. He kept his eyes closed when I approached, but now opened them and stared at me.

"Madeline Bean. Would you believe you are my first visitor? And I don't even know you, do I?" He took a moment to adjust his wire-rimmed glasses and smooth a hand back over his thinning hair.

"I wish I had had time to bake," I said, feeling awkward, "but I stopped at Urban Epicurean." I held up a large tote filled with the assortment of gourmet treats I'd picked up on my way over.

"Oh, goodie. Real food." He said it in a most sarcastic

tone, but I think he was pleased. "Set it down over there." He gestured to the bedside table that was moved a few feet away. "I'll get one of the slaves, or would that be nurses? Yes, I'll get one of the nurses to put it away in a refrigerator. Probably the last time I'll see it, too. Thieves, the lot of them. Oh well, no matter."

I smiled. And he very grudgingly let his eye twinkle. But only for a fraction of a second.

"I've come, of course, to talk about the business. If you think you are up to it. There are some things that need to be dealt with, the sooner the better, but I don't want to bother you if you are too tired."

"The business? By that you mean *my* business, don't you?" Whisper Pettibone looked me over. "We hardly know each other, Miss Bean. And truth to tell, I really didn't think I liked you at all. Not at all."

"I got that impression, yes."

"But here you are, coming to visit me like I'm your sick uncle. Wearing that ghastly little dress. Bringing store-bought food." He clucked his tongue, annoyed at himself. "But quite respectable store-bought food, I must admit. And you don't gush, do you? You didn't go all wimpy asking about the nasty details of my injuries. Admirable. I may have to change my opinion of you . . ."

When it's a toss-up between being amused or being insulted, I take amused every time. Life is short. And where's the fun without the occasional kook, crackpot, or scalawag getting in the jambs? I sat there appreciating one of life's sincerely oddest old kooks, and smiled.

". . . which, of course, I never, ever do. Because I'm always right, naturally, so it's never necessary. You see what a pain in the ass you have become to me, Miss Bean? So vexing. I begin to wish you had never shown up at all. However, seeing as how you are the only one likely to make this sacred pilgrimage to my sickbed, I must rise to the occasion. Do sit down."

I did.

"Have the police figured out who did this to you?" I asked, concerned.

"Don't make me laugh. Not a bloody clue. I mean, they are without a single brain cell between them. They're savages and good for little else than beating poor defenseless things about with their billy clubs. You only have to imagine how they dealt with a man of refinement and culture. I was bloody and unconscious, being rolled into the x-ray, and they were after me like hounds, trying to get information. I couldn't speak. How could I? It wasn't my own injuries, Miss Bean. I am not talking about mere pain of the body.

"It was from a much sharper pain that I was struck silent. You see, those bastards told me about Vivian. The first moment I recovered consciousness, they told me. I fought my way back from the depths of oblivion, only to be told I had lost my soulmate, my dearest companion, my very best friend in a wretched and desolate world. My lovely Vivian has been killed, they told me. I really cannot be expected to take this all in. I am an artist, with an artist's soul, and an artist's sensitivities." He closed his eyes.

It was quite a speech and had clearly exhausted him. His labored breathing began to sound more and more like snoring. Just as I was sure the man had fallen asleep, he spoke up.

"I hope you will not leave just yet, Miss Bean."

Startled, I sat back down.

He opened his sunken eyes and looked at me. "I'm worried," he said.

"About the business?"

"It's all I have, Miss Bean. Are you still determined to take it from me?"

"No. Absolutely not. Don't you give it another thought."

"What's that? Are you toying with me? What, dear lady, are you saying?"

"I never wanted Vivian's company. I am not sure why she fixated on the idea, but she approached me and kept after me. I thought she might have needed the money."

"Nonsense. We are doing well, naturally. And Vivian is worth a fortune. Everyone knows that."

"Are you sure? Sometimes people give the impression . . ."

"Hush!" he interrupted me, "I see her books. I do her personal finances. I know where her offshore accounts are kept. I pay the bloody insurance premiums on her jewels and furs. I have a key to a joint security deposit box, which is filled with cash, if you must know. We are not in any way low on funds. And Vivian came into the business with so much capital she barely knew what to do with it all. Have you seen her home on Courtney Road? She bought it with cash. Shortest escrow in the history of Beverly Hills."

"I see."

"I should hope so. Be sensible. In all the time I've known Viv she has never made a decision based on money. My word, we were above all that."

"Then I can't understand why she was so insistent that I buy her out. I told Vivian no at the wedding, but she didn't want to listen to me."

"I'm not sure I believe you, you know," Whisper said, upset. "Oh, I don't know what to believe. It was most unusual from the start." He looked at me, as if to decide how much he wanted to confide. "Should I tell you?"

"That has to be your call," I said.

"You don't beg, do you? You don't pry and you don't insinuate. Most amazing in a girl like you."

"Actually, I prefer being referred to as a woman."

"I'm sure you do. The problem I'm having is with Vivian's behavior, don't you see? It doesn't seem at all Vivian-like. It troubled me then and it troubles me now. She was secretive. Well, that wasn't so unusual. Viv liked to have her little secrets. Silly woman. Of course I found out every single one. Why wouldn't I? I was in charge of the purse strings. I kept the accounts. Let me tell you it is very difficult to keep a secret from the man who balances the books.

"When Viv was seeing that young waiter, who did she imagine was paying the Visa bill that listed all those single-night stays at the Hotel Bel Air? And did she imagine I bought the story that all those clothes she charged at Saks were for Ralph? I think not."

"Are you saying Vivian was seeing someone?" I asked.

"Of course she was. She was a very complicated woman. Ralph couldn't begin to understand her. Why she kept him around is a question for the gods, but she wouldn't hear a word against him."

Vivian's husband. Vivian's boyfriends. Any of these people could have motives to have murdered Vivian. Even Whisper himself. If he really believed Vivian was planning to sell him out, what would he have done?

Whisper must have been figuring things out, too. He looked startled, and then reached up his thin hand and touched his mouth. "Oh, my word. Don't tell me you are trying to solve Vivian's murder, my dear? Can that possibly be what is going through your brain? Stop it this instant. *I* have been going over it all, again and again, and believe me, if anyone were able to get to the truth, it would be me. And it's all nonsense. No matter what you think of any of us. No one would kill Viv, no matter what they may have hoped to accomplish."

"You said her husband . . ."

"No balls! That man is not very good at anything but drinking scotch rocks, my dear. He would simply not have the appropriate gonads to pull off such a stunt. And if Ralph somehow surfaced from his Glenlivet haze long enough to have done the deed, how in the world do you imagine he discovered the courage to drag her poor body across half a museum, up a bloody staircase, and toss her across that heap of bones?" Whisper's eyes blazed at me, challenging me to disagree.

"That's the million dollar question."

"So you are trying your hand at playing detective. This is too rich! And who, pray tell, is among your other suspects?"

"Please don't take this personally, Mr. Pettibone, but I find just about everyone suspicious."

"How wise. How young and how wise you are, Miss Bean. And by that I suppose you mean to say you suspect me?"

"I hope that doesn't make you too uncomfortable," I said, pleasantly.

"Pish-tush! Let's not quibble about niceties. Not when we are beginning anew, Miss Bean. Not when we have a whole delicious relationship to embark upon. Not when you assure me, as indeed you have assured me, haven't you? That you have no intention of taking our wedding business away from us. So let's put our heads together, shall we? Let's think deep thoughts. What if, as you suspect, I had been upset and angry with Vivian? Let's even say I had a very good reason. Can you guess what that might be?"

"Perhaps you hadn't been consulted about selling the business?"

"Excellent point. See how well we are doing? So there I am, distraught over the thought of losing a business I had worked for twenty years to build up. A business, I might add, that had been promised to me all these years. Well, if not promised, then implicitly pledged, as anyone would assume after I had traveled such a long and hard journey building the business up. Even if one imagined I had ample reason to work myself up to *hate* Vivian, which is pure nonsense—I simply worshipped and adored her—but *should* I have felt thrust out, as surely you must have suspected, as you wisely suspect everyone, would I have it in me to kill her? Well?"

"I don't know."

"Good answer. You don't know me at all. But I know me. I could never do such a thing in a million years. But let's say you don't take my word on it. All right, then, let's look at the question logically. Since you have cleverly worked out a possible motive upon the notion that I covet Vivian Duncan Weddings, why then, dear lady, you can't believe I would harm the business. I wouldn't. Had I any motive which involved keeping and preserving and running the business which is Vivian Duncan Weddings, the last place I'd commit a murder would be at one of our own weddings. Don't you see? It would be exactly like pissing in one's own Jacuzzi. Simply not done."

"Excellent point, Mr. Pettibone."

"Whisper to you, now that we're friends."

"Why do people call you Whisper? Your voice is quite booming, really."

"Another time, perhaps," Whisper said, playing at being elusive. "A gent must keep an air of mystery. Now, I wonder if you would be good enough to pour me a glass of water. No, no, not that awful stuff they put in that pitcher. It's from the tap, for the love of God. No, I have a bottle of San Pelegrino here, somewhere. Ah, yes, that's it."

I poured out a glass for Whisper and then, in the brief lull as he drank, grabbed the chance to get a word in and ask one of the questions I was really after.

"I'd like to know more about the day Vivian's car was stolen. Would you mind filling me in a little?"

"I'm sorry? When was that?"

"When her Mercedes was car-jacked." I sat down and I looked at him. "Don't tell me that doesn't ring a bell. Three weeks ago. The day she was supposed to meet Sara Bell and her fiancé at Darius for their tabletop. You called me later that day, remember? You had been worried because you couldn't reach Vivian."

I could tell, as I spoke, that it was the first time Whisper Pettibone had heard of the car-jack incident. And he had claimed it was impossible for Vivian to keep a secret from him. Hah. On the other hand, just exactly why would she have kept such a traumatic crime quiet?

"This is most alarming." Whisper chewed his lower lip. "That is not the story I heard at all. Vivian took the Mercedes to the shop, she told me. Some gizmo gone wrong at the worst possible time, that sort of thing. Certainly, if she had been robbed, I would have known. And she came home late that night, as I remember, driving her own car once more. This is very disturbing. I would suggest a car-jacking never happened, but I believe you would only contradict me."

"I was there. I saw it. I was almost run down by the car as it tore out of the alley." I looked at Whisper, shocked he didn't know what I was talking about. "Didn't Vivian tell you I found her on the pavement?"

"No." He looked at me, shaken. "But now you mention it, dear girl—scratch that—woman, I do recall that I found Vivian's poor pink Chanel wrapped up for the trash. Snagged something tragic! Vivian said it was ruined as she scrambled under a car to fetch a child's fearful kitty. The snags. The oil. The tiny rip. These she explained away as the inevitable consequences of helping this crying tot."

"And that sounded like Vivian to you?" I asked.

"Not on your life. No. Sacrifice a two-thousand-dollar Chanel? And this season's, no less? For a child? I knew it wasn't the truth, but I figured she was keeping one of her boyfriends somewhere messy. This would have explained her sorry excuse for an excuse. I let it go. It was our way. But now you are telling me Vivian had been attacked weeks before the evening of the wedding?"

This was big. I pulled out my phone and dialed Honnett's private line. When he didn't pick up, I left a message.

"Unless . . ." I could see Whisper Pettibone puzzle it out in his mind. "Unless she was indeed covering for some reprobate boyfriend she was seeing at the time. I hadn't thought she was into that riffraff scene anymore. Frankly, it has been years since I've known her to take on a new friend. But if, indeed, she had found a young man who hung with the wrong sort . . . well, it's possible he or one of his sordid little mates stole the Mercedes. If Vivian recognized who took the car, she would never have wanted to report it to the police."

"Yes. Whoever did this would have counted on her

silence. She feared bad publicity. She was the perfect victim. She'd never tell the police."

Whisper said, "Of course. But, really, I can't think this is possible. I would have known. She might have kept a brief car disaster from me, but never a love interest."

"Do you think you could find a picture of her old boyfriend—the waiter you mentioned? And any others. I'm sure she'd have pictures somewhere, and only you could probably find them."

I thought it over. If Vivian had gotten herself mixed up with an immoral lover, who knows what he might have been capable of? Had she somehow threatened him to keep him in line? After all, she got her car back almost immediately. Had he gone a step further and murdered Vivian? Oh, yes, this was promising. Except for the fact that we had absolutely no evidence "he" even existed.

"Aha! Entertaining a visitor this morning, Mr. Pettibone? Lovely!" A cheery nurse, the size of a cement truck, entered the room, carrying a tray with needles.

I knew my cue and stood up. "I'll leave this list with you. The messages on your answering machine."

"No need," Whisper said, briskly. "I got them this morning. First time I wasn't drugged up to kingdom come. I'll take care of the business, now, don't you fret."

"Fine. If you're sure. I know Beryl was worried."

"Beryl? Worried about the business? That is such a laugh, my dear lady, I cannot begin to tell you. Little Beryl worried about mummy's business. Ho-ho-ho."

"She's working on a very big case and she seems like she might snap. I guess mother and daughter had a difficult relationship."

"Tell me about it," Whisper said, as the nurse came around to tidy up his table. "It was simply vile. I talked to Vivian about it. Constantly. But what could one do? Viv was simply *not* maternal. It was regrettable, but there it was."

"And you don't think that Beryl . . ." I let the sentence hang, in view of the bustling nurse.

"My, my, my. You *do* suspect everyone, don't you? Who would ever guess that a pretty little thing like you had such a nasty, nasty imagination?"

The nurse was raising one of the needles, checking it in preparation for a stick. I made for the door.

"Miss Bean! Madeline, if I might? Don't run away. I would hate to think you were offended, now that we've become such fast friends. I meant no offense, dear lady. Your nasty imagination is one of your most charming qualities."

Chapter 18

"All I ever wanted was my own house." Sara Silver sat on the floor of the large living room of her grandfather's house, cross-legged. "Didn't I?"

"Well, that and a man," the thin redhead said, giggling.

"Denise!" the tall brunette hissed. "Cut it out."

Sara was not alone. Three former bridesmaids sat with her offering support in her time of need. Or if they couldn't actually provide support, they seemed determined to stick by her side, come what may.

"I thought I was getting out of *here*, anyway." Sara sighed. "Would you want to live here?"

I looked around. The four walls were paneled in dark mahogany. The wood floors were covered in fine antique oriental carpets. The furniture, in burgundy and brown, was of the heavy, tufted leather variety. Accessories like the brass spittoon and the large alabaster ashtray finished the masculine look. But I almost missed noticing any of it, so overwhelming were the room's central features.

"Well . . ." What was the polite thing to say?

"I'm afraid I'd feel the souls of these animals stalking my dreams," Denise said, clearly not one to give the niceties a second thought.

"They're hideous!" Sara said, referring to the stuffed heads of Africa's slain species mounted all around the two-story-high room. A rhino and a hippo, a giraffe and

144

a lion. They stared down in dismay. "I hate them."

"Why don't you just leave here and move into the condo?" asked one of her friends, a young lady with Asian features and blond streaks in her dark hair.

"No. That was supposed to be for Brent and me. If I moved in there without him, it would be like I've given up."

"That's the point, Sara. Give up. The guy disappeared. What kind of freak leaves his wife before their wedding night? It's abnormal. What could be more jerky than that?" The redhead spoke in a matter-of-fact tone.

I watched Sara. Her hair, black as coal, was tied back, giving her young face a classic look. Her dark brown eyes flashed at Denise and then she stood up.

"Thanks, you guys. It was great of you to come over and cheer me up. But now I've got to talk with Madeline."

"Hey!" one protested.

"What's that?" asked another.

"I thought we were gonna go get our nails done?" The third, a brunette, scrunched a freckled nose. "I've gotta get this little one mended or it's history."

"And *your* nails are shot, Sara. You've picked them right off. You've got to take care of yourself," counseled the first.

"If you stay here, you're just going to get all down on yourself. You've called everyone you know seventeen times and you still can't find Brent. So give up," demanded the second young lady.

Number two was the alpha-bitch of this group. She stood and straightened her charcoal slacks. "Okay. Here's the plan. We'll go to Sara's room and get ourselves fixed. We'll be back in fifteen, and then Sara will be done and we can all go do nails. Come on," she ordered, and the others, chattering away about nail polish, followed her out of the room.

"Sorry about that," Sara said. "I should probably offer you something to drink."

"No need. I got your messages and I figured I'd better stop by. It sounded urgent."

I took out my little notebook, expecting some question or other regarding security deposit money, or thank-you note etiquette, or some other odd or end.

"Oh, Madeline." Sara instantly went into tears mode. "Remember back when we first met at the flower shop? Remember how Brent looked at me. Tell me you remember how much he loved me then."

I put down my pencil. "Of course I remember. You were a darling couple, Sara."

She smiled at me, tears streaming. "I know we were. I know it, goddamn it! We had everything. I had the perfect dress. He had the perfect hair. It was supposed to be the perfect wedding. So how did it all fall apart?"

She was only twenty-two. She hadn't learned, yet, about the risk of insanely high expectations. But why should she? Her wedding planner had been the best in the business. She virtually guaranteed her brides would have a perfect day. Dangerous word, perfect.

"You mean you really haven't heard a word from Brent in all this time?"

"Grandfather even called the police. They said Brent wasn't really missing. We'd have to wait another day or something to make an official report."

I began to worry that this might be more than a case of a bridegroom with cold feet. After all, a murder had happened right at the wedding reception. Anyone might have accidentally seen something and become the target of a killer. Is that what happened to Brent Bell?

Sara used her hands to wipe the tears from her cheeks and I noticed the large engagement ring, now joined by a wedding band, and recalled that I had been impressed by its deep green stone the first time we'd met at Darius's shop.

"Do you think something might have happened to Brent?" I asked carefully.

She looked down at her lap and shook her head.

"Are you sure, Sara? What if the same person who hurt Vivian . . ."

"No." She said it quietly, but I could tell she was holding something back.

"You know where Brent is, don't you?"

She looked up at me. "I want you to go see him. Please. Tell him to come home. Tell him I don't care why he left me. I want him back."

"Are you sure?"

"Yes."

"Where is he?"

"I think he moved into our condo—the one we bought in Santa Monica. Grandfather gave us the money as a wedding gift. We were supposed to go on our honeymoon for three weeks and then when we got back, we would have moved in together. It was so romantic. I had just finished furnishing it, you know? Nothing like this disgusting place. I picked light colors, you know? Brent said I should pick out anything I wanted."

"You *think* he's there? Or do you know for sure? Did you go over and confront him?"

"No. I've been calling there, dozens of times, leaving messages on our answering machine. I imagined that he might be there, standing in the hall next to the machine, listening, and he would hear my voice and . . . I don't know. I figured he was just upset. But he never called me back. And none of his friends have heard from him, not even his brother. So then, pretty soon, I didn't know what to think. I doubted he was there at all. And I couldn't just go there. Don't you see? What if he was there, after all, just hiding from me? I couldn't face him like that. I couldn't. And I couldn't ask my friends to go. They don't want me to get back together with Brent. They think he's a terrible loser, and they won't even let me talk about us fixing it. So last night, when it was really, really late, I decided to call the condo again. And that time, Madeline," she said, breathlessly, "that time somebody picked up the phone."

"Brent?"

"I have to think so. He didn't say anything, but who else could it be? Maybe I woke him up and he just instinctively reached for the phone. But what am I going to do? I can't go there myself. It would be terrible. What if he hates me? I just can't face him."

"Sara, I have to ask this. Could Brent have been involved in Vivian's death? Is he hiding from the police?"

"No way! How could he? That's impossible. He was with me every single minute from the instant I walked down the aisle and met him at the altar until the second I left the table to go to the little girl's room and saw Vivian hanging up there." She began to tear up again.

"I see. That makes it clearer. Thanks."

"My life is ruined."

"I know it must seem awful right now. In fact, it is awful. Really totally crappy. But things change."

"Yes. I know," she said with sarcasm and pain. "That's what Grandfather keeps saying. I'll get over it. Right."

That hurt. My great advice. Since when had I gotten so lame that my words of wisdom matched that of a seventy-year-old geezer? I tried again. "I'm sure that isn't very much comfort to you at the moment, but it's true. I feel so bad for you, Sara. You don't deserve any of this. Your wedding was . . . well, it didn't go as well as you'd dreamed. And Brent's behavior is so extremely bizarre . . ." I let it trail off. I felt so damned useless.

"I wish there was a way to fix it, I really do." I shook my head, frustrated. "Vivian would have figured out a way to help you. Vivian would never have stood for one of her brides being unhappy." I had to admire Vivian, once again, and oddly enough, I missed her.

"By the way," I continued, "your grandfather said he'd known Vivian for a long time. I was curious about that. Did Vivian plan your mother's wedding?"

"Oh, no!" Sara grew quiet.

"Sorry," I said, feeling instantly like I'd trespassed upon some taboo topic. "None of my business. I just wondered about Big Jack Gantree's connection to Vivian."

"It's all right. It's you mentioning my mother like that. I guess it startled me. The thing is, I didn't really know my mother. She died when I was a little girl."

"Is that when you moved in here with your grandfather?"

"Oh, no. We always lived here, I think. My father had died before I was even born. He worked for the Museum of Nature, actually. He was a senior natural biologist, I guess. He did an awful lot of field work. And my mother met him in Africa. They married there. Anyway, it's a long time ago and I don't really know all that much about their wedding. But you are right about one thing. Grandfather did insist we use Vivian to plan our wedding. When she first came to the house to meet with Brent and me, she told us how she used to dance with Grandfather at some officers' club. So, wouldn't that be from World War Two or something? She wasn't very specific."

"I see."

Sara checked her watch, and again I caught a flash from her emerald.

"May I ask about your beautiful ring? I couldn't help noticing how deep the green is."

"It's really too large, I know. Denise says I'm just waiting to get ripped off. And Anita thinks it's so big it looks fake. Imagine that? But, as a matter of fact, Vivian Duncan helped us find this ring."

Emeralds. Vivian Duncan. "How?"

"She knew a gem dealer or something. Grandfather worked it all out. In fact, if you can keep a secret, I believe Grandfather paid for the ring as well. He wanted me to have it, you see. He said it was meant to be. But Brent wasn't real happy about it."

"What did *you* want?"

"I love it, of course. Who wouldn't? And emeralds are my birthstone. May. But I know it must have cost a fortune. I thought Brent shouldn't spend so much right now. But Grandfather likes me to have whatever is best. Next thing I knew, Brent was giving me the ring." She thought it over. "Oh my God! Do you think that's what's bugging Brent?"

"Well . . ."

Sara stood up, shaking with emotion. "I don't care about any of this! I only care about one thing, now. Remember what you told us? That no one is ever guaranteed that there is going to be a tomorrow. You were right."

"Sara . . ."

"Talk to Brent! Go to the condo and tell him I don't care about this stupid ring. I don't care about what my grandfather wants. Tell him I want to start over. Tell him I'll do whatever he says!"

"I'm not sure this is something I should get involved in . . ."

"Please, Madeline? Please? I love him."

Just then, the three friends came rushing into the room, ready to handle any emergency. "Sara, darling, what is the matter?" one asked, alarmed.

"We took too long. It's all our fault," said another.

"Damn it, Denise, I told you we didn't have time for you to try on Sara's wedding gown!" said the third.

"What are you doing to Sara?" asked the first friend, as she came to put her arm around her sobbing friend's shoulder.

"It's not Madeline's fault," Sara said, trying to pull it all together. "She's helping me. Shut up, all of you."

The girls shut up.

"Here's the paper you need," Sara said, pulling a folded note from her pocket. She handed it over to me in a way that kept the prying eyes of the others from catching a glimpse of its message. Held between the note I felt a hard object, a key, which I slipped into my bag, and walked quickly to the front door.

Just as I opened it to leave, there stood the man of the house about to enter. Startled, he just stared.

"Don't I know you? You're not one of Sara's friends. No."

"I'm Madeline Bean. Excuse me, Mr. Gantree, but I was just leaving."

"Madeline Bean? Ah, yes. The caterer. You're the one who is taking over Vivian's wedding business, if I recall." He looked me up and down and burst out in a chuckle—one that I actually remember from his old T.V. series—and said, "And that, I'm afraid, is your tough luck. Because I can tell you right now, Miss Bean, I have absolutely no intention of paying the bill!"

Chapter 19

I pulled my thin jacket tighter around myself. There was a definite, early-June-in-Santa-Monica chill to the air. The sky had been overcast for days. But I was happy. I had managed to park smack in front of the building I was looking for, a three-story architectural statement just a few blocks from the ocean. The ultramodern, concrete-colored structure featured odd flying angles and strange tubing railings and sheets of glass here and there. At the entrance, a small board displayed the numbers of each deluxe condo. A phone allowed one to call up and announce one's arrival. I pushed the button marked S & B BELL for several long, insistent seconds.

No answer.

I used Sara's key.

Soon, I had slipped past the lobby elevator, jogged up the stairs to three, and begun prowling an interesting hallway that was half indoors and half out. Wrapped around the corner, I found 3C. Sara and Brent's new condo.

Okay, I thought, looking around for inspiration, now what do I do?

Was, as Sara hoped and suspected, anyone home? Had Brent really deserted the lovely Sara and hidden himself away in their deluxe condo? Only one way to find out. I stood in the hallway and knocked. No sounds came from inside.

Brent, Brent, Brent, I thought, why have you bailed on your bride? The obvious thought was, because a woman had been killed at the wedding and he was afraid of being arrested. But I'd been over this a dozen times. Brent *couldn't* have murdered Vivian. I was sure of it.

One, it would have been too unfair. I admit, this reason is based purely on principle. I think it's an outrageous notion that a party planner could be done in by the host when that wedding was going perfectly! Well, okay, that's my bias.

Which brings us to *two*. Even if Brent Bell did have some reason to hate Vivian, which I doubted, he was seen by hundreds of witnesses all throughout dinner. But something was surely up. Facts are facts. Brent did take a powder. So what, I wondered, was the problem?

I knocked again, several good, loud knocks. I called out, "Hello, Brent? Are you home?"

Maybe Brent bolted for a more personal reason. Maybe he had some other secrets that had nothing to do with Vivian's unfortunate death. I thought that one over. With my philosophy—you remember? *people are weird*—it was hard for me to be shocked at anything another being might do. I was therefore blissfully free to consider just about any weird thing.

Maybe Brent had a criminal past and when the cops showed up he was afraid they'd recognize him. Hmm. That wasn't bad. Maybe some former girlfriend showed up, unbeknownst to any of us, carrying a three-year-old she now claimed belonged to the groom. Possible. Or, maybe, after spotting my new friend Whisper Pettibone looking sharp in his tux, Brent had chosen the worst possible night in his life to realize that he was secretly gay. Oh, I give up!

I beat the door rather loudly and worried about what the neighbors would think. What they probably thought was: why had they plunked down their million dollars on a condo where aggravated caterers could make so much noise in their hallway?

Enough, already, of that. I used Sara's key.

"Brent?" I called out, closing the door softly behind me.

From where I stood, the condo appeared spotless and unoccupied. The living room was done in shades of mint and white, and looked like it had just been delivered from Ethan Allen, whole. I stepped into the dining room and noticed the same air of undisturbed newness. I continued through the deserted house.

"Anybody home?"

Down the hallway, looking in this room and that, I found no signs of life. In the kitchen, I opened the refrigerator and found it bare except for a large fruit basket. A ribbon across the plastic read CONGRATULATIONS AND WELCOME HOME! I reached out to see if the cellophane wrapper had been opened.

"TURN AROUND!"

I gagged on my gum.

"TURN AROUND! NOW! DO IT!"

My heart had leapt and exploded, and I was barely able to turn around, let alone speak.

Brent Bell stood there, blinking. "Wait a minute. You're . . . you're the caterer we met."

"That's right!" I said, by now gushing adrenaline. "We met at the flower shop, remember? I'm Madeline Bean. Please," I said, still in shock, "put that thing down."

Brent Bell stood in his stocking feet holding a raised baseball bat.

"What the hell are *you* doing here?"

I noticed he did not lower the bat.

"Sara gave me her key."

We stood like that in the brand spanking new kitchen for a few more seconds. My racing pulse made a stab at slowing down. Where the hell had he been hiding? I had looked in most of the rooms. Finally, Brent lowered the bat and I could feel my heartbeat begin to drop below 300 beats per.

"Look," Brent said, with a lot of force, "I don't know what you think you're doing here, but you better leave."

He was breathing pretty hard, making me guess his adrenal glands were surging just like mine.

"Okay," I agreed. "Okay. Let's be calm." I took a few measured breaths. "I want you to know," a few more breaths, "I did try knocking."

"I thought you were somebody selling something. I thought you'd gone away."

"Sorry."

"Yeah, well . . . shit!" Brent gestured with the bat like he'd really like to smash something. "I'm sorry, too. I've been sacked out in the laundry room, and . . ." He rested the bat down again. "If you don't already know, I've split with Sara. Look, I don't really want any company right now. I don't want to talk about this."

"Everybody is worried. Can't we sit down for a minute, as long as I'm here? Would you care for a drink or something?"

My mesh bag, which featured an unopened two-liter bottle of soda along with a few chocolate bars, seemed to catch and hold Brent's attention.

"I haven't really been . . . eating anything, I guess."

"That's not good."

As my initial shock was wearing off, I began to notice little details. Like, for instance, young stud Brent Bell looked like last Thursday's leftovers. He stood there in a dirty T-shirt and those formal tuxedo pants with the black satin stripe up the sides. In stocking feet. Looking at the blond stubble of his unshaven face, I had to guess he'd either been overly influenced by some *Miami Vice* rerun, or he hadn't changed in days. He looked pretty dazed.

"There's fresh fruit," I said, trying not to spook him. "Why don't I get you some?"

I opened a few of the sleek brushed aluminum cabinets and drawers and discovered about fifty place settings of brand new Royal Crown Derby wedding china and an equally impressive supply of designer silver and Waterford crystal. The never-been-used refrigerator's new icemaker provided the perfect half-moon cubes for our Diet Coke, and soon I'd fixed up a relatively humble fruit plate on a thousand-dollar English platter. I added the Nestlé Crunch bars, for fiber. From a gourmet's standpoint, I had committed sacrilege, but I was positively desperate for a shot of caffeine and Brent needed some carbs, quick.

He watched me slice up the last of the ripe cantaloupe. As soon as it was cut he grabbed a piece, popping it into his mouth.

"You don't have to do this," he said, eating off the platter with his fingers.

"It's fine," I said. "Let's go sit down in the dining room."

"*No!*"

I stared at him, alarmed.

"It's just," he said, looking worried, "I shouldn't be here. I'm trying not to use anything. What I mean is, I don't want to mess anything up. I've been staying on the floor of the laundry room."

"Brent," I said, "isn't this your place, yours and Sara's?"

"I shouldn't be here. Man, if Sara found me here she'd have me arrested. I just needed a place to think. I'm out of school, you know. And I wasn't ready to . . . I didn't want to talk to anyone. Promise me you won't tell Sara I'm here."

"Brent, honey . . . she already knows."

"Damn it!" Brent Bell looked as much like a man who is at the point of tears as I've ever seen. "*Damn it!*" He picked up the bat again, gripping it hard, and for a moment I thought the gleaming new toaster might be history.

"May I make a suggestion? Why don't we sit down? Maybe we could just sit here at the counter."

"*No!* I don't want to touch the chairs or anything."

"Then we can sit on the floor."

"What?"

As I moved the plates and goblets to the kitchen floor, I kept talking. "You know, a picnic on the floor. You've gotta eat, Brent. You look . . . well . . . not great."

I sat down and unwrapped a Crunch bar.

He stood there staring at me. I took a bite. Then he sat down on the green tile next to me and grabbed a plate.

"Oh, God." He picked up a strawberry and ate it whole.

I kept my eyes on him and took a sip of Diet Coke. What the hell was going on here? Bride heartbroken. Bridegroom acting weirder than shit. I was at a loss. What, I wondered, would Vivian Duncan have done if confronted with this loony? I couldn't imagine. But one thing seemed certain. Vivian would not be sitting cross-legged eating chocolate on the cold floor.

"This is good. Thanks." He reached for the grapes. "I guess I was a little out there."

"Just a little."

"This reminds me of when I used to work parties and we'd get to eat all the leftovers back in the kitchen. Thanks."

"Brent, may I ask you a question?"

The guarded look returned, but he didn't say no.

"Are you really sure about this breakup with Sara?"

"Listen, it's not like that. It's just gotten out of control, you know? I don't want to hurt anyone. I mean, I love Sara."

This was not sucking. I must have a gift.

"So you love her. And you married her. But, well, something must have gone pretty wrong because now you're living in a laundry room, starving yourself, and attacking people with a baseball bat."

He stopped eating and looked ill.

Oops. Perhaps I had to work on my technique.

"I'm desperate," he said. "I have no other choices."

Desperate? What if . . . ? For a moment there, I began to have a second thought.

"Please don't tell me you killed Vivian Duncan, Brent, because I quizzed Sara on the subject and she explicitly assured me you have an airtight alibi!"

"Me? What are you talking about? I didn't kill Vivian. Are you nuts? But I couldn't stay married to Sara when . . . ah, shoot! I am trying to do the noble thing here, okay? I am trying to protect everybody. There's stuff I can't tell you. Stuff I wouldn't want anybody to know. Leave it alone."

"Stuff about you?"

"Maybe."

"Stuff you didn't want to talk to the police about," I said, starting to get excited. Of course! He was not expecting the police to arrive at his wedding and start asking questions about . . .

The rollers tumbled into place.

"Oh my God, Brent, did you ever work for Vivian when you were home from school?"

"What? What did she tell you?"

"Did you work as a waiter for Vivian's weddings?"

"So? What if I did? Lots of college guys pick up waiting gigs. The party circuit is fun. You can work whenever you're in town, no problem."

Didn't I know it. That's the sort of help I usually hired, myself, when I was catering parties. No problem with that. There had to be something more that Brent couldn't stand to have come out on the night of his wedding.

"Please," Brent said. "Please, leave this alone. I can't say any more. This is the whole reason I had to get away."

"Well, maybe this is something that will blow over. Maybe the police will find the man who killed Vivian soon, and you won't have to answer any questions."

"Do you think so?" Brent asked. "That's what I was hoping."

"So, aside from that 'stuff,' which we just won't talk about, is there any other reason you and Sara have to be apart?"

Brent looked at me, a slightly older woman drinking Diet Coke, sitting on the floor in my tight jeans and tan suede jacket. How much of a threat could I be?

"Well, there's her grandfather, Jack Gantree. Know him?"

"We've met."

"I've always hated the jerk, but I could never explain it to Sara. All those animal heads he's got mounted all over the house. Have you been there?"

I nodded.

"Well, then, you've seen them. They're disgusting. I don't get it. Their whole family was supposed to be these famous naturalists, or something. And instead of protecting and preserving all these animal species, her granddad ends up stuffing them and displaying them like trophies. It always bugged me."

Well, I could see his point.

"But that isn't the worst part. Jack was always buying things for Sara. He could afford to buy everything in the world for her and he usually did."

"That must have been hard to deal with."

"Hard? I told Sara I could never marry her. I said I couldn't live up to all that wealth she'd been brought up with. But she kept pleading with me. She begged me not to be prejudiced just because her family had money. What was I supposed to do?"

I let him go on talking, letting the anger roll out.

"When we finally did decide to get married, I told Sara I wanted to elope, just the two of us. Who needs everyone else? But then her grandfather got wind of it and that was the last time I ever heard about our simple, private little wedding. The next thing we know, Big Grandpa Jack brings in *Vivian Duncan*, for God's sake! Just what was I supposed to do? And then Vivian swept right in and we're planning the wedding of the century."

What power did one young and handsome man have in the face of the bulldozer that was Vivian?

"Man, I don't know how it could have spun so far out of control so fast. First it was the wedding at the museum. Then it was this condo—a little wedding gift I never wanted us to accept. Then there was the surprise honeymoon, all planned by Grandpa Jack. We were supposed to go on safari or something. More of Jack's money. And what am I supposed to do? Just live off the fat? Just beg Grandpa Jack for another favor?"

The thing is, I really did know how he felt. I'd seen more party budgets spin wildly out of control than most. Families who spend more on one party than on their children's education. Money, even when there's a lot of it around, can cause some serious grief.

"So why didn't you tell Sara how you felt?"

"Are you kidding? You should have seen her face. She was like a princess. Every time I suggested we should turn something down, I could see the way she looked at me. She thought I was being silly. It was 'only a wedding' or it was 'only a gift.' Anyway, I told her it all ended after we were married—the gifts from Jack, the money."

"I realize there are problems, and they're none of my business, but you *love* each other. It doesn't seem . . ."

"Look, it's gotten too crazy. I think maybe I know who killed Vivian and it's somebody who is very close to Sara. Okay? Are you satisfied now?"

I looked at him, amazed. "You think Jack Gantree killed Vivian?"

"Don't you tell her that! He's the only one she's got. Don't you tell her I said . . ."

"But why?" I interrupted. "Why would Gantree . . . ?"

"He could turn on people. He could be buddy-buddy one minute and then slam a guy the next. I heard him talking to Vivian, right before dinner, and he was really way over the top. He kept saying how he'd found out something. Well, I overheard that and I got worried. What had Gantree found out, you know?"

I could imagine how that might have made Brent nervous at his own wedding.

"He called Vivian a 'lying whore.' Nice, huh? But when I heard enough to figure out it had nothing to do with me, I stopped paying close attention. Then later, after they found her, I remembered one thing Jack had said. He said she'd wind up dead."

I felt a chill. Brent Bell may have had some sad connection to Vivian Duncan that he preferred his new bride never find out about, but what had really been upsetting him were his suspicions. He believed his grandfather-in-law committed murder. Now *that* could spook anyone into hiding out and thinking things over.

"Do you remember anything about their argument?" I was sure this would be the information I needed to make sense of Vivian's murder.

"He was upset about something that happened twenty-three years ago. And Vivian kept saying, 'Calm down, Jack. He's not going to say anything.'"

"I wonder what that was about."

"Jack is a tough guy. He likes to threaten people. But this time I think he lost his mind or something. An hour later, they found Vivian's body."

"So you took off," I said. "But why didn't you tell Sara?"

"What? Was I supposed to tell her that I was pretty sure her grandfather had just killed somebody? No way would she have believed me. I figured I was doing her a big favor just to disappear."

Big Jack Gantree, murderer. Could it be? Just the firepower to bring down the rhino he displayed over his fireplace was enough to make me believe the man was not only capable of killing, but he was good at it.

"So," Brent said, sounding a lot better for having talked it out. "Have you seen Sara? How is she holding up?"

"Well, she's been better."

Brent looked pained. He said in a soft voice, "Man, I really miss her."

"Okay," I said, gathering our empty plates and glasses, "how about this? You're not solving anyone's problems by disappearing. Right? No matter how this thing is going to turn out, you have to think about getting your life back together and moving forward. Hadn't you better talk this whole thing over with Sara? She's your wife now, Brent. And she loves you. You have to realize you have a partner. Let her help you. Together, you'll decide what you do."

Brent picked up the remaining dishes and empty chocolate bar wrappers. "Yeah. Maybe you're right."

Chapter 20

*T*he rest of the day was packed. I owed calls to everyone. Upon hearing that the wayward Brent had been found, Sara sounded relieved. I guess somewhere, in some dark corner of my heart, I'm still pulling for romance to triumph. I'm not actually putting money on it, but still.

Beryl called and seemed more stressed than ever. Her mother's death was weighing her down. In her entire career, she told me, she'd never had the opportunity to handle such an important divorce. Kip England owned a football team and half of southern Orange County. He was waving a ridiculous prenuptial agreement in their faces. And just when the about-to-be-ex-Mrs. England needed her attorney to be at her sharpest, Beryl admitted to being distracted and worried. She complained that she was about to blow it, she should be working on it right now, but she wanted desperately to know if I'd found out anything to help her father. I told her about Gantree.

"What did the police say? Will they arrest him?"

"Slow down, Beryl. This is hardly . . ."

"Madeline, we're hanging on by a thread here and I don't have time for you to get offended. I thought you wanted to see Vivian's murderer brought to justice." She actually had the nerve to sound exasperated.

"Of course I do. And things will work themselves out. But you've got to stop pushing so hard. People," I informed her with great subtlety, "don't like it."

"You're right. You're right. Sorry."

"Perhaps you should think about taking a break from work."

"I can't. Not now. Thanks so much, Madeline. I mean that. I'll tell my dad you'll talk to the police."

She was right about one thing. Honnett needed to hear the story about Jack Gantree.

But as things worked out, I don't know why I bothered. My hearsay of an overheard conversation that may or may not have taken place was just another note in his murder book. Honnett was, not to put too fine a point on it, skeptical.

"So whatever became of that African, Nbutu? You were pretty sure *he* was the murderer last time we talked."

"I didn't say that. I just said it was very suspicious that he dropped out of sight!"

"Madeline, did you ever stop and think maybe these people aren't all disappearing. Maybe they just missed the memo ordering them to check in with you before they leave the house?" Honnett thought he was pretty funny. I heard the smile in his voice come over the wire.

"This conversation is over."

"Wait. Wait a minute. Don't get sore. I'm sorry. Look, I know you're trying to help. Okay? But this story you heard about Gantree threatening Mrs. Duncan is just not relevant. We don't really think Jack Gantree is a possible suspect."

"Why not?"

"If you'll settle down, I'll let you in on what we discovered on the videotape."

"What videotape?"

"From the wedding. The videographer turned over all his videocassettes. He had several cameras going during the reception. In fact, one camera was set up on a tripod aimed at the head table and it rolled all through dinner. The cameras were programmed to record timecode. You know what that is? It's those running numbers on the bottom of the screen that editors use when . . ."

"I know what timecode is," I said, my heart sinking.

"And we took the tapes right out of the videocams ourselves, so I figure this is pretty reliable. Checking all the tapes, your murder suspect Jack Gantree never left the dining hall. He's at the head table eating his dinner or standing not far off in every frame. There is simply no way for Gantree to have left and killed Vivian Duncan and still appeared on those time-stamped tapes."

Oh. I hate it when that happens.

"Don't give up, slugger. There are still a large number of wackos and oddballs in this case. I'm sure you'll pick up on another one of them soon and off you'll go. Have you tried tracking down the clergyman? For all we know, maybe he's disappeared, too."

"It's nice to know you haven't lost your polite respect when dealing with members of the public, Detective Honnett."

"Come on. You know I like talking to you."

"My luck."

"Okay, okay. If we can step out of weirdland for a minute, let's just talk about what might have happened. Hypothetically. Let's say Vivian Duncan's husband was broke. Let's say he and Vivian didn't have a pleasant marriage and maybe even his wife had a history of seeing extremely young men. Then, add to that, the guy was present at the scene of the murder. We found Ralph Duncan in the men's room, actually. And then, hypothetically speaking, we find he was under investigation for forging frequent flier upgrade certificates and had lost his travel agent license a few weeks ago."

"Oh."

"I admire your imagination, though. I do."

"Honnett, after giving me all this crap about my theories on Nbutu and Gantree, if it turns out that Ralph Duncan did *not* murder his wife, you are going to owe me more than an apology."

"If Ralph Duncan is innocent? Name it."

"You will apologize to me. In front of witnesses."

"All right. But not if he's just acquitted. That doesn't mean anything."

"Right. But that's not all. You will be my slave, Honnett. For one entire day."

"I'll do anything you ask."

"You will?"

"Hell, yes." I heard the smile again and just hung up.

Violin music wafted out of the entrance to The Gardens restaurant of The Four Seasons Hotel. Zelli Gentz was waiting nearby. Before he saw me I had a chance to check him out. Tan suit. Black shirt. Slim build. Dark mustache. Ah, yes. Strings played softly in the background as I watched him push back that black hair which had a sexy habit of falling into his eyes. He looked phenomenal, very Euro-man.

"Madeline?" He saw me and came over at once. "You look lovely. I like your hair like that, all down."

The maître d' left us at a secluded table. This was an important little test. I am tremendously fascinated to learn how people order their food. What Zelli ordered would be supremely revealing. Was he the type who would order the plainest beef dish off an elaborate menu? Or, would he fuss and specify ingredients? Would he take more trouble with the wine list than with the food? I was like the world's cagiest foodie analyst and he, with menu in hand, was on my metaphorical couch. I was excited with anticipation. How lovely to be with a new man.

At The Gardens, each day's menu consisted of whatever the chef felt like creating from the freshest market ingredients. I took a look at the printed listing.

"Ah, how splendid! I must have the speciality. Would you object if I ordered the lobster?" my companion inquired.

First, I love that he asked my opinion. Big points. And lobster? How decadent. How money is no object. I checked my menu sheet. *Maine Lobster*, I read. Good.

Steamed. Excellent. It was served with *Pea and Wine Polenta*.

"So American," Zelli said, with a blush. "I suppose you think me quite the tourist, now, don't you?"

"No, no. It sounds wonderful."

I admired a man who went straight for the most expensive item on the menu. This was not what Honnett would have selected, I thought with a satisfied sigh. Honnett was more the porkchop type. This was certainly not what Arlo would pick, I knew. Arlo would ask them to grill him a burger, medium-well, and bring a wedge of iceberg with thousand island. But lobster! Lobster was so no-holds-barred. Succulent white meat dripping in butter. It was primal, sensual, manly. I was getting turned on by his goddamn dinner order!

The waiter came to the table and Zelli ordered a bottle of wine. A California Chardonnay. He was doing the U.S. thing.

When we had been poured our wine and made our final dinner selections, Zelli leaned forward and said, "I'm so sorry about your friend, Vivian Duncan. I am sorry for your pain in this very sad event."

"Thank you. But, actually, Vivian and I were not close."

"Really?"

"We had only recently met. It was about business. I'm afraid the last thing I ever said to Vivian was that I would not buy her company. She wasn't happy about it. Now I wish that hadn't been the way it ended."

"I see." Zelli Gentz pushed his hand over his forehead, finger-combing his hair back. "So that is sad, still."

"What about you? How did you know Vivian?"

"Well. It was a long time ago. I was young then," he said, flashing very white, even teeth. "I did a lot of traveling for my work, you see, and I knew Vivian quite well in Rhodesia—that was before the country changed its name."

"How fascinating. I had no idea Vivian ever lived in

Africa, although I thought she must have some connection to Rhodesia. Her dog, you know . . ."

"Ah, yes? Well, back then, back in the seventies it was, I spent a good deal of time traveling to Africa. This was just before the wars there, you understand."

"I'm afraid I don't know much about that. Would you tell me? I'd love to hear."

I didn't actually bat any eyelashes, but I did have the absurd feeling I was flirting my way, if not into bed, then into getting a lecture on recent civil war activity in emerging African republics. A first.

"If you are interested," he said, flashing another self-effacing smile. "Of course. I'm Swiss by birth, but my family sent me to school in London. Indeed, I have a house there, still. But my offices are in Zurich. For my work I would go down to what was then Rhodesia fairly often."

"What is it that you do?"

"I'm a gem dealer."

"Amazing." Who *was* this guy?

Zelli Gentz smiled and sipped his Chardonnay.

"Please go on."

"Well, Rhodesia was a source in those days for some extremely fine gem quality stones."

"Emeralds?"

"Why, yes. Emeralds have been around for thousands of years, but they are still quite rare. Exceptional emeralds have been found in Colombia and Egypt, of course, but they were only discovered in Rhodesia in 1956."

"You're kidding."

"I would not lie to you, Madeline," Zelli said, with a smile. "Back in '74 and '75, in the Sandawana Valley in the Mberengwa area that is now part of Zimbabwe, fine stones were being mined. I used to go down there to buy them and visit with friends of mine. Many of the farmers, you know, the landowners down there, had large plantations. We had a wonderful time in those days."

"I've never met a gem dealer before," I said, looking up at Zelli Gentz. "Tell me, how did you buy the emeralds?"

"Ah, well that took a bit of ingenuity, but nothing terribly difficult, really. The native people had the stones and they would get word to us that they were available. My friends would set it up. Then we'd go out into the jungle and make the deals."

"You'd buy the gems in the jungle?"

"Oh, certainly. They didn't want to be caught, naturally. And, of course, neither did I."

"It was illegal?"

"Absolutely." He seemed pleased with the startled look in my eyes.

I *was* startled. By Zelli's frankness and his daring. I had become, I realized with a sudden, sharp dismay, accustomed to the company of conventional men. A man like Zelli rarely crossed my path in citified old L.A. He relished a life of danger and sought adventures more thrilling than crossing town at rush hour. He seemed amused to have an audience so apparently mild and civilized. His manner, while modest, was also rather pleased to show off his daring of long ago. And why shouldn't he talk about the past? There was no long arm of the Rhodesian law any longer who would know or care about what happened twenty-five years ago. He was charming. But was he also dangerous?

"May I take a moment to discuss the politics of mining? Or would this bore a lovely lady too much?"

"Please tell me."

"You see, many of the world's great supplies of precious gems are found in rather primitive countries. In some cases, these mineral deposits are among the nation's richest resources. The governments of these countries are poor, naturally, and their people are not as sophisticated as you and I. They mistakenly believe it is in the best interest of their government to nationalize all mineral rights. You see?"

"Um . . ."

"It was basically illegal for *any* private party to mine or sell stones. That was the policy for years in Rhodesia. After the first emerald was discovered, the country claimed all mining rights and granted no licenses. And this, of course, was most inconvenient for the poor African people. You see, it turns out the crystal is very easy to find. You don't need a professional mining operation. Just scratch the earth at the right spot and a man who is working the land might find a very valuable rough stone."

"You're kidding."

"I am not. And what do you think this very poor man does with this stone? It could be worth, if sold privately, enough to support his entire family for ten years. Twenty. Does he turn it in to an agent at the Ministry of Mines as the law requires?"

"I guess not."

"Look. It was bad economics, you see. Rhodesia owned all the mines. And yet, with several nationalized mining operations in production, the mine workers never reported finding any emeralds! The mining reports were laughable. Some years, not one stone was claimed to have been found."

"Because of poor management?"

"Because, you see, no one could profit by it. On which side of the piece of toast, as the saying goes, was the bread buttered? I assume you, as a good American, believe in free enterprise? Well, the mismanagement of Africa's mineral resources was in setting up a policy which gave the worker no incentive to turn in his findings."

As if it hadn't been radical enough to realize I was dining with an international Euro-guy gem dealer, I now discovered he was something of an armchair social economist. My, my, my!

"It was only to be expected that all the finest emeralds would disappear. They were hidden and taken off to be sold privately. It was very common."

"So all the emeralds were sold on the black market."

Zelli poured another glass of wine for us both, astonishing me with his global nonchalance.

"It is a wiser policy to allow free trade in the gem quality stones, regulate the market, and add a substantial export duty to profit the nation. In that way, the individual African would have incentive, you see, and the country would prosper. I believe it is only now beginning to be recognized as the most logical solution. But back then . . ." Zelli shook his head. "Perhaps it was more fun that way, eh?"

The waiter came with our food, but I was mesmerized by the story of jewels and black market sales and was afraid this interruption would spoil his telling it.

"And that's what you did?" I asked, when the waiter had left. "You smuggled emeralds out of Rhodesia? Zelli," I said, smiling, "I'm shocked."

"Well, you know," he said, playing along. "There is always a market for the finest gems. There is a demand, you see? We had to acquire the stones somehow. That was simply the way it was done back then. And we had many wild adventures. I remember, once, a time when a friend I played polo with told me about some rough."

That word again. "Rough?"

"Excuse me. Yes. This is what we in the jewelry trade call the rough stones. Uncut and unpolished. Rough emeralds look smudged, like they're dirty, but that's actually a veneer of other minerals that will eventually be polished off. To differentiate a fine gem quality stone from a stone that's less desirable, one must look at the size and the color . . ." He broke off and sampled a forkful of perfectly moist lobster, swirling it in the small pot of drawn butter, and raising it to his mouth. "Do you know about emeralds?"

I shook my head.

"Ah, well this is where the skill comes in. A stone may be of great value or it may be almost worthless. You have to know how to read the rough. Size is not the only rule. In fact, a large inferior stone is worth next to nothing to my clientele. The color is very important, yes. A dark, deep green is the most desired, and so most expensive. But then you must look into the stone and read the occlusions. And you must know how a given stone can be cut to best advantage. I trained as a jeweler, so these are things I studied."

"You can do this? You can read the rough?" I barely tasted my own dish, a beautiful Chilean sea bass in a sweet garlic crust tucked in a light tomato basil sauce.

"Well," Zelli Gentz said, displaying an attractive tendency to downplay himself a bit, "that is what we tell ourselves we can do. That is the myth. Sometimes, it's a gamble. Nothing about viewing stones in the rough can be a certainty."

"Just like life."

"Precisely," Zelli said, pleased. "We agree."

I watched his eyes take a trip south and I blushed.

"You don't wear much jewelry," he said as his eyes slowly met mine.

"Haven't got any. But after tonight, I may have to go shopping. I find I'm unexpectedly interested in looking at emeralds."

"Perhaps you'll permit me to guide you. The main mineral that forms the emerald is called beryl. It's, in fact . . ."

He went on discussing the chemical formations that compose the crystals, but I was suddenly jarred back to my original quest, following a clear path of clues leading from Vivian Duncan to Rhodesian emeralds. My God, she named her daughter after the stuff!

". . . is the same material, basically, that is the aquamarine."

"My birthstone," I said. "And it's the same mineral?"

"Yes. The difference is in the trace minerals that give the stones their unique color. The blue stones we call aquamarine, but the green are emeralds, you see?"

I ate my dinner and wondered if he would tell me any more details of his forays out into the wilderness of Rhodesia.

"It must have been dangerous when you went out to the jungle to purchase the rough stones."

"Most of the time, no. But there was risk, certainly. I remember a most amazing event. We were going to meet a very old woman at a point. I must tell you, most of the negotiations were handled by the women, I'm not sure why. My friend drove. And when we got there the old woman climbed aboard our Land Rover to show us her stone. The reason they liked to do trade with us was that we offered U.S. currency, which was of real value. American dollars were worth twice the value of Rhodesian dollars, and these natives knew it. These women were talented negotiators. And, they had a unique way of storing the stones, these Africans. They would wrap each stone in shiny silver paper. They took the foil wrappers from cigarette packs. I used to think this was a local custom, because all the gems I saw came wrapped like this."

"Strange."

"Yes. But you shall see what it all means at the end of my tale. So I looked at the old woman's rough emerald and it was good. Very good. One large, dark green stone that, when cut, might weigh over five carats. This big a gemstone was extraordinarily rare. The rough was maybe the size of a Scrabble tile, but some was always lost in the cutting. We haggled a bit, and finally agreed on a price. The next thing we know, our Land Rover was surrounded by soldiers. Government troops yelling at us with their semiautomatic weapons drawn. But just before they yanked open the door, this woman calmly wrapped up her giant emerald and swallowed it."

I sat there, happy as a child being read a story.

"That's right, she swallowed it rather than be found with it on her. In the end, they had to let us go. They could not arrest us. How could we be charged with dealing for an emerald that they could not produce?" He laughed.

"But the emerald?"

"Remember I told you that you would learn the reason

that Rhodesians put silver paper around their stones?"

I thought about the route that particular emerald would have taken.

Zelli continued smiling at me. "Easier to find once it passed, you see."

It was not, perhaps, the most fortuitous digestive moment, then, for the waiter to approach our table to tempt us with dessert.

"What would you suggest for us?" Zelli asked me. What a charming man. If Arlo could only take lessons.

"Is Mr. Wresell in the kitchen tonight?" I asked the waiter.

"Certainly."

"Then," I said, looking into Zelli's large brown eyes, "I would recommend we have the *Delice*. Donald Wresell is the pastry chef here and he's famous for this amazing dessert. He brought the bronze medal home from France for creating it. Are you interested? It's a sort of cream pie with strawberry marmalade inside and . . . well, trust me, it's brilliant."

"Let's have two. With coffee, black. And for you, Madeline?"

"Hot tea," I said, content.

"You know so much about cuisine," Zelli said. "I find that terribly interesting."

None of this polite "date" nonsense! I had just made a majestic leap in logic and I was hot to try out my ideas on a gentleman who would not greet them with laughter. Now that I had actually met one.

"But I really hoped you'd fill me in on Vivian," I said. "I know Vivian must figure into this somehow. Was she involved in the black market activities?"

"She had relatives living in Harare at the time, did you know?"

I shook my head.

"She came to visit her brother there, regularly. He was part of my polo set, although naturally quite a bit older. But he had money. Lots of money. And he owned some very fine ponies. Well, I met Vivian through this brother of hers, Stephen Mills. And she was very persuasive. Since I needed to find a way to bring hard currency into the country, and I also needed a reliable way of getting the rough emeralds out, we formed a pleasant partnership. Vivian was an American and found clever ways of getting U.S. dollars into Rhodesia. She traveled quite a lot. With all my trips, the authorities knew what I was up to. I was no longer able to come and go freely across the borders. At the airport in Harare I was always searched in the most intimate fashion. But a middle-aged American woman whose brother was a wealthy Rhodesian landowner was another story."

"I see." My tea arrived and I began to sip it slowly. "This is all making sense. Now the only thing that would tie it all up with a bow is figuring out how Jack Gantree fits into this. You were at Sara's wedding. Tell me that Big Jack was part of this, and I'll kiss you."

Oops. We exuberant Americans. Heh-heh.

"Ah, a challenge, yes? Well, perhaps I will win it. I told you we always needed sources of hard currency. American dollars, to be exact. It was Vivian's idea to bring in Jack. He was often on the continent filming his television program. He brought us cash. It was easy, because Jack visited Stephen's home regularly."

"Jack Gantree stayed with Vivian Duncan's brother in Rhodesia?" I knew this was it. I knew I was on to something.

"Yes, of course. They were not exactly in-laws, but close. Stephen's wife and Jack's wife were sisters, so when Jack Gantree came to Africa, he and his wife often stayed at Stephen's house. They usually brought their daughter, Gazelle. She used to hang out with my crowd."

"I can't believe this! I knew that Jack Gantree and Vivian went back, but I never . . ."

"That was before the trouble, of course. That was back in the early seventies."

"You mean the civil war?"

"That, of course, but actually I was referring to the trouble that Jack's daughter got herself into."

"Sara's mother?" I paused with the forkful of *Delice* almost at my mouth.

Zelli's eyes crinkled as he smiled. He had another good tale for me and he was a most indulgent raconteur.

"This was the scandal, back then, you understand? It was not talked about. But somehow, some way, Gazelle Gantree arrived in Rhodesia one July a virgin girl of sixteen and left pregnant. When her father found out, months later, he flew out to Africa and confronted his brother-in-law, Stephen. I remember because I was there that night, and so was Vivian. Jack demanded to know what had happened to his daughter. Gazelle would not tell him anything, you see. Jack was determined to discover who had been allowed to go into Gazelle's bedroom while she had been staying under Mills's roof."

"My God. I heard a very different version of Sara's parents. She told me her father worked for the Los Angeles Museum of Nature. The museum where the wedding was held. But is that just a story?"

"They had to tell the child something. Her mother, Gazelle, was not strong and I believe she died soon after the baby was born."

"You were at the wedding, Zelli," I said, watching as the man pushed his long hair out of his eyes once more. "Pardon me for being so curious, but I wonder. Was that because you wanted to see your daughter get married?"

"Ah, you suspect me of being that rascal? After I openly told you the entire story? But no, dear Madeline, I did not have an affair with Gazelle Gantree. She was younger than I was and much more naïve. No, Gazelle's baby was not mine. I tried to convince Jack and Stephen of it back then, all those years ago, in Stephen's study. It was very unpleasant."

"What happened?"

"Vivian came to the rescue. She talked to her brother and Jack. She knew how to convince them. Whatever it was she told them I never learned, but at once they called on me to apologize. They humbly requested my forgiveness. As a gentleman, I had to give it."

"What could Vivian have told them?"

"What do you think?"

I thought it over. "Perhaps Vivian knew more about the men Gazelle had been seeing than the rest of you."

"Perhaps." He smiled his appreciation. "You are very clever. *The only woman worth winning is an intelligent one.* A Bantu proverb."

I appreciated the compliment, but I was also charged with where this thread might lead. "Perhaps Vivian told Jack which man his daughter was seeing before she turned up pregnant."

"I have always imagined that was so. And now, Madeline dear, I wonder if you would care for an aperitif? I have a lovely bar up in my room and, for your amusement . . ."

"Yes?" How bold would this very smooth European dare to be?

"If you would like, I would be most happy to show you a pair of . . . very rough stones."

Chapter 21

*T*here was nothing wrong with the offer. I actually considered it for two or three brief seconds. But the truth was, I was not ready for an alliance with a new man right now. Not even with a terribly handsome, endearingly flattering, international gem smuggler. And Lord knows, there were not a lot of those banging down my door. Timing, as they say, is everything. And with my feelings for Arlo and Honnett so unresolved, how could I begin something new?

Zelli took the rebuff with a warm smile, charming me where another man might have turned cooler. These Swiss guys are something. We stood at the hotel entrance, talking for a few more minutes while the valet got my car. And when the parking attendant pulled up smoothly in my black Jeep, Zelli Gentz gently pulled me closer to him.

Payment in full for winning my challenge. And a little bit more. The kiss was warm and tasted of coffee.

When I drove away from the hotel, I checked to see Zelli in my mirror. He stood there, still smiling, smoothing back his long black hair. Spending time with him had felt like a passport to a different world. Zimbabwe. Reading the rough. Polo. How exotic his world seemed when compared to mine.

I was amazed at what I had learned about Vivian's past. Not only had she gotten involved with smuggling emeralds out of Africa back in the good old seventies, but she'd been a partner in crime with Big Jack Gantree. This was the link I'd been searching for. There had to be something that went sour between them which would explain why Gantree would want to see Vivian dead.

I thought that over as I drove back to Whitley Heights. And I also thought over the other stunning news Zelli told me at the Four Seasons entrance, with his arms around me to keep me warm. The valet attendant saw our heads together and discreetly left the Jeep parked out front. We didn't appear to be in any hurry.

I had finally remembered to ask Zelli Gentz about the phone message he'd left for Vivian, on Sara Silver's wedding day.

"Oh, that," he said, amused, never showing a flicker of offense at any of my inquiries. "It had to do with my work."

"Something you're working on now?"

"I am searching for some special gems, yes, for a client. This client is from the Middle East, a wealthy man. I cannot name names, of course, as he is well known, but this is rather an amusing tale. If you'd like . . ."

"Please."

"It is his tradition to present a gift to each of his senior ministers. At the New Year. So, to show his favor, he would give each man a watch of enormous value. You know the sort of thing, very big, very overdone, with jewels on the face. Very ugly, in my opinion, but . . . Each of these watches would cost in the neighborhood of one hundred thousand dollars."

"That's an outrageous neighborhood."

"It was my task, each year, to acquire the timepieces, and so, earn a fee. But after many years of this, as you may imagine, a problem developed. It seems that after so many years of the same gifts—watches, watches, and more watches—his men began to feel . . ."

"They had too many watches and not enough wrists?" I suggested.

Zelli flashed me a smile. "You see the point precisely. Very good. These Middle Eastern ministers and generals were loyal, of course, but they began to see the gifts as, shall we say, less desirable than currency. Can you imagine? It got so bad, that each year about a week after the New Year's presentation, you could stroll through the bazaar and buy a huge diamond-faced Rolex for a tenth its cost, only ten thousand dollars."

"They cashed out," I said, shaking my head. "That's funny."

"Not to my client."

Ah, the sultan had not been amused. I shook my head. The rich really do have problems.

"To stop this degrading practice, my client has decided to change his tradition this year. Instead of presenting wristwatches, he turned to me and commissioned seven rings."

"Do you mean you design them?"

"Of course. But the design is something you wouldn't like, I'm sure. It's to satisfy this Arab leader's taste that I have to make the rings large, naturally, and each must feature one perfect gem. It is not easy. You see, each ring must look enough like the other to ward off envy among the generals. You understand the problem? I have been traveling to many countries in search of seven brilliant gemstones fit for princes."

"Fascinating. You're hunting for treasure."

"You could put it that way. I'm afraid it is elusive treasure. The stones I must find are rare. Since each one must be valued at one hundred thousand dollars, naturally I'm thinking of emeralds."

"And that's where Vivian came in," I said, shivering a little.

"Yes. Are you cold?"

"Please go on. I must know about Vivian."

"All right," he said, putting his arm around me for warmth. "This part of the tale goes back to that time I was telling you about in Zimbabwe. You remember?"

I nodded, my head close to his.

"It was a very dangerous time, in 1976. The British had agreed to Zimbabwe's independence, and among the celebrations, the country was plunged into chaos. Various African factions were fighting to take control of the government. Well, just before the civil war completely overtook Zimbabwe, I told my partners we could only stand to do one more transaction before it was simply too risky to continue.

"There were ambushes every day. There were mutilations, rapes, every kind of atrocity. I don't like to speak to you about this. It is too upsetting."

"I'm fine. What happened?"

"The black Africans were the targets, mostly, by other black African factions, but the streets were becoming unsafe. And for those Europeans who were left, the country had become a very uncomfortable home. The newly formed government was in a constant state of crisis and there was always a threat of an overthrow. Each week, the country was swept with new rumors. Supporters of one faction would be beaten. Supporters of another would be found slaughtered. Many people would simply disappear."

"So what did you do?"

"It was time to leave Zimbabwe for good. So, I worked for a month, buying up as many emeralds as I could find. The government troops had begun to wield their guns without any checks. Any suspect, you see, could be shot on sight."

"Were you crazy? Why didn't you just go?"

He looked at me and smiled. "Yes," he said, "I must have been crazy."

"What happened?"

"By that late date, all the other gem buyers had left. The Africans who still held onto valuable rough stones were becoming desperate. African rule, they saw as a victory over the English, true, but their new government was in upheaval. The coming war meant they were losing us Europeans who bought their gems."

"They could kiss the black market goodbye."

"Exactly, and the most unbelievable stones came to me from out of the bush. Never in my life, Madeline, had I seen such raw treasure as these. I bought and bought and bought."

"How much?"

"Gantree gave me eleven thousand American dollars and I spent it all."

"Wow. And how many emeralds did that money buy?"

"Well, at the time I believed the emeralds might be worth a thousand times what I'd paid for them when cut."

I was shocked. "How did it end?"

"I had been very lucky, but I knew it was time to quit. I had collected fifty-two very large stones. They were magnificent. I told Vivian and Gantree it was over."

"Did they agree?"

"Let me tell you what happened on my last trip out to a village to buy. The last two stones I bought were from an old lady—the same old lady, as a matter of fact, I told you about at dinner, the one who years earlier swallowed the emerald."

"Yes. You saw her again?"

"This time she was showing me stones found by another family member, I think. Anyway, I paid her for the emeralds in almost the last of my reserve of U.S. dollars. This time there were no troops to interrupt us. Afterwards, she ambled off into the bush. My friend who was driving and I watched her disappear into the trees."

Zelli paused in his story, and I didn't want to push him to talk about his memories. He rubbed my arm, and stood in thought.

In a few moments he went on. He said that it was only a few seconds later that the young men felt the earth jump, heard the low eruption, saw the flash. The calm old lady who'd been sitting next to him in the Land Rover only minutes before, agreeing on a price, counting out the dollars, must have stepped on the wrong patch of jungle, trod upon a land mine, and died on the spot.

The fierce guerilla fighting had turned the very earth into a death trap.

It had been Zelli's last gem deal in the new Zimbabwe.

"The problem came when Vivian tried to leave the country," Zelli continued. "She was not permitted to board the plane out of Zimbabwe. Her luggage was searched. Her clothes were searched. Even her body. These black Africans were now in charge and Vivian told us later that the Zimbabwe militia enjoyed stripping a white woman. The airport security officers tore through her personal things. In her wedding album, they found a large section which had been cut out and the space filled with a box. Fifty-two rough emeralds were confiscated."

"Oh my God," I whispered.

Zelli looked at me, taking in my reaction, and then went on. "It was only due to the fact that she had two thousand U.S. dollars hidden in a fake shaving cream can, I believe, that she was able to pay off the soldiers and escape Zimbabwe."

Vivian, strip-searched in Africa. The mind boggles.

"At least," Zelli said, with his arm around me at the curb, "that was the story that Vivian told us when we all met up again in the States."

But all these years, Zelli had kept tabs on Vivian. He kept an eye on the emerald market, noting the sale of any gems larger than three carats, examining several over the years, looking for distinctive occlusions that told an expert gemologist they were from the Sandawana mine district of Zimbabwe. In the past twenty years, he had not seen many turn up, and that handful he carefully traced back to other known gem hunters from that earlier time.

I had followed this story very closely.

"It's suspicious that the missing emeralds haven't shown up on the market in all this time, isn't it? I mean, if the officers in Zimbabwe had really confiscated them, they'd have tried to unload them to cash out. And if they turned them in to their government, then why weren't they put on the market by the Ministry of Mines?"

"You have a very fine mind, Madeline." Zelli seemed to be enjoying this conversation enormously.

"The only reason those emeralds would be out of circulation is if they were destroyed . . ."

"Unthinkable," Zelli agreed, smiling.

"Or . . ." We both thought the same thing. "Vivian kept them all along."

Zelli took my hand and whispered, "I so admire you American women."

But I needed to hear the end of this story. I begged him to tell me the rest.

The years went by, he said. Each of the partners prospered. His own business became established in the highest of international circles. He designed custom pieces for royalty, what there was left of it, and did well-paid errands for oil-rich potentates and Far Eastern billionaires.

And then, out of the blue, he received the wedding invitation. All these years later, Jack's baby granddaughter had grown up and was getting married. And he knew Vivian would be there. He thought it would be a fitting time to bring up the subject of the emeralds once again. He was determined to fulfill his Arab commission and wondered, perhaps, if Vivian might be ready to cut a deal. Time had passed, he figured. Gems of that quality were almost impossible to unload quietly. If she did still have the rough emeralds, she'd really have had no way to sell them without him.

He talked with her briefly, by phone, upon arriving in Los Angeles the day before the wedding. If she was ready to cash in, he told her, they could let bygones be bygones. As far as their third partner, Jack Gantree, was concerned? Why would he have to know?

Vivian had not exactly confirmed that she had the gems. But she didn't deny it outright. Zelli told her to bring seven matched gems to the party and he would look them over. If they were as fine as those two he remembered so clearly from the day a poor old African woman had her life blown away, walking through the wrong field, in the wrong country, at the wrong time, he thought his picky buyer, the Sultan, would be very pleased indeed. It was business, he explained to me. As if this type of business went on every day.

Alas, Zelli's business deal never had time to resolve itself. Vivian died before she ever had a chance to show him the rough.

I drove back home, flushed, my breath coming quicker. Vivian's office was searched. She was killed. It had to be tied to Africa, to the missing rough emeralds. I was beginning to get a pretty good idea of why Vivian's office had been turned upside down. Someone was looking for them. I'd bet on it.

Chapter 22

It was nearly eleven, but I was buzzed. When I got home I found a message from Paul on the machine. He'd managed to arrange some sort of settlement offer with Five Star's attorneys. I called him quickly and asked him to come over. I wasn't planning on sleeping any time soon, and Paul stayed up half the night himself. The only problem was how he was going to get here. One of Paul's eccentricities is that he refused to get a driver's license. He didn't want *them* to have him in their system. And I always wondered whether he just didn't enjoy having all his associates have to drive him around. Luckily Wes was home and, as it turned out, Holly had another broken date with Donald. They offered to pick up Paul and bring him by.

I threw my jacket on a chair and walked into the kitchen, thinking I'd put together something to sustain us through the upcoming summit meeting. Now, what was the perfect thing to serve while discussing a three-million-dollar lawsuit? Caviar? Ah, that's positive thinking.

I searched through my CD collection, looking for the right music. Odd. As I flipped through the stack, I discovered I had several discs of Arlo's mixed in. I had thought I'd gathered up all his stuff and returned it by now. I started pulling out the ones I needed to send him. When I got to Peter Gabriel's *So* I felt a momentary pang of loss. I flicked the case open and put the CD on. Loud. One last time.

Several minutes drifted by. I flipped the light off in the kitchen and went to my office. A framed photo of Arlo and me sat on my desk. Wesley, in an effort to help me over the breakup, likes to turn the picture face down when he thinks I'm not looking. I turned it up and studied it. I had certainly looked happy.

Maybe it had been building. Maybe it had been the flirting with Honnett which was going nowhere. Maybe it was resistance to the new. Maybe I just missed the jokes.

There was a buzz at the door. What a strange mood I was in. I set the picture back on my desk. Then I turned it face down, and hurried back out to the entry hall. Had Paul arranged another ride and arrived early on his own?

"Hey, Mad. Is that my Gabriel CD you pinched?"

Standing at my front door, like I'd conjured him up out of my sad swirl of emotions, was Arlo.

"Hi."

"Please, Mad. Don't tell me you've got company."

"I'm expecting some."

He gave me a hangdog expression.

"Really," I said, smiling.

"So I have to stay outside? Is that our new rules? We're supposed to be friends, now, but only if I remain curbed?"

I laughed. And he knew he'd hooked me.

"So what you're saying is, my CDs may enter your house, but not my cute little body. Am I getting the hang of it?"

"Are you saying it sounds harsh?"

"If I promise to keep my hands off of you, will you invite me in for a drink?"

I opened the door wider and he passed quite close, sneaking in a quick, charming kiss on his way in. It was in the mouth vicinity, but it was chaste, like a good friend. Since that was what we were trying to evolve into, good friends, I let him follow me to the kitchen where I kept the booze.

"No date tonight?" I asked it lightly, as I poured the bourbon he liked over a few cubes. I hadn't bothered to turn on the blazing overhead lights, and we stood together next to the center island, in the low glow of the light coming from the glass door of my Traulson refrigerator.

"It's hard, Mad," he said, looking adorable. "I shouldn't have broken up with you."

I poured myself a fresh glass of Chardonnay and sighed.

"It had been coming for a long time," I said, comforting the guy. Which was really such a good joke, I wished I could laugh. He'd broken up with me, and now I was the one he turned to when he needed consolation.

"Maybe we should just take a break," Arlo said after sipping from his glass.

"From breaking up?"

"Sure. Am I nuts? Everyone needs a little breather. Why shouldn't we just give the breakup a rest?"

"For how long?"

"As long as it takes," Arlo said, putting down his glass on the counter and putting his hand on my waist, just underneath my sweater.

"Oh no, sweetheart." I put down my wineglass and removed his hand, gently pulling it out from under and placing it over the knit fabric. After all, a woman needs to draw clear boundaries.

At first it had stung me. After all we'd been through, Arlo was the one to suggest we were going nowhere in a limp balloon. It wasn't so much that I disagreed with his assessment. I loved him. But not, I suspected, in a totally fulfilled way. It was more that I hadn't been courageous enough to break it off. I'd been too happy to have the status stay indefinitely quo. And I wasn't proud of myself, either.

"Look at it this way," Arlo said, slipping his hand underneath the back of my sweater. "We've been going at this breakup for a few months now, and has either one of us found anyone new who could do it for us? No."

I was relieved he hadn't waited for my answer.

"I've grown up, Mad," he went on most sincerely. "I'm not the silly kid you remember."

He was a comedy writer and couldn't help going for the laugh with that one. I had to chuckle. He was some 36-year-old kid.

"I know it's only been a matter of months. But think of those weeks in dog years, Mad. You love dogs. If I was a poodle, I'd have gained like a year or two of wisdom already, just since we broke up."

"That's true." I felt the heat of his hand on my back as he moved it a few inches higher and to the side, just below my new lace bra.

"I'm really grown up now, Madeline. I'm ready to talk about stuff."

"Stuff?" Arlo had never, since I'd known him, been comfortable talking about stuff.

"Grown-up manlike stuff." He nudged his finger beneath the clasp to my bra.

Uh-oh. This was one of his great talents. He had this special gift for unsnapping bras. When Arlo was in junior high, he'd stolen one of his older sister's bras, fastened it around a beach ball, and at night in the dark of his bedroom, he'd practice unsnapping it in one swift move. I think he came up with the whole idea from the Playboy Advisor. And now, twenty-five years later, it was still a skill that served him well.

As I felt a sudden, well, freedom that meant the master unsnapper had worked his magic, I was ready to protest. "Arlo . . ."

"I wuv you, Maddie."

What was that? In four years Arlo Zar had never come close to using the L word.

I pulled his hands out into the open and held them there. As his mouth met mine, I said, "Did you just say you 'wuv me'?"

"I tried to stop. I tried to date other women. I tried, Maddie, but I'm not happy. I've been talking about it to my shrink and she agrees with me."

Oh, of course she did. That's why Arlo paid her for three sessions a week, on top of which he had her on retainer for sudden Arlo-emergencies. But no matter how many sessions he took, he had never seemed to change. I'd often wondered if he was capable of hearing any suggestions other than his own. But, now . . .

Arlo had been leaning me back against the cold marble top on my center island. Now he lifted me up and seated me on it and, without so much as spilling his drink, he jumped up beside me.

"What are you doing?"

"Nothing."

"Hey. I thought we were going to talk."

"We are talking." He tried to pull my skirt up, and soon we were both laying on top of the kitchen counter on my enormous center island, with my sweater now flung somewhere, I think maybe over the toaster, and my skirt moving higher.

I laughed and pulled it down. "Talk, Arlo. More stuff."

"You are an incredible woman, Mad. I will do whatever you want me to. If you want me to prove my wuv, I'll do it. I've grown up, I tell you. Why you wouldn't know me, I've changed so damn much." I felt him unzipping my skirt, and sliding it off, felt it slip away, down onto the floor. "I'll do anything you tell me to."

"Anything?"

"I'll even eat broccoli." Arlo did not eat vegetables, so I was duly shocked.

"Tell me how you really feel about me, then."

Arlo stopped his steady progression of unzipping and unsnapping, and pulled up on one elbow to look me in the eyes. In the low glow of the refrigerator bulb, I saw how sweet he was, how sincere. He found the bottle of bourbon and refilled his glass while I lay seminude beneath him. After a fast swig, he was ready.

"I want you back. I need you. I wuv . . ."

I raised my hand to his mouth, touching his lips.

"I love you, Mad. I am crazy when I don't have you to . . . talk to . . . oh . . . and to . . . play with . . . ah . . . and to . . ."

By then, I had a pretty good idea of what exactly else he was getting at. So it was, well, *reconciliation interuptus*, to say the very *least* about what was going on on my countertop, that at that very private moment, my phone began to ring.

Chapter 23

"*M*adeline, it's Honnett. Am I calling too late?"

"Uh. No. I'm always up late. You know that."

I adjusted myself by propping up on one arm. Arlo, who understood all about work calls, moved over a bit to make more room.

"I've found your African. I thought you'd like to know."

"Albert Nbutu? Where?"

"He's staying with another Zimbabwean refugee in Altadena. I was going to go over and talk to him."

"I'm shocked. I thought you were just shining me on about Nbutu."

"On the contrary. The LAPD awaits your every command."

I laughed.

"I told you I'd look into it."

"Yeah, yeah. So what gives?"

"Nbutu is in the country without documents. Perhaps he's got information on our case and forgot to come forward, seeing as how," he said with sarcasm, "he probably doesn't understand how our justice system works here."

"So you're going to question him?"

"Correct. I thought you'd probably like to ride along. You could fill me in on what you know about the guy on the way out there."

"You mean right now?"

Arlo turned and began to listen more closely. He may have heard the distant death knell to our reconciliation recreation.

"You up for it?"

"Sure. By the way, do you have dubs of the wedding videos I could take a look at?"

"That's what I mean about you," Honnett said, "I find this African, Nbutu, you've been hot about, and do I hear any thanks? No, right away you ask for more."

"Well?"

"Yeah, I've got a copy you can look at. Still don't believe Gantree has an alibi, do you?"

"We'll see. So you're coming by now?"

"On my way. I'll see you in ten."

I hung up and looked at Arlo.

"Okay," he said, "so where were we?"

"Uh, see, wait." I disentangled a bit. "I've got to get dressed and . . ."

"What? Are you going out with this Honnett geek?"

"It's this murder I'm involved in. Vivian Duncan. I'm right near the end, Arlo. I've almost got it. The answer is so close. I just need to concentrate for a little bit longer."

We both heard the key turn in the front door lock down the hall at the same time.

"Aw, shit!" I said, grabbing for my sweater.

"Damn!" Arlo said, zipping up, disgusted.

"This always happens!" I found my skirt.

Arlo helped me button. "Remind me to buy you a chain-bolt."

"Anybody home?" called out Holly, amid a nearing herd of feet.

"Welcome," Arlo invited the guests, "to Maddie's and my sex life. Come one, come all."

"Oh, you two." Holly turned on the full blast of the overhead lights, exposing Arlo shirtless and me just barely presentable. "Can't you ever just do it in the bedroom?"

"What did I miss?" Wesley asked, hurrying in behind her and then stopped cold. "Oh." Wes took in the little drama. "If it isn't Arlo."

"I missed you too, buddy," Arlo told Wes, only muffled since he was pulling on his shirt over his head.

"So does this mean we need to Lysol down the countertop?"

And then Paul entered the kitchen, still talking on his cell phone. He had, thankfully, missed most of the teasing and by the time he rang off his call, we were more or less straightened up.

"Last-minute stalling tactics from the other side," Paul said, referring to the call. "I can't believe these putzes. First they tell me they have a settlement in mind, and then they call back and say hold up before telling my client. That's bullshit! Oh, hello Arlo. Are you back?"

Arlo smiled. "Yep. Anyone want bourbon?"

Wesley, who'd been fairly quiet in the presence of the raw evidence that Arlo seemed to be back, just stood there giving me that funny look. Like, oh, we have to talk! But he turned to Paul and asked, "It's after midnight. Do you mean you're still negotiating with some corporate attorneys at this hour? Jesus! How much are they going to charge Five Star for this?"

"Beats me. I just wish the assholes wouldn't start jerking me around. I told them we had a firm deadline— midnight. And it's forty minutes past and they're giving me grief."

I found my bag and pulled out my lipstick just as the doorbell rang.

They all looked at me.

"That's Honnett."

Holly looked amazed. She pulled me to the side and held up three fingers, whispering "*Three?*"

Zelli, Arlo, and now Honnett. Yes, I was having a busy night.

"Why not?" I whispered back, and then turned to the group assembled in my kitchen.

"I think I'm onto something in that Vivian Duncan

deal. I have to find out. If I'm right, this should be over soon. I just have got to go."

Wesley turned and asked, "So what about our meeting?"

"Can you stick around? Holly, you'll find some homemade ice cream in the freezer. And I just put on a fresh pot of coffee before . . ."

The doorbell rang again.

"She's crazy," Holly said conversationally to the room, dismissing me.

"Nutty as a jar of Skippy," Arlo agreed.

"Did someone say Maddie made some ice cream?" Paul asked.

"One scoop or two?" I heard Wes ask, ever the pleasant host, as I ran to answer the front door.

It was almost one-thirty in the morning when Honnett turned his old Mustang up the quiet street in Altadena, cutting the engine and gliding to a stop at the curb in front of a small house. The corner streetlight didn't reach this far down the block. A neighbor had left his back porch light on and a house across the street had a car parked in front of it, full of teenagers. It took off the moment our car slowed down.

"Making out, probably," I suggested.

From the backseat of the Mustang, Detective John Martinez laughed softly. "It's sex, drugs, or rock 'n roll."

Honnett, in the driver's seat, said, "John's just reciting the three reasons kids hang out in their cars. Hey, you ready to go?"

"Sure," I answered.

Honnett looked at me, amused, and he kept his voice low. "Not you, Bean. John and I will go up and check it out. This house belongs to a cousin of Nbutu. She lives here alone. Her kids are grown. If Nbutu is in there and if the place is cool, we'll bring him out to talk. If you can keep quiet, you can stand over there and listen."

He gestured to the only tree in the small front yard. "If we need any information, we'll ask. Otherwise, keep yourself contained. Got it?"

"Right."

I stood by the car as Martinez and Honnett approached the front door. After a few minutes of knocking a light came on over the porch. I saw a woman tightening a blue robe around herself in the doorway and then the formalities of badges being shown amid a low rumble of voices. The next thing I knew, both men had been admitted to the home.

Then all was quiet.

I began to hear a faint sound at a distance and strained to make it out. Then louder, I could feel the pump of the rhythmic bass to some rap song as the sound filled the street, louder and louder. I turned to see the same car we'd seen earlier, roaring up the side street, windows down, music blasting.

The car slowed to a stop. The blare of the radio pierced the quiet night, a rapper screaming about "da bitch wid da attitude," as the car idled a few feet away. I saw two young girls in the back, with a boy in a tank top, his arm around them both. The driver leaned out his window, pounding the door along with the driving rhythm, and yelled to me.

"Hey, mama. You want to go for a drive with me? We'll have some fun, you sweet thing."

"You boys want to spend some time talking to cops tonight?" I jerked my hand toward the house, and smiled pleasantly.

"I told you," the boy in the back yelped.

"Hey, your loss, *chica*," the driver said with a smirk, and then the rap-mobile peeled off down the deserted road.

A few minutes passed and I became accustomed to the sounds of the night. The simple landscaping around the yard next door and the yard next to that became familiar shapes I could now decipher in the dark, cool night. The gentle wind rustled the shrubs, moved through the slender trees, chilled me. My eyes adjusted to the low light, filtering dark gray bushes from darker gray fence. There. What was that? I saw a strange movement near the front door of the small house. There in the thick plants. I stared at the area, watching closely.

Nothing. Then a rustling movement, again, from among the sharp, jutting leaves.

An animal, I thought, worried. A pet, perhaps. Or a rat. I looked to the house, but the door was shut tight. Honnett and Martinez were inside and I and the rats were out.

I stared intently, gray upon gray upon gray, watching that porchside bush rustle again. A cat, I thought. Maybe a . . .

A hand covered my face. Another arm strangled me. I tried to scream, but I couldn't. I could hardly breathe. I had been grabbed, all at once, from nowhere, grabbed from behind.

My God, I thought. Oh my God! Those kids. Those damn kids had sneaked back and attacked me.

I tried to squirm free, to see who held me so tightly. But the assailant had pinned both of my arms with one of his. His hold was strong, unyielding, fierce as iron. This man was taller, larger than those boys had been. More cunning, silent. I tried to kick, but the tree trunk of a man against whose body I was trapped felt none of it.

In an instant, I was overpowered. Completely helpless. Completely vulnerable. I was caught in the night and unable to move or fight back or yell, not forty feet away from the illusory protection of two cops, now inside.

The hand that held my face was hot, rough-knuckled, enormous. I was sure, now, it must be Nbutu.

"Please," his voice whispered from behind my ear. "Please, not a word, not a sound."

I stopped fighting, tried to control my breathing, get my heart to stop racing, my brain to think.

"I mean no harm," he whispered in my ear.

I squirmed harder then, kicking back with my heel into his shin, almost twisting my head away from his tight grip. It was only due to the fact that he was not intent on smothering me that he almost lost his grasp, but he pulled me back firmly and I could tell I'd never again have that slight chance. Surely, I thought, surely Honnett would be coming out. Now, I thought. Now! Come out of the house!

"You must stay still. I will take you somewhere and leave you there. I do not wish to hurt you," he said.

Leave me somewhere? I could imagine my dead body, left somewhere, some ravine. Some landfill. Some . . .

"I don't want to hold you, you see? I don't want to hurt you. But I must leave now. I must escape."

Nbutu pulled me back into the bushes that bordered on the yard.

No, I thought, this was getting worse. Not back into the bushes.

"Don't be frightened," he whispered. "I will let you go."

And then, remarkably, he did just that.

I spat on the ground as his tight fist released my mouth.

"Don't scream," he pleaded with me. I spun around and faced him, shocked to be free. Stunned to have a chance to run.

"I let you go," he pleaded. "Do not turn me in!"

The large black man stood cowering in the bushes and something stopped me from yelling my lungs off. Something in the way he stood there, trembling, not able to go through with the abduction.

"I must get away," Nbutu said, staring at me. "I can't take you, just let me go."

I trotted several feet away, out of his range and then stopped. "Turn yourself in right now," I said, "and I won't say anything about you grabbing me."

"No."

"Turn yourself in *RIGHT NOW!*" I yelled. "I'll get you a lawyer."

"I can't," he pleaded. "I can't. I can't."

The front door opened and Honnett and Martinez came running.

"That him?" shouted Martinez, gun drawn.

"Back away!" Honnett yelled to me. "Get away!"

Somehow, I couldn't. I was afraid, suddenly, of the police. What would they do if they suspected I'd been held by this man? If I stepped away, would they shoot him? What was really happening?

Quickly, Honnett was there, spinning Albert Nbutu around, pushing him face first into the tall bushes, handcuffing him behind his back.

"Did he hurt you?" Honnett asked me, his voice husky. I'd never seen him treat anyone as roughly as he handled Nbutu. Was this emotion I was watching? The cool Honnett coming a bit unglued?

"Nothing happened," I said, meeting Albert's eyes. "He seems scared."

"What are you doing out here, Albert?" Martinez asked him, his voice aggressive. "Trying to run?"

"No," I heard myself saying. "He must have been taking a walk."

The men looked at Nbutu and then looked at me.

"Are you arresting him?" I asked.

"We're *talking* to him. If he cooperates, we may not have to drag him downtown. It's up to him."

"But the handcuffs?"

"Albert doesn't mind the cuffs, do you, Albert?" Martinez was not as tall as Honnett, but he was powerfully built.

Just then two patrol cars turned up the small street, flashing lights but with their sirens cut. The officers walked up and talked to the detectives. Apparently Honnett had a search warrant and the men entered the small house. I could hear the protests from Albert's cousin as she wailed from inside.

"What we want to know about, Albert," Martinez said, "is what happened at the wedding at the museum? You dropped out of sight, pal, which is very suspicious.

But you . . . you probably got a reasonable explanation, don't you? So why don't you just go ahead and explain."

Albert Nbutu was frightened. Very frightened. In the dim light given off by the front porch and the open door, he looked to be older than I'd first guessed.

"About what?" he stammered.

"About what? Now you see, Albert. That's the kind of smart answer that gets us ticked off. You don't want to tick us off, do you, Albert?" Martinez sounded pissed, all right.

"No. No, sir. I don't know what you are asking about. At the wedding I made the ice sculptures. For each table. Do you want to . . ."

"Forget the ice animals shit, all right? We look like fools to you, Albert? We're interested in the death of a lady named Vivian Duncan. You *do* remember that she was murdered that night, right?"

"Yes," he said, his head bent.

"Okay. Are we through fucking around? What we want to know is did you see something, Albert? Or did you, maybe, get angry with the lady and do the job yourself?"

"*Me*? No. No. I had nothing to do with it. I am innocent. You . . ." The African began to stutter in fear. I was not sure I could watch it anymore. He was being questioned in the middle of the night, out on the street, with his hands cuffed behind his back.

"Honnett!" I yelled his name sharply.

Chuck Honnett looked up, startled, meeting my eyes and holding them for a beat. And then he put his hand on Nbutu's shaking arm and tried to calm him down. "Look, let's just go sit you down in our car. How about that? I can't take the cuffs off, but maybe you'll be more comfortable. Okay? Easy there, Albert."

When Albert had been put in the back seat, Honnett began to talk. "Here's what we know. You are in this country, Mr. Nbutu, without papers. You are an illegal alien, and we will be sending you over to our friends at INS to deal with. But, before we do that, we have got to get to the bottom of this Duncan murder. You know who did it, or you wouldn't have run. It's best to be truthful."

Albert Nbutu sat there, looking out at us, the two detectives next to the car and me, standing in the rear.

"And you?" he said to me, meeting my eyes. "I saw you at the party. Are you INS? That is what I thought. So I gave you a card where they would not tell you how to reach me. I am sorry, but . . ." He looked down, disheartened. Caught. "Are you also a police woman?"

"No," Honnett answered for me. "Now what do you know, Albert?"

"At the wedding? I was working outside. What could I see?"

"And you're saying the only reason you've been in hiding out here is because you were afraid of INS? Come on!" Martinez had that macho sarcasm that made me want to punch him.

"I came to this country two years ago," Albert said, quietly. "How do you think I could stay here so long and not get into trouble? It is because I am so careful, you see."

"You come from Zimbabwe?" I asked.

Albert nodded.

Honnett shot me a look to cool it and continued his questions. He and Martinez kept asking Nbutu to talk about the night of Vivian's murder. They asked him where he was standing and what he could see from there. Over and over they asked him to account for each minute of the evening. But all Albert would say is he knew nothing.

After thirty minutes of getting nowhere, Martinez left us and joined the officers conducting the search of the house.

"How old are you?" Honnett asked. The change in subject was a surprise. Albert carefully responded.

"I am forty-nine years old. I was born in a tiny village in Rhodesia, as it was called then. My family was poor.

My father worked to build the national mine, so this brought in some money."

"Sandawana," I said.

Honnett looked at me. "Yeah, I noticed that tattoo. So that's the mine where you worked?"

Nbutu nodded. "When I was a child, yes. We would all go down to the mines and search for the emeralds. It was a game. And when I grew older I worked there, too."

"And you got that tattoo in prison?" I asked. Honnett looked at me.

"Yes." Albert hung his head.

"In prison? What were you in for? Assault?"

Honnett was such a cop.

"No, no," Albert said, his voice strained. "It was a mistake. I was arrested by our government."

Honnett was going to make another scathing remark, I was sure of it, so I put my hand on his sleeve to stop him.

"Is that why you are so frightened now? Because of what happened to you in Zimbabwe?"

He looked at me. "It was a terrible time, miss. Many were imprisoned. So many people, so many men just . . . disappeared. There was very bad corruption. We were free of the British Commonwealth, but our leaders fought. And then I was arrested. They accused me of stealing emeralds but that is a lie. They made this story up! There was never any proof. There was no trial. There was no witness. It was just done."

"And you stayed in how long?" Honnett asked, more subdued.

"Ten years. From 1976 to 1985."

"And then what?"

"The government changed again. And it became a little more stable. My relatives saved their money, and . . ."

"They bought your way out of prison?" I asked.

"Yes. It was very difficult. If the wrong man was in charge, he could have taken their money and had them arrested as well. But this time they let me out."

"And why did you come here?" Honnett asked, seemingly resigned to talking about the past.

"The United States is a great land," Nbutu said.

"Right," Honnett said. "But why here? Why Southern California?"

"I have family here," Nbutu said.

"Your cousin," Honnett said, and then he looked at me. "There's nothing else he's going to tell us here. We'll have to take him downtown anyway, so I'm going to . . ."

"Can I ask you a few more questions, Mr. Nbutu?" I said, turning to the man in the car.

I could imagine what had pushed him near the edge. As a young man, Albert Nbutu had been savagely arrested, illegally thrown into some primitive African jail to rot for a decade, and then he'd had to watch his family barter away their small holdings and risk their own safety just to bribe his way out. I could understand why he'd been driven almost crazy to escape from more police.

"What things do you want to ask?" Nbutu seemed unsure.

"Back in the old days, who sent the militia to arrest you? Was it a white man, perhaps?"

Nbutu looked at me, shocked.

"Was it Jack Gantree?"

Now Honnett looked at me, puzzled. "Are you saying that Gantree knew this guy back in Africa?"

"Gantree was there, in Zimbabwe. His wife's sister lived there with her rich husband. Gantree stayed there all the time."

"When he was making his television series?" Honnett asked, catching on.

"Yes. But he also had a lucrative investment scheme on the side. Big Jack financed an emerald-smuggling operation."

"You know this for a *fact*?"

I nodded.

Honnett turned to look at Albert. "Did you know Jack Gantree, like she says?"

"Everyone in Rhodesia knew Mr. Gantree. He made the television films."

"Is that why you came to Los Angeles? To get back at Gantree for something that happened to you twenty years ago in your home country?"

"No! I swear to you. I did nothing wrong. I did not hurt anyone. Please, I am not lying. I . . ."

Before Nbutu could finish, Detective Martinez came out of the house, all smiles. "We got it! We got the bastard!"

He walked over to the car and held up his clenched fist. "We just found this in the toilet tank, wrapped in a nylon stocking."

We all watched as he opened his hand to reveal the damaging evidence.

There were two small, shiny objects. The first was a silver tube of lipstick, a MAC color I was familiar with called Spirit. And the second object was a beautiful gold cigarette lighter with the initials V.D. in tiny emeralds. Vivian's lighter.

Chapter 24

*L*et me explain why a trained chef like me is so good at solving crime, in my opinion. I've been thinking about it quite a lot. The answer, I figure, goes back to how we eat. Well . . . and what doesn't?

When I first taste a brand new dish, with the very first bite, I feel a splendid joy. I close my eyes, in fact, just to better appreciate the sensuous pleasure of the palate. Is there anything better? But next, almost without my conscious choice, I find the second bite brings with it a puzzle. I must, it seems, know how and why and where and what it took to get this unique result. I find myself deconstructing the tastes, solving the puzzle, if you will, of how a few ingredients could have been coaxed into such a unique melange. A dozen thoughts occur to me, all at once, as I ponder what type of cooking method performed at which precise degrees combined with what particular dough made from which exactly right grain, and mixed in what specific order and proportions had wrought this fine éclair, for example. It's how my brain works, overanalyzing its neurons to a frazzle, working out the recipe from the finished dish backwards.

It is not that different, I was finding, with murder, and I had sampled too much of this particular "dish" to dismiss it. I knew all the ingredients. I had only to reconstruct the timing and temperatures, the motives and movements, and I felt I was close to knowing who had killed Vivian Duncan at the disastrous Silver-Bell wedding.

Albert Nbutu had not done it. I was certain of it. Let the police take him in if they thought they must. He'd be out.

Honnett had a car drop me at my house and I jumped into my own car as soon as my escorts left. I drove across the city from east to west. Traffic was nonexistent at three A.M. and I was cruising fast down the wide, black streets, slick now with a sudden unseasonable downpour.

At home, Holly and Wes were still hanging out with Paul. On the phone with Wes, I could hear Paul in the background playing his sax. But after I filled them in, Paul, of course, was gonzo to take on the authorities and see what he could do to help out Albert Nbutu. Wes and Hol were still wide awake and agreed to meet me in Beverly Hills. Arlo, I was told, had gone to bed. My bed. It was a territory thing, Holly tried to explain to me, but I was too jazzed with what was pinging around in my head to pay much attention.

Some cities are known for their nightlife. Not ours. Bars close at two in the morning in L.A., so there isn't much reason for anyone to be out late. And if Wilshire Boulevard going west into Beverly Hills was any example, nobody *was*. I sped through my share of yellow lights, wondering if I would beat them all.

I turned left and pulled up in front of the custom tailor shop and cut my engine. Mine was the only vehicle parked on either side of this commercial block. Rain fell softly and I let my wipers run as the car idled.

Soon I could see a pair of headlights coming up the street from the opposite direction. The car slowed, then pulled a wide U-turn to park directly behind me at the curb. When the car cut its lights, I could see in my rearview mirror a white Lincoln Continental. The door opened slowly and a hobbling figure hunched beneath a large hooded rain cape emerged.

When he got to my car I rolled down the window.

"I'm soaking wet," grumbled Whisper Pettibone.

I jumped out of the Jeep and we walked up to the street door that led to the stairway to his office. Whisper used his key on the outer door lock and then I insisted I help him climb the steep staircase one floor up.

At the top were the two doors facing each other, just as I remembered. Only this time, there was crime scene tape across both Vivian's and Whisper's doors.

"You want me to . . ." Whisper stared at the yellow police tape.

I tore some of it off. "Open it."

Soon, Whisper's key had unlocked the heavy door to his own office and we were inside. Whisper flipped on the office's overhead lights.

It had been a mess before. Papers every which way, drawers pulled out and dumped. Files slashed. Everything now seemed almost exactly as it was, except added to the picture were the black powder reminders that the fingerprint squad had been here with a vengeance.

"I simply cannot cope," Whisper said, unmanned by the sheer enormity of the destruction.

"Madeline?" It was Wesley. He was calling up from the bottom of the stairs.

"Come on up," I called back. And to Whisper I said, "Have a seat. We've got reinforcements."

Holly and Wesley entered and we all four tried to find a place to stand where we weren't trodding upon sliced wedding photos or ripped invoices or, I pulled one intact slip of paper from the shredded mess, a recent California Lotto ticket.

"Loser," Holly sniffed after checking it out. She keeps these things in her head.

Wesley took charge and righted a tan velvet loveseat, pushing aside the drifts of defiled papers.

"Please sit down," I said to Whisper.

"Thank you. Oh, and by the way. When we spoke earlier, you asked me if I could find some photos, do you remember?"

"Yes. I was interested in seeing if we might recognize one of Vivian's young, um, employees."

"Well look around, dear," Whisper said, sad and grumpy. "Here are our files and photos. Watch where you step or you might destroy some vital clue."

We all contemplated the extraordinary mess around our feet.

"Actually, I am interested in finding something much more important, now."

"I'm sure I told you," Whisper said, "the police have already spent a day here, trying to see what might have been taken. They aren't sure if anything has. They say it may have just been vandals looking for a kick. Someone who hated Vivian, perhaps, but not a thief."

Wes perched next to Whisper and asked, "Was there anything here of value?"

"I do beg your pardon. Clearly you do not remember to whom you are talking. All, I repeat, *all* of our parties were written up in the newspapers. We had files of our clippings going back to 1977. Miss Taylor's weddings," he said, "and I do mean in the plural. Miss Streisand's wedding. And now look at them. So," Whisper held back a sob, "so, was there anything of value here, my friend? I don't know. *You* tell *me*."

"Gentlemen," I said, hoping to get back on track before Whisper tore off on another rant. With the trauma of seeing his precious "things" so messed up combined with the shock he must be feeling to reenter the location where he had been recently attacked, he was getting less steady by the minute.

"Which reminds me," Holly put in, "how did you ever get the nickname Whisper?"

We all looked at him. His voice had been raised most of the time I'd known him.

"Ah, that. When I first began working with my lovely Vivian, she told me I spoke too loudly. It upset her. And so every time we'd be having a talk, she'd remind me, over and over, 'Whisper, whisper.' In fact, her daughter

Beryl heard her mother say that to me so often, she just figured it was my name."

I had not been expecting a sweet story. Somehow Vivian had grown into a caricature in my mind. I realized again how real and human Vivian Duncan had been to her grieving partner and friend. It made me more determined than ever to find out the truth.

"I believe there was something here. Something Vivian may have been killed over."

"But nothing much was missing," Whisper protested, sitting forward. "I assure you I had a detailed list of the company's assets and . . ." he looked around, miserably, "they are all pretty much here."

"Perhaps, but we intend to search."

"We do?" Holly did not sound optimistic.

"What? Through all this rubble? Do you have any idea what time it is?" Whisper asked. "Don't any of you young people sleep?"

"Calm down. We can do this. Now, Whisper, can you tell us the general layout of your offices? What rooms were used for what?"

"We had both sides of the stairs. Viv's office was on that side, of course, along with a bridal parlor where we display wedding photos from some of our past triumphs. That's where our clients come for their meetings with Viv. I remember now, the police officer told me the hooligans destroyed even the furniture in there. They broke the back off the television monitor, if you can imagine that. And they hacked up the VCR and even pried open the videocassettes we had in our wedding memories library." He stopped with a sniff.

"Steady there. And are those all the rooms across the hall?"

"There is a little powder room on that side, as well."

"Good. Now what about your side?"

"I've got this little entry," Whisper said, gesturing. "And then down the hall is my office. I have my own bathroom off of that."

"But there is another room in the back," I said, "where you were found."

"The supply room, yes. It's also where we keep the Xerox machine and those sorts of things."

"So you were knocked unconscious and then locked up in a supply closet?" Holly asked, fascinated.

"It wasn't as much fun as it sounds, dear child," Whisper said.

I thought it all over again and asked Whisper about my one insistent memory. "The other day, when the police rushed out of nowhere and scared the soufflé out of me, I didn't notice anything. But afterwards, after they found you and took you off to the hospital, I do remember getting a quick look through the open front door into Vivian's side of the office. There was a small desk. And on it was a silver dish. Am I right?"

Whisper looked at me. "Why yes. Vivian always had candies in a sterling candy bowl for her clients. It was one of her trademarks. You know, that kind of thoughtfulness."

Wes spoke up. "Maddie, are you saying you remember seeing an expensive silver dish which the thieves left behind?"

Whisper jumped in, "That does seem peculiar. That candy dish was an antique, worth over a thousand dollars. I would certainly imagine even a *cretin* would know silver could be melted down." They all thought it over, but I was interested in something else.

"Whisper, quick! What sort of candy did Vivian keep in that dish?"

They all turned and looked at me.

"Chocolate," Whisper said slowly, not following my train of thought at all.

I got excited then. I *knew* it would have been chocolate! I made Whisper give Holly his master key and sent her across the hall to find the candy dish and bring it back to us.

A few minutes passed and then Holly returned, holding a beautiful Sheffield dish, the one I remembered noting, but nothing more.

"This was on the desk," she said. She turned to Whisper and asked, "What kind of chocolate was kept in that dish, anyway?"

But before Whisper had a chance to respond, I spoke up. I had to be right. I said, "Kisses!"

Whisper nodded. "That's right. Viv always insisted we keep Hershey's Kisses in that dish. It goes with the theme. Naturally, we were very aware of that sort of sentiment. Our brides appreciate it, you know."

Wes looked at me, excited. "What's up, Mad?"

But I was too excited to slow down and explain. I jumped up and said, "Come on." Jogging down the short hallway to the back of the offices I pushed open the door to the supply room. On one side a counter ran the length of the room. A broken coffee maker sat tipped over. I stepped over the cord to the copy machine, which had been shoved over against the water cooler, which had in turn spilled over the mess of papers on the floor.

Wes and Holly were right behind me. Whisper discovered renewed energy as well, and pushed past them. I pulled open the supply closet door, the one that had recently housed the unconscious body of Mr. Pettibone himself. In the closet were several cardboard cartons of kitchen supplies. One box contained packets of coffee for the coffee maker. The carton had been slit open by the intruder and its contents checked. Nothing but coffee.

In another carton was a supply of tea bags. This box, too, had been roughly ripped open and a few dozen tea bags had been yanked out and were now on the floor of the closet. No doubt the thorough search had left no box unchecked.

I bent down to pull out the brown cardboard box that was marked in black with the name "Hershey's." Its top had been ripped open, revealing a few dozen bulk-sized cellophane bags of Hershey's Kisses.

"Oh my God," Holly said, squeezing her arms together and bouncing on her heels. "Oh my God. What is it?"

After feeling around to the bottom of the box, I pulled out one individual cellophane bag. From the look of it, it was identical to all the others.

"You've been filling up the candy dish for how long, Whisper?"

"Years. Since we opened. Why? What is that you have?"

"It's a bag that was at the very bottom of this carton. But it wasn't just on the bottom," I said, turning it over. "It was taped to the bottom." I showed them.

"Each month when I order fresh supplies for the office," Whisper explained, "I put the new bags of candy right in there." He gestured to the carton I was holding.

I ripped the cellophane top off the bag and poured several dozen silver-wrapped Kisses out onto the table.

"Hey, there are some smaller ones. They're not the right shape," Holly said, reaching for a candy. She untwisted the foil and pulled out a dark green rock the size of a Milk Dud.

"What is it?" she asked.

"One," I said, "of fifty-two missing rough emeralds from the Sandawana mine district in what used to be Rhodesia. Wrapped in silver foil."

I began unwrapping another one.

"Oh, mercy me!" Whisper Pettibone said, collapsing in the room's only chair.

"What do we do now?" Wes asked.

We had to know for sure.

I handed them out to the group and said, "Count them."

Chapter 25

"*I*t's almost seven," Wes said, playing his usual role of timekeeper in the kitchen. Oh how I had missed this. Cooking for guests is so therapeutic. That is, it is for me. For others, I'm often told, cooking drives them up a tree. Which is why there will always be a place on this earth for chefs, I thought happily, as I checked the oven to see how the salmon was doing.

"You're loving this," Wes said, annoyed. He'd been nervous all night. In fact, he never went to sleep. I, on the other hand, was too busy to sleep. I'd been to the Santa Monica farmer's market just after dawn and, of course, I had all those telephone invitations to take care of. Luckily, none of my guests had a previous engagement for a Wednesday night. They were, in fact, due to arrive in thirty minutes.

"You like this?" Holly had been arranging flowers for our table.

We were expecting a party of twelve, counting ourselves, and for the evening's décor, I'd suggested Holly pick up several pots of African violets and do groupings down the center of our long table. Now, she held up her work, simple terra cotta pots, upon which she had painted bold golden stars.

I nodded my approval and she swooped them all away.

The food for this party would be special. In truth, I

had been yearning to do a dinner party while it was still wild salmon season and luckily we had just made it. These special fish are line-caught by boats from San Francisco north to Alaska and they are only available for about a month, from mid-May until mid-June. After that, fish markets offer the milder farmed salmon for eleven months more.

Tonight, I chose to use a cooking technique called oven-steaming. This method is extremely simple and the cooked fish comes out a most startlingly bright orange color. It's also incredibly moist and rich. Best of all, because you cook it in a slow oven on a cookie sheet over a roasting pan filled with boiling water, you can easily make enough for a large crowd. My favorite fish-monger is a dear, and he skinned a whole side of wild salmon for me. Then, to give Wesley something constructive to do, I asked him to remove all the pin bones with a pair of needlenose pliers.

While Wes worked over the salmon, I prepared the cucumber salad featuring rice vinegar and sesame oil, with snipped chives and chopped cilantro and a sprinkling of toasted sesame seeds to give it snap. But by now, the salad was ready and the salmon was in the oven so we were doing just fine on time.

"Uh, Mad, sweetie?" Arlo poked his head in, sniffing the air for something, *anything*, that he might find edible. "I'm here."

"Don't worry," I told him. "You can eat this salmon. It's plain."

"Well . . ." He didn't seem too happy.

"The new you, remember?" Wes suggested, helpfully. He and Arlo had had a long talk last night, man to man. Kind of.

"Right," Arlo said. "Anything I can do to help?"

"Nope," I said, checking again and finding the salmon done to just flaking perfection. I pulled the tray out of the oven and put it on the counter. "But go ask Holly to fix you a drink. We've set up a new tequila bar."

"Tequila?" Arlo sounded enthusiastic.

"Yes. I intend this evening to be positively psychotropic."

"Did you get *Patron*?" He mentioned one of the premium bottles available from Mexico.

"We got *Patron* and *Herradura* and *Casta* and *Porfidio* . . ."

Somewhere along the list I lost Arlo as he departed in search of one of these high-prestige spirits.

Then he poked his head back into the kitchen and asked, "Hey, Mad. You want me to get you a drink?"

Wes looked at me and I looked back. Is it always so good when you make up? And, conversely, why does it have to get so bad, first?

"Later," I answered Arlo, and then, after carefully moving the deep orange/pink wild salmon onto a large, turquoise-colored, oval platter, I began to decorate the fish. The traditional design suited me, and I lightly painted the fish with tarragon mayonnaise and began covering it with thinly sliced cucumber fish scales.

"Everyone is coming," Wes said, for the fourteen millionth time.

"What can go wrong?" I asked, humming happily in my busy kitchen. "Honnett will be here. Relax."

"You don't have a nerve in your body," Wes mumbled. "That's what's the problem. You aren't concerned a little that Honnett is going to sit down to dinner with Arlo?"

"Well . . ." I thought it over. "Nah."

"Guests are arriving," Holly said as she sailed into the kitchen. "How are we doing?"

"I'm done," I said, adding the last cucumber slice to my masterpiece. I pulled off my long white apron, and tossed it on a peg. "It's showtime."

I left Wesley muttering and walked with Holly over to the large living room at the other end of the main floor, where our guests were gathering. So far, Arlo was standing near the bar setup, and Beryl and her father, Ralph Duncan, had just arrived and were trying to make

small talk with Arlo. As I entered the room, Beryl spun
around and smiled.

"Hello, Beryl," I said, approaching. "I'm so glad you
could make it at such short notice."

"Madeline Bean, this is my father, Ralph Duncan.
Daddy, this is the woman who has been helping us."

Vivian's good-looking husband held out his hand. His
were the type of looks that made excellent news anchors.
I shook his hand a moment, and then said, "I'm glad
you've come. I think Esmeralda has been a little home-
sick."

"Daddy's ready to take her home, aren't you Daddy?"
Beryl flashed a smile at her father, who nodded.

In the past two minutes I'd seen Beryl Duncan smile
more often than in all the encounters we'd ever had.

"You seem happy," I said, feeling her out.

"I am. I heard from the police that they have arrested
the man who killed Vivian. Thanks to you, I hear." She
almost beamed at me.

"Is that right?" They were holding Albert Nbutu on
charges stemming from his illegal entry to the United
States and his possession of stolen property. To my
knowledge, they had not yet charged him with murder.
But Paul said it was only a matter of hours.

The doorbell rang and the next to arrive was Det.
Chuck Honnett. At the same time, Big Jack Gantree and
the newlyweds appeared. Sara was stunning in an Ar-
mani dress without a back. Her deeply tanned skin was
set off by the gown's pale pink color. Her new husband,
a man with whom I'd shared canteloupe on the kitchen
floor, stood by looking uncomfortable, although I noticed he'd managed to get out of that wedding tux and
into an expensive suit.

Next, Whisper Pettibone joined our group, looking almost jaunty in a pearl-gray ensemble and leaning heavily
on a silver-tipped cane. There was that pleasant cacoph-
ony of small talk and joking that makes such sweet social music, the sound I instinctively listen for at all my
parties. People having a good time. Excellent.

Holly took over at the bar, offering tastings of several of the potent tequilas we had purchased for the evening. And I joined her there, pouring myself a deadly and delicious watermelon margarita made with fresh-squeezed limes and melons.

"Listen here, Madeline," Big Jack Gantree said in a manner that I imagined passed for gruff charm to those who appreciate it. "We got off on the wrong foot. Big guy like me and a modern young lady like yourself, we just got off to a rough start."

"Then here's to a new one," I toasted. I took a sip of my margarita while Jack downed a shot of straight *Paradiso Anejo*, which, at $95 a bottle, was one of the most expensive in my collection.

"My granddaughter told me how hard you worked to help her and Brent-boy. We appreciate that. We don't forget a favor, either."

Or an insult? I wondered, sipping from my broad-rimmed glass.

"A toast to the happy couple!" Big Jack boomed. The white-haired T.V. mini-legend lifted his glass.

All the others, with the exception of Arlo, had been present at the wedding and were happy to help a bride and groom get a steadier start to their marriage. This tequila bar was going great guns.

"To their life together," Big Jack said. "May they be healthy, wealthy, and . . . come to think of it, that's enough!"

The last of our group arrived just a few minutes past seven-thirty. The doorbell rang once more and in walked Zelli Gentz. Luckily, a business opportunity had kept him in town a few more days. I had a pleasant little buzz going, just enough to smooth out the rough edges of my brain, where the anxiety over having the three men I'd recently kissed all about to dine together would have been itching to freak out.

"Would you all please join me for dinner?" I sang out, leading the way to the dining room where a long French pine table was set for twelve. The African violets looked lovely, set amid a dozen glowing votive candles. As the guests took their places, mindful of the place-cards, I began to relax. I watched Arlo sit just far enough away from Honnett, who was seated just far enough away from Zelli.

Wesley whispered in my ear, "I warn you, if you had made out with even *one* more man here—say Whisper or Big Jack?—this seating plan could have never handled it."

I tried to take a swipe at him, but missed. It was time for me to set down my watermelon margarita.

"Everyone . . ." I looked over the assembled party with their polite, expectant expressions and smiled. "Please enjoy yourselves."

"If you can . . ." whispered Holly near my ear as she began serving the guests.

For several minutes there were only the sounds of oohing and ahing. To any cook, this is the sweetest sound there is, so I took a moment to enjoy it.

Whisper adjusted his wire-rims and offered his stiff compliment, "Well, at least you really can cook." Which I got a kick out of.

As I dragged my brain back to a more alert state, I overheard Brent tell Sara he wished she could cook like this. Well. The man had some taste, after all. The lovely Sara made a joke that someday they'd hire a cook who could do any damn dish he'd like.

Arlo was trying his best to fit in. The only one of all our guests he'd met before was Honnett, and Arlo was clearly annoyed to see him at the table. The triumphant seating chart, however, was my salvation, as it prevented Arlo from using his legendary wit to cut the detective to shreds. Beryl, meanwhile, was acting a trifle too gleeful for a woman whose mother had recently been killed. Yes, she had her issues with regards to her mother. But in public, I wished she'd stop laughing quite so loudly. I shot a look to Holly just in time for her to skip over Beryl's glass as she refreshed everyone's watermelon margaritas from a large green glass pitcher. Beryl never even noticed.

Another loud peal of laughter came from Beryl's end of the table. Honnett was taking note of it. Well, I thought, reconsidering. Perhaps my seating plan had not been perfect, after all. I should never have placed the "grieving" daughter right next to Arlo. He makes such a point to be amusing.

I watched as Whisper spoke across the table to Big Jack Gantree. Jack was smiling, enjoying himself now. I overheard Jack say, "I worked it all out with Madeline. I won't be paying for that big wedding because you won't be billing me."

Whisper looked at me and I nodded.

"I think Vivian owed Jack that much," I said, and then I turned to look directly at Jack Gantree. "At the very least."

He sat there, smiling for a moment. Then, his expression changed as he thought over just what I'd said. Then, he shot a look over to Zelli Gentz. Perfect.

The party was going so well, I was almost sorry I was going to spoil it. Imagine that. Me, spoiling my own party. It was an amazing stretch.

I turned to Zelli and asked him, in a voice loud enough to carry, "Do you remember telling me that you were interested in purchasing some emeralds?"

"Yes," he said, with perhaps just a hint of hesitation. I imagined that Zelli Gentz was not used to talking about his business dealings, delicate as they were, at a noisy dinner party. As I had expected, the general hubbub dimmed a level or two, allowing more ears to hear our conversation.

"Did, by any chance, those seven rare stones ever turn up?"

Jack Gantree rested his fork on his plate. Beryl, named for the mineral itself, looked at her father. Brent and Sara stopped giggling together. Honnett studied my face. And even Whisper failed to keep up his end of the conversation with Wes.

"I wonder why you ask that?" Zelli said, quietly.

"I would be happy to tell you. Only first, may I assume that you have been contacted by an individual who offered to sell you those stones for seven hundred thousand dollars?"

Zelli stared at me, as did everyone else at the table. Things had gotten deadly quiet.

"It's the oddest thing, really," I continued, "but last night I found these."

I took the bag from my lap and emptied it onto the starched white tablecloth. Forty-five large dullish-green rocks tumbled out.

"Good God!" Big Jack Gantree's voice had suddenly gone hoarse.

"What are they?" Beryl asked, her voice shrill.

Brent Bell stood up and said, "Excuse me," and quickly left the room. Sara turned around, uncertain, but stayed in her seat, fascinated with the pile of rough emeralds in front of her. I looked at Honnett and he gave a nod. I knew no one would be making any unexpected exits from the house.

"My word, Madeline!" Zelli said, licking his lips as if they had suddenly gone dry.

"Do they look familiar?" I asked.

Zelli's eyes searched mine.

"Beryl," I said, turning to the daughter. "Did you know where your mother got her seed money to start Vivian Duncan Weddings?"

She shook her head and looked uncertain. She turned to her father, who was staring at the stones.

"I think your father does. Aren't these the rough emeralds you were searching for, Ralph, the night of Sara and Brent's wedding?"

"What are you talking about?" he asked, in a soft voice.

"When Vivian Duncan came back to California after her years traveling to Rhodesia, she brought home several souvenirs. More than fifty of them, actually. It was by using these raw gems as collateral that she was able to have enough cash to buy a house in Beverly Hills. It was also with this ready supply of cash she went into business. But surely, Ralph, your wife told you about the legendary emeralds she managed to bring back with her to America?"

Jack Gantree spoke up. "Is this true, Gentz? Did Vivian have the stones all along?" He was huffing a little, shocked.

"It appears to be so," Zelli said, and then turned to me and asked, "May I?" before he reached for one of the large green stones on the table.

"Please do."

Zelli pulled out a jeweler's loupe and held it in his eye as he lifted one of the largest stones from the table and examined it.

"I better go see what's happened to Brent," Sara said, nervous perhaps to let her new husband out of her sight for too long.

"Wait just another minute," I suggested.

"Daddy," Beryl said, "you didn't go to Vivian's office that night. You didn't!"

"*You're* the one?" Whisper screeched, offended. "You dared to lift a finger to me? Why I ought to . . ." He raised his silver-tipped cane over his head.

Honnett helped Whisper settle down while we all looked on.

"Daddy!" Beryl grabbed her father's hand. "Don't say another word. Don't speak. I'm your attorney now, Daddy. You have done nothing wrong."

I would have loved to have heard Whisper's reply, but I turned my attention back to the rest of my dinner guests.

Meanwhile, Arlo, who was the only one present who didn't have a stake in all the dramatic goings on, was mesmerized by the pile of rough stones on the table in front of him. He picked up one that was the size of a small olive and turned it around over the candle. It glinted dully from behind its wash of mineral soot.

"Man, these are amazing. I counted forty-five emeralds. Are they the real deal?" Arlo asked Zelli.

But I answered for him. "Of course they are." I looked over at Zelli and asked, "Are they as beautiful as you remember?"

His eyes lit up as they met mine. Zelli Gentz knew at that moment that I did truly understand him.

"Hey!" Arlo looked from Zelli back to me. "What's going on?"

"This is a story that goes back almost twenty-five years, Arlo. Vivian Duncan said she had been forced to give up fifty-two exceptional emeralds, eleven million dollars in raw gems, to corrupt Zimbabwe border guards. She said she barely escaped Zimbabwe with her life. A tragic story. But Zelli always suspected Vivian of running her own scam.

"Then, a few days ago, she had begun to change her tune. The timing was right. She was ready, perhaps, to cash out. She was planning to sell her wedding business. That's where I came in. Because it had become time to collect her big prize. She was prepared, finally, to admit to Zelli that seven of the rough emeralds might be available. That was, until she wound up dead before they could complete their new deal."

I turned back to Zelli Gentz. "But it was only a minor setback for you, I think. You always expected to get another call about those gems. Perhaps," I met his gaze, "you even thought *I* had them?"

Gentz smiled, his dark mustache emphasizing his beautiful white teeth. Everyone else at the table was silent.

"When we found the stones this morning," I continued, "seven were missing. I knew they hadn't been found on Vivian. And I was certain Zelli didn't have them, yet. I expected whoever might have taken them would call you," I said, turning back to Zelli, "possibly even today, offering to sell you those seven perfect stones."

"Let us say for the moment," Zelli commented, "that is true."

"And Sara," I said, turning to the bride, "don't you think now is the time to tell Detective Honnett just how you got the seven emeralds which you offered to Mr. Gentz?"

Sara looked up at me, startled. "Me? Why, I never . . ."

"The emeralds, Sara. That's why you killed Vivian Duncan. At your own wedding." I shook my head. No party planner enjoys a hostess who sabotages her own affair. All that planning and painstaking hard work and then the bride doesn't have sense enough to restrain herself from committing murder!

Sara stood up, but then so did Wesley and Honnett.

Big Jack bellowed, "Sara child! What the hell is all this about?"

And Honnett, who had remained remarkably quiet all evening, said, "Let's just let Madeline finish what she wants to say. Settle down."

"Somehow," I continued, "that night at her wedding, Sara must have learned about the emeralds," I explained. "She probably overheard a private conversation between Mr. Gentz and Vivian. Earlier, they had agreed to just such a meeting. Vivian planned to bring seven wonderfully matched rough emeralds, which Zelli intended to purchase, to the Museum that night. They set a price at near seven hundred thousand dollars. Perhaps Sara had even overheard Zelli suggesting the money was already deposited in a Swiss bank account that could easily be transferred to her name. Simple for a man from Zurich."

Zelli nodded and I went on. "So much money. Right in front of her. And Sara needed money. She had just married a man who didn't have any. And from the way Brent had been behaving, he was just about through accepting the tokens and bribes that Big Jack kept at the end of his leash. How could Sara have the lifestyle she needed and the husband she wanted? I think she just took it." I turned to Sara. "Didn't you?"

"Me? You are insane!" Sara looked at me through slits of eyes.

"And what made me realize you could have done it, Sara, was the videotape from your wedding reception. I checked the tape taken from the fixed camera that covered the bridal table. Your table. Funny thing. The bride wasn't there."

"Yes, I was . . ."

"Sara," I interrupted her. "The police have the tape."

"So I couldn't eat that horrid food, okay? I was mingling with my guests and . . . I didn't kill anyone. That's just crazy!"

"When we saw you that night," I said, staring her down. "When you came into the foyer, Sara, when Honnett and I had just discovered the body. You knew it was Vivian, didn't you?"

"No, I . . ."

"You knew she was dead."

"I . . ."

"Sara," I continued, "look around. Brent has ditched you. He must realize whom he has married by now. Perhaps he suspected you even then. And today, I had a sneaking suspicion that you asked him to drop off a package at the Four Seasons Hotel, so I checked with the front desk. Don't you think he's got to know you were using him to deliver the seven emeralds you took off of Vivian Duncan's dead body?"

Sara stared at me, biting her lower lip. She was cornered.

"You hated Vivian. You must have suspected she knew Brent very, very well."

"She was a disgusting, old hag!" Sara shouted.

"So you cornered her outside, while she was having a smoke. You hit her with something hard and found her bag, found the stones."

Sara stood up, her eyes wide.

"And before you attacked her, did she perhaps tell you who your real father was?"

"Shut up!" Sara yelled, her eyes filled with alarm. "How could you know? Who are you, anyway? Did Vivian tell you? That horrid old witch! Did she tell you *all* my secrets? How could she? How could she try to destroy me?"

Cool Sara had finally broken down.

"You stupid bitch!" screamed Beryl Duncan, startling us all with a breakdown of her own. "You killed my mother, you stupid little fool!" Beryl stood up, tipping her chair, and lunged for Sara's thick black curls.

"Ooh. Cat fight," Arlo observed, grabbing his shot glass of tequila and stepping out of the way.

At that point, it seems just about everyone else jumped into action, all talking at once. Big Jack Gantree pulled Beryl back just as Honnett stepped up to Sara and slipped on a pair of handcuffs.

And all the while, Whisper Pettibone sat back in his chair and clapped.

Chapter 26

I had prepared a spectacularly light, three-layer high, lemon curd cake for the evening. Unfortunately, no one seemed especially interested in dessert.

Honnett, of course, was on the job. He had to take Sara, along with her shocked grandfather, to the police station to charge her with the murder of Vivian Duncan. A back-up patrol car, which had been stationed in my cul-de-sac, had rounded up Brent Bell as he had tried to make an early departure. The patrol officers now watched Sara as well, as Honnett returned to my house for one more thing.

He said we still had personal business he needed to finish up. He didn't require any prompting. He flat out told me that he had been wrong about Ralph Duncan. I asked him to speak loud enough for Beryl Duncan and Ralph to hear. And it did my heart good to see Honnett take responsibility, in front of everyone, for the sin of, well, of underestimating me.

He turned to go and pulled me aside.

"You have your own way of doing things," he said.

"That I do."

"Sorry if I came down on you too hard, before."

"Don't mention it," I said, happy to be the one who gets to be big enough to forgive.

"And I won't forget," Honnett said, winking. "I'm your slave. You pick the day."

"What?" Arlo said, coming into the entry just as Honnett left to go. "What was he saying?"

"He bet on the wrong horse and now he's going to have to pay up."

"Hey," Arlo said, taking my hand, "I sure hope that dweeb isn't calling my girlfriend a horse."

"Arlo."

"Wild night, Mad. You sure can throw a party."

"Aren't you sticking around for cake?"

"I better take off," he said, looking sheepish. "I should go home and work."

"Arlo, your show is on hiatus. What work?"

"Oh, I've got scripts to read. You know."

He left, and I was pretty sure I knew where he was headed. To McDonald's for a couple of Big Macs and a super-sized fries. Such are his epicurean standards, humble though they may be.

As I turned to go back to the dining room, Zelli Gentz came out, putting on a black leather jacket.

"Oh no, Zelli," I said, suddenly sad. "Are you leaving?"

"I'm afraid I must," he said. "I had a very exciting evening, Madeline. You are an excellent chef. Thank you especially for preparing such a fabulous North American dish. You knew I would enjoy it."

"I'm glad."

"And I must thank you for reuniting me with all those stones from so long ago. I had never expected to see them again, all together."

"Perhaps not," I said, "but you are quite worldly, Mr. Gentz, and I am certain you expected to come across those stones some day, didn't you?"

"You are wise. With such a rare commodity, it is true, we learn that every stone will eventually turn up one day. But what a treat that you would find them for me tonight. I shall never forget the sight when you sat at your dinner table and poured them out on the table, like a magician. You are truly an amazing woman."

"Thank you. And you are pretty amazing yourself."

Zelli put a hand through his hair and smiled a roguish smile.

"Would you like to visit Zurich, Madeline?"

"What did you have in mind?"

"We shall see. Alas, I have work to do that keeps me away. I now go to Colombia where I have my cutters."

"To cut the seven emeralds for the sultan's rings?"

"Yes. The best emerald cutters in the world are in Colombia. They pass this skill down from father to son, working in the most primitive conditions imaginable. But they are artists. And an artist is what is called for."

"Are you serious?"

"Yes. Why wouldn't I be?"

"Those emeralds. The ones you purchased from Sara Silver today. They will make you give them back. You don't expect you can just leave the country with them."

"Ah, Madeline. You do not remember all that we discussed last night. Do you think those rough stones are still in the United States?"

"No?"

"They are gone, of course. Would I be so foolish to carry them on me? I expect I will be searched quite thoroughly this time when I leave your LAX tonight. But, of course, there is nothing to find."

Of course. There wouldn't be. He was something.

"What will you do with the money? Will you pay it to Sara Silver?"

"Ah, yes. The seven hundred thousand. I suppose I have to think about this. Sara stole those stones, so it is not right that she should profit."

"It certainly isn't," I agreed.

Zelli put his arm around me, standing there at the front door, and thought.

"But when you stop to think, Vivian stole those emeralds, too. According to our agreement, ten percent belonged to Vivian, ten percent belonged to Gantree, and eighty percent belonged to me. So you see, I might as well claim that these seven stones were part of my eighty percent and pay no one."

"Ah, but let's think a little bit further," I said. "It seems to me that under the conditions you originally acquired those stones, it could be argued that you obtained them illegally yourself. Perhaps they really belong to the country of Zimbabwe."

"Yes, I can see your point. So do you suggest I send the payment directly to their government?"

"Let me think about it, and I'll let you know."

"Yes. I will do that. And now, since your Police Detective took the other forty-five stones away, I have no further business in the States. Goodbye, dear Madeline. Thank you so much for inviting me to your charming home for dinner."

What manners. I would miss Zelli Gentz.

When I got back to the dining room, Wesley caught me up on what had been going on. Apparently, Beryl Duncan was brokering a settlement between Whisper Pettibone and her father, Ralph. If Whisper could convince the police to drop their assault case against Ralph Duncan, they were offering Whisper the chance to own Vivian Duncan Weddings outright. Whisper was a man who expected justice to be served, but on the other hand, what could be more just than for him to finally own the whole show?

Holly and Wes were clearing the dishes and told me that the three of them had gone out to my courtyard to discuss the details. That's where Esmeralda was napping, and Ralph had suddenly realized how much he missed her. The dog-Dad reconciliation was currently in progress.

I looked at the tower of lemon cake and turned to my friends.

"Holly?" I asked her, "A little slice?"

"I've been eating way too much." She gave me an apologetic smile. "Sorry."

"Wesley?" I looked at my friend.

"I couldn't eat a thing. My stomach is still doing the Macarena from the scene we just witnessed."

"Maddie, why don't I cut you a piece of cake," Holly

suggested, picking up the silver cake server.

"No, wait," I said, stopping her. "Our guests are gone and I just don't feel in the party mood any more."

"That will happen," Wes said, philosophically, "when you invite a murderer to dine."

The doorbell rang and I ran out to see if someone had come back. Instead, I found my dear lawyer Paul at the door, surprised to see all the cars parked in the street.

"Am I intruding on a party?" he asked, hesitant.

"Not at all," I said. "Come right in."

I showed him to the dining room where Wes and Holly had just finished clearing up the dishes.

"Paul," I said, trying once more to be the hostess. "Would you care for a piece of cake?"

"Maybe later, Madeline. I'm too worked up right now. I just got back from downtown. Those poor bastards never knew what hit them."

"What poor bastards?" Holly asked.

"The law. The cops."

"What hit them?" I asked.

"Me," Paul said, proud of himself. "I'm hitting them on every single charge they are holding Albert Nbutu on. The INS, I hope to stop cold. Mr. Nbutu is a political refugee seeking asylum in the United States."

"Are they buying that?" asked Wesley, pouring cups of coffee.

"Actually, I don't think he will have a leg to stand on. The government of his country is much more stable than ever before. But this is a war of inches. They have to check it out, and while the paperwork gets filed, they cannot deport Albert."

"But they'll keep him locked up," Wes said, worried. "I don't know how he will be able to stand that."

"What about the possession of stolen property charge?" I asked, sitting down at the table.

"Says he found those items," Paul explained. "And since there is no one claiming those items were stolen, I'm telling them they have to let him go. Of course they aren't ready to listen to me yet, but when we get before a judge I'm going to dazzle them."

"But poor Albert stays locked up. Do you think that could be true?" Holly wondered. "Did he just find that stuff? I mean, if Sara Silver killed Vivian, how did this Albert guy get Vivian's jeweled lighter and lipstick?"

"I believe my client," Paul said, with a bit of bluster.

"So do I," I agreed. They all looked at me. "I think Sara followed Vivian outside, where Vivian was taking a break. She was smoking a cigarette and Sara started a conversation. That's when, I'm afraid, Vivian mentioned she knew who Sara's real father was. Sara had been thinking about how she might get her hands on the rough emeralds she knew Vivian had on her, but when Vivian began telling Sara the truth about her birth, she went totally nuts. Sara picked up something heavy, maybe one of the folding chairs that were stacked out there next to the building, and swung. I imagine Vivian went down easily. She was not very heavy. And then, perhaps because she didn't want Vivian ever to tell the story of her parentage, Sara swung again, this time breaking Vivian's neck and killing her."

"It's awful. How do you know all this?" Holly asked.

"Honnett told me they got to the rental company and found the chair they believe may have been used. They're doing tests and whatever it is they do. But mostly because of what Sara said at dinner tonight. She admitted that Vivian taunted her about her real father."

"Have you got any idea who Sara's real father was?" asked Wesley.

"Yes. I believe he is Paul's new client."

"What?" Paul stopped sipping his coffee with a jerk. "Albert? Albert Nbutu?"

"Vivian knew that Sara's mother, Gazelle Gantree, was spending time with some of the younger people who played polo at their club in Rhodesia. That fall Gazelle met a young man who worked in the stable."

"Oh my God," Holly said. "How do you know?"

"This afternoon, when I was setting up this evening's

event with Honnett, he let me speak again with Albert. I told Albert I knew he traveled all the way to Los Angeles to find the daughter he had never known. Gazelle Gantree's daughter. He had spent a lifetime trying to get his life back and he desperately wanted to see this lost child.

"That's why Jack Gantree had Albert thrown in an African jail for years. After learning from Vivian that Albert Nbutu was the real father of his grandchild, Big Jack paid off some officer at the Ministry of Mines all those years ago to arrest Albert and make him disappear."

"Holy shit." Holly was dazed.

"So how did Albert finally meet his daughter?" Wesley asked.

"Albert asked his friend, Chef Reynoso, to contact Vivian and suggest she hire Albert to work on Sara's wedding. Albert said Vivian never recognized him from the old days. But at the wedding, he approached Vivian and told her the whole story. She claimed she never knew what became of him. That she and Gazelle had been told Nbutu was killed in the fighting.

"But Albert never believed her. He remembered seeing Vivian once when he was with Gazelle in the Polo Club. He had always known that she was the one who betrayed him. After he confronted Vivian, Albert planned to tell Sara the truth."

"My goodness, Madeline," Paul said, "Albert told you all that? Today?"

"Yes. You know that old technique they call good cop-bad cop? Well, Albert had just spent last night with a pack of really bad cops, and then he got to speak with me. I think he was so traumatized by being in a cell again, locked up, that he was ready to talk to anyone."

"You underestimate yourself," Paul said, seriously.

"She always does," Wes agreed, and then turned back to the fascinating tale. "So did he tell Sara he was her father, face to face?"

"No. Vivian insisted she should be the one to tell Sara

first. She was a woman, she told him, and Sara would listen because Vivian had been in Africa with her mother."

"But," Wes picked up, figuring out the logic of what must have happened, "when Vivian told Sara the African ice sculptor was really her dad, she got hysterical."

"Exactly what I think," I agreed. "Whatever her mixed-up reasoning, she'd been brought up by a racist pig who had possibly passed his prejudice down to his granddaughter. Perhaps she couldn't absorb the news that her father was black."

"That's sickening," Holly said.

"Poor Albert," Paul said.

"His whole life has been so tragic," Wes said.

"I know," I agreed. "And later, when he walked back outside to the area where he had been working, he discovered Vivian's body lying there. Dead."

"Shit!" Holly shook her head. "What a shock."

"He really didn't want to talk about this part. Maybe he figured out what had happened. Maybe he saw Sara walking away from the area. He wouldn't say yes or no to that. He's still protecting her."

"So is he the one who moved the body?" Wes asked.

"Yes. He was scared to death. He didn't want the body to be found, especially so close to his work area, so he carried Vivian's body out to the foyer while all the guests were busy dining in the closed Hall of Small Mammals."

"But why toss her onto the *Triceratops*?" Holly asked.

"In Rhodesia, they have a custom of displaying the bodies of those who have been executed. In public. Hung on a stake. In the town square. As a warning to others."

"So you think Albert Nbutu was applying that quaint custom to Vivian?"

"I do. And when he moved her body, he discovered a tube of lipstick and a jeweled lighter."

"The lighter was Vivian's. That makes sense," Paul said, figuring out how this might impact his client. "But he could have found it any time after the body was moved, Maddie. There's no evidence to the contrary."

"Not that the police have, no," I agreed. "But the lipstick is another matter. That shade of MAC lipstick was never worn by Vivian Duncan. She was a Chanel addict down to her makeup. That MAC lipstick belonged to the bride, Sara Silver."

"Holy cow," Holly said, "I'm sure you're right!"

"And when I mentioned that to Honnett this afternoon, he checked it out. They won't be able to connect that exact tube of lipstick to Sara, but that is the same shade she buys. They're convinced it was hers. And if they can make a deal with Paul here, I believe they are prepared to allow Albert to walk out of that cell if he'll testify he found the lipstick underneath the body. And they may even deal on the INS issue."

"This is too good!" Paul said, relishing the thought. "The police asking our permission to let our man go. Well, I gotta run, children. I'm on my way to make Albert Nbutu a free man."

Paul kissed Holly and me on the tops of our heads and left.

Holly and Wesley stood up, too.

"Where are you guys going?" I asked. I was high on getting answers and didn't want to be left alone.

"I'm going to put this beautiful cake away," Wes said, ever the fastidious one. "Whipped cream frosting, you know, needs to be kept cool."

"I'm going to make a phone call," Holly said, moving towards her desk in the entryway.

"Who are you calling at this hour?" I asked.

"My dad. I suddenly miss him a whole lot."

Chapter 27

A week had come and gone, allowing all the events fit to print, to be printed. The arrest for murder of the ward of one of T.V.'s favorite oldies was custom made for L.A. T.V. news, so we had little trouble keeping up on Sara Silver's arrest and confession. Or on the revelation to the press that poor Sara had been addicted to prescription painkillers and was requesting permission to attend a detox clinic before her trial.

Maneuvering, Paul had called it. If Sara had claimed she was addicted to hummingbird wings, Paul would have found it more believable. He could be so cynical, sometimes. And for very good reason. Sara was working on her case the way rich lawyers advise, spinning some tale to take the heat off her selfish, foolish self.

We sat around the living room downstairs, Wes, Holly and I, recapping the events, since so much had been resolved in one short week. Paul Epstein would soon be joining us to announce the third final settlement agreement he'd hammered out with Five Star. So we were fairly apprehensive.

"Oh Maddie, tell Wes what we found out about that car-jacking thing," Holly prompted me.

"Oh, yes. Remember when I first met Vivian?"

"No," Wes said, deadpan. "Of course I do. Who did the car-jacking, anyway?"

"She was never car-jacked, really."

"What?"

"That's right. When Ralph Duncan was talking to the police, he admitted that he and Vivian had been quarreling that day and she had insisted he get out of the car and find his own way home."

"So he stole her car?"

"Well, not exactly. But they did start scuffling, I guess. He said he drove off in a hurry."

"I'll say. Didn't he barely miss you?" Wes asked. "What are these people thinking?"

"Yes, but because she was Vivian Duncan, she manufactured a whole song and dance about car-jackers. How do you like that? It was a much more glamorous story than that she had finally pissed off her poor husband to the point where he had shoved her down onto the pavement, trying to get into the car and get home."

"She was fairly clever at spinning tales," Wes said.

"Which didn't end up winning her any contests," Holly commented.

We all shook our heads.

"Madeline, I talked to Beryl Duncan this morning," Wes said.

"You did?"

"I was wondering how Esmeralda was doing. We had sort of bonded, you know."

Wes was a real dog person. I understood he had become attached.

"She said her father was doing okay. He is selling the house, he decided. It seems too big for him and Esme now that Vivian is no longer there to fill it up. And Beryl was pretty excited, really. She had just closed that Kip England divorce settlement she'd been working on."

"That's right," I said, recalling how worked up she had been over it. "She represented the wife."

"So you'll love this," Wes said. "She got Kip England to give his ex 20 million dollars."

Holly whistled. "That's my dream amount of money," she said.

I looked at her. "You have a dream amount of money?"

"Sure. You know, if you had that much you'd never worry about money again. That sort of thing. What about you, Mad. What's your dream amount of money?"

"I don't know," I said. "I think maybe it's not too good to get too comfortable."

"Glad you said that," Paul said, entering the room. "Hi Maddie, hi guys."

"Paul! What's happening already? We're going nuts. What does Five Star want from us?"

"Your bank statement, for a start."

"I beg your pardon," Wesley said.

"Here's the deal, kids. We take it or leave it. It's totally up to you. Five Star understands that you have had expenses this year. They are willing to sell you back your company . . ."

"Oh, no. Here we go again," Wes said, looking grim.

"Eh, eh, eh . . . let me finish. They want some of their cashola back, naturally. But they figure, if you deduct what you spent for reasonable expenses, including the party you did for the pope and so on, they will drop their lawsuit and you may go back to business as of tomorrow morning."

"Do we get to keep the money we spent paying off Maddie's mortgage?" Wes asked, concerned. "And there was an equal amount I used for a down payment on the house I'm remodeling."

"That was three hundred thou for Maddie's mortgage and another three hundred for you, right, Wesley?"

"Right."

"Sorry, no. They won't accept that. It must go back."

"Holy cow," Holly said, worried.

"Do you think this is the best offer we'll get?" I asked, trying to readjust to being poor again.

"I do," Paul said. "But we can go on and fight them in court. That's always an option. It will take time because they are bastards and they know the more time it takes the longer you're out of work, but that doesn't mean we might not win in the end."

I looked over at Wesley, who was coming to terms with our reality. Perhaps it would have been best had we never had a taste of the rich life.

"Holly," I said, "I changed my mind. In answer to your question, my dream amount of money is three hundred thousand dollars."

Wes smiled. "Mine, too."

"Well, then," Paul said, with a smile, "you may like to hear what I've arranged."

We all stared at him.

"See, Five Star's attorneys understand the world. Especially they understand bloodsucking lawyers, you should pardon that expression. They easily agreed that a reasonable expense would cover your attorney's fees for this litigation."

"Well, good," I said, feeling a little better. At least Paul would be paid. I could feel less guilty for all the time he'd given us.

"No, Maddie, I don't think you fully appreciate what I'm saying. Five Star will allow an expense of eight hundred thou for attorney's fees."

"Eight hundred thousand dollars?" Holly was stunned. "Paul! That's wonderful! You're rich!"

"Hey, what do you take me for? Come on, now. I mean I will bill you for eight and you will pay me eight, and then I will send you each a check for four hundred thousand dollars."

"What?"

"Oh, come on, Maddie. It will be perfect. You'll get to keep your house and so will Wesley, and you can start up Madeline Bean Catering again."

"You mean Mad Bean Events & Catering," Wes corrected, but he and I were so excited we could hardly quibble about a name.

There was hugging and congratulating. Holly ran to get us all drinks.

"But you will bill us for real," I insisted, as I gave Paul a big hug.

"Don't worry about me," he said. As always. "Oh, and I have news. They finally released Albert Nbutu."

"Well, it's about time."

"The INS have agreed to allow him to stay in the country for now, but they are tough mothers. We're still working on it. The police have dropped the other minor charges, so that should help."

"What will he do?"

"Right now he wants to stay in Los Angeles. He wants to get to know his daughter," Paul said, shaking his head.

Holly returned, hearing this last. "Oh, man. That's going to be difficult."

Paul said, "We'll see. Who knows, once Sara is treated for her poor, unfortunate *addiction problem*, she may eventually accept him."

I rather doubted it, but I was not willing to share my dark opinion of human nature with the group when we were busy celebrating our good fortune. Back in business! How sweet that was.

"I spoke with Zelli," I told everyone. "He called."

"So what's up with that?" Paul demanded. "Is Arlo back, or is it going to be this Zelli character?"

"Don't forget Chuck Honnett," Holly added. "What is going on there?"

"Hey," I said, with affection, "give a girl a break. I'm just playing the field. Anything wrong with that?"

"What did Zelli say?" Holly asked.

"He is so odd," I said. "I cannot believe how blasé he is about the most bizarre events. He seems to have managed to get away with those seven matched emeralds."

"Good for him," Paul said. We looked at him. "Well, why not? He took the risk and he beat the cops at the airport."

"But he and I had some unfinished business. He still

had the payment from this client of his for the jewels. The money has already been deposited in a Swiss bank account and Zelli was willing to let me decide to whom he registers the account."

"I love this guy," Holly said, breathing deeply. "I could marry this guy."

"So what did you say?" Wes asked.

"Well, first I told Zelli that Honnett will hold onto the rest of the stones, those forty-five rough emeralds we found in Vivian's office. He's not sure if Ralph Duncan will ever get his hands on them, though. It seems the State Department wants to get involved and they may just turn them over to The Republic of Zimbabwe."

"Really. Imagine that," Paul said.

"The thing is, Zimbabwe has been strengthening its friendship with the United States recently. They've even sold a license to mine emeralds to a U.S. mining company. Zelli was philosophical about the loss of those other stones. He said the Zimbabweans would eventually put them on the market. He expected he would see them again. And he's even talking about doing a deal to represent Zimbabwe in the sales."

"This is a man who seizes every opportunity," Wes said, thoughtful. Perhaps he was worried I'd move to Switzerland soon.

"Oh, yes. And the best part. He agreed to transfer the Swiss account with the payment of seven hundred thousand U.S. dollars to the name of Albert Nbutu."

That last announcement got quite a rousing reaction. The only one who was in the least subdued seemed to be Holly.

I sat down next to her, as Wesley and Paul discussed the ramifications of all these new business deals.

"Holly, you look a little down. What's the matter?"

"With me? Nothing. No, I'm not down. It's just that it's so wonderful that Albert will get his dream money, and that you and Wesley will end up with the company intact and still get your dream money."

"But where is *your* dream money?" I looked at my sweet assistant and sighed.

"Everyone," I announced, catching the men in mid-discussion. "In honor of the restart of Mad Bean whatever we're gonna call it, I'd like to propose a promotion. I think we need to promote Holly Nichols to Vice President and Manager."

That started everyone talking about how we were going to go forward and what new parties we were suddenly free to pursue.

Interrupting our chatter, the phone rang and I picked it up.

"Hello, Madeline? It's Darius, darling."

My friend and florist. I hadn't spoken to him for a while.

"I'm totally swamped, sweetie. We're doing more weddings this June than ever before. Luckily Whisper Pettibone has taken the reins of Vivian Duncan Weddings and we are going strong. Do you know, he didn't lose one bride? Amazing. So I was just calling to find out how you are doing."

"Me? I'm fantastic. I just got the news that our company is back on track. We should have several events booked by next week. I'll call you."

"Thanks, pet. Oh, and I've been following the news about the Sara Silver thingie. Can you believe it? We met her together, and I swear, I could never see it coming."

"I don't think everyone who is capable of murder looks like a raving lunatic, Darius. In fact, it's scarier to think they look like Sara Silver."

"So true. And I was hoping you weren't getting too down on yourself. Not depressed, are you?"

"Depressed? Why would I be depressed?"

"Good for you. Just don't go there."

"Go where?"

"Well, I just meant that when you were in my shop last month, when you were doing that tabletop for Sara and her fiancé, didn't you talk those two into getting married? I mean, wasn't that match breaking apart and then you glued it back together? I just thought you might be feeling some regrets, not that you *should*. But if you hadn't done such a brilliant job of patching up that dishy young man with Sara Silver, it's more than likely they'd not have gotten married and Vivian might still be . . . well, no good to moan about what could have been. No reason at all. Just wanted to stay in touch." And then Darius, realizing he'd said way, way too much, rang off.

I slowly replaced the receiver.

"What now?" Wes asked. "Bad news?"

"Not exactly," I said, but I was not ready to talk about the issue Darius had raised.

Here we all are, unwitting accomplices to all of life's agonies. We turn left, and we are almost killed by a wildly out-of-control car whirring by. Lucky we stopped. We turn right, and we never realize that by taking just one step, safe and well-meaning as we may be, we may have allowed a deadly chain of events to keep rolling by, taking with it another's life.

But surely, even had I not gotten involved, Vivian would have patched up the Sara Silver–Brent Bell union. She would have had her wedding. But would she have met the same fate? I wondered. Would just the extraction of one element, me, have altered the course of events to such an extent that the results would not have been fatal?

"Hello," Holly said, waving a hand.

I looked up, back to the present, still unsettled.

"Did you ever tell Wesley about your gift?"

"Oh," I said, snapping back. "I almost forgot. Holly found a box left for me this morning."

"You're kidding. It's not your birthday."

"That's right, it isn't. But here's the thing. Arlo was very inspired by our dinner last week." I pulled a small box from out of my pocket. "He sent me a get-back-together gift."

I opened it and the group crowded around to see. Inside the little box from Tiffany's was a pair of earrings.

They were classic little studs made from two beautiful emeralds set in yellow gold.

"Where'd he get the taste?" Wes asked, approvingly.

"You don't need taste when you've got money," Paul said, joking.

"You scored!" Wes said, happy for me.

"Yes, but that's not all she got." Holly would tell all my secrets if I didn't watch out.

Holly held up a card she'd opened that morning, as she opens all of our mail. It showed a large emerald on the cover.

"Appropriate," Wes said. "This from Arlo, too? I swear, that man is turning over a whole new leaf."

"No," Holly said, tattling. "This is from Honnett."

"Honnett sent you a card?" Wes was intrigued.

"Oh, it's nothing. Just a payoff on a bet we made a while ago."

Holly steamrolled on. "He says he'll be over at seven in the morning on Sunday. He says he'll be her slave . . ."

"Oh my," Paul said.

". . . for twenty-four hours," Holly finished.

"My, my, my," Paul added.

"Hey, we're just fooling around," I said, laughing.

"Which reminds me," Paul said, after everyone had had his or her laugh about how popular I had suddenly become. "When I came up the steps I met the UPS guy. I signed for this."

From out of his pocket he pulled a small UPS envelope.

"It's for Mad," Holly said, reading the label. "Of course it is. Whatever your horoscope is for today, frame it."

I looked at the label and blushed. It had been sent from Colombia. From Zelli Gentz.

Inside was the most amazing jewel we had any of us ever seen. It was, of course, a perfect emerald. Mounted on a gold ring.

"It's got to be ten carats," Holly whispered, shocked.

"I'd say it can't be real . . ." I said, losing it, ". . . but I don't think Zelli would . . ."

"Of course it's real!" Wes said, gawking. "I think it's worth more than the house."

I read the note.

"The sultan has had a shakeup in his staff. One general has lost his position and probably his head. Lucky for me, the business arrangements had been settled in advance, as this one perfect stone was destined to be yours."

The good and the evil. The love and the rage. Life was a study in contrasts. It reminded me of the wedding vows I don't like to sit through. The vows I avoid like the plague. "For richer or poorer, in sickness and health . . ." Perhaps we are not meant to obsess on the small decisions, the tiny steps we are always taking. Perhaps we are only supposed to walk on.

3

Dorothy L. Sayers

One of the greatest mystery story
writers of this century.
Los Angeles Times

GAUDY NIGHT	0-06-104349-4/$6.99 US
STRONG POISON	0-06-104350-8/$5.99 US
HAVE HIS CARCASE	0-06-104352-4/$6.99 US
BUSMAN S HONEYMOON	0-06-104351-6/$6.99 US
IN THE TEETH OF THE EVIDENCE	
	0-06-104356-7/$5.99 US
CLOUDS OF WITNESS	0-06-104353-2/$5.99 US
MURDER MUST ADVERTISE	0-06-104355-9/$6.99 US
THE UNPLEASANTNESS AT THE BELLONA CLUB	0-06-104354-0/$6.99 US
WHOSE BODY?	0-06-104357-5/$6.99 US
THE DOCUMENTS IN THE CASE	0-06-104360-5/$6.99 US
UNNATURAL DEATH	0-06-104358-3/$6.99 US
THE FIVE RED HERRINGS	0-06-104363-X/$6.99 US